PREHISTORIC

EDITED BY S.J. LARSSON

SEVERED PRESS
HOBART TASMANIA

PREHISTORIC

ISBN: 978-1-925840-87-2

TABLE OF CONTENTS

THE KELDOS

By David Achord

Fred Menske's car slid off of the icy roadway, down an embankment, and came to rest against a battered guardrail. He tried in vain to get his car unstuck, but there was no use. He shoved the gear shift into park and began shouting several invectives while slapping the steering wheel. He was interrupted by someone knocking on his window. He looked to see a man with a scraggly beard standing beside the driver's door, staring at him with seeming concern. He was obviously homeless.

"Are you okay?"

His voice was muted somewhat by the closed window. Fred rolled it down partially.

"Why don't you be a pal and give me a push?"

The homeless man looked at Fred for a moment with bloodshot eyes before straightening and walking to the front of Fred's fifteen-year-old Ford. Snow was gathering on the top of his black knit cap and in unkempt whiskers as he looked things over before walking back to Fred's window.

"I don't think so," he said. "Your front fender is smashed up against your tire. You ain't going nowhere."

Fred scowled at the man, as if the accident was somehow his fault. "Well, thanks for nothing," he said and rolled up his window, ending the conversation.

He didn't have insurance, so calling the police was out of the question. He retrieved his phone and demanded Siri locate a tow service. The line stayed busy for several minutes before he finally got through. A gruff speaking man told him he'd gladly put him in line for the next tow, but it would be a wait of at least four hours. Fred hung up on him and then called the lab.

"Keldo Laboratories," a man answered.

"Who is this?" Fred demanded.

"I give up, who are you?" the man responded with a snarky tone. Jerry, it had to be Jerry. Why did it have to be Jerry? Fred rubbed his face in growing exasperation.

"Jerry, is that you?" he asked.

"Oh, my Lord, is that you non-doctor Menske?" The same snarky tone.

"Jerry, I don't have time for your nonsense. I've been in a traffic accident and I need someone to come get me." He held back a sigh as he looked over to the homeless man. He was standing under a bridge with a couple of other men. They were surrounding a barrel, smoke and an occasional lick of lame coming out of the open top and passing around a bottle which was still in a brown paper bag. Fred curled a lip in disgust.

"Oh dear, the non-doctor is stuck in the snow, how awful," Jerry said in mock consternation.

Fred found himself rubbing his eyes. He could feel a headache coming. "Please, just stop," he pleaded. "I am in need of assistance. If you don't want to help, please put someone else on the phone."

"Sorry, non-doc, there's nobody else here but me," Jerry said. "The boss man had everyone go home early. And I ain't coming to get your sorry ass."

Before Fred could respond, he heard the distinct click of the line being disconnected. He sat there stewing, wondering why nobody bothered to call him and tell him to stay home as he put his phone back in his jacket pocket. Home was almost ten miles away. The office was only a mile. He scoffed. Only a mile. Fred was not an athletic man. A mile was a long way for him. And, he was wearing loafers, not an appropriate shoe for hiking. His first inclination was to sit in his car with the heat going and wait for the tow truck, but when he turned the ignition, the car sputtered and died. That made the decision easy.

He stepped out of the car and was immediately hit with a gust of cold wind. The snow was coming down even heavier now. The news lady on the radio said it was a nor'easter. He turned the collar up on his jacket before grabbing his briefcase. He glanced at the men as he walked by them. The one who checked on him held out the bottle.

"Do you want some antifreeze for the road, brother?" he asked.

"Like I'd drink from the same bottle as you," Fred muttered as he walked by.

It had started out as sleet, then turned to ice, and then snow. Fred's shoes and socks were soaked and his feet ached from the cold by the time he made it to the security gate. Realizing his I.D. card was in his briefcase, he chose to push the signal button, hoping someone inside would remotely open the gate. He pushed several times with no response. He gazed down the parking lot and only saw one car: Jerry's four-wheel-drive truck with the disgustingly large redneck tires.

"Oh, joy," he grumbled through rattling teeth.

Fred did not want to lay his leather briefcase on the snow-covered asphalt, so he tried to balance it on the post containing the security card reader while he fumbled with the three-digit combination locks. Alas, as soon as he opened it, the briefcase slipped from his grasp. He tried to grab it, which caused him to lose his balance. Fred and the briefcase both fell to the ground. Fred landed on his ample buttocks, the contents of the briefcase spilling into the slosh and snow.

He heard someone howling in laughter and looked up to see the security guard, Jerry, sticking his bald, watermelon sized head out of the main door.

Fred gathered his belongings, stood, and slid his card through the slot. A moment passed before the security gate rattled open. He did his best to maintain a semblance of dignity as he trudged through the deepening snow. Jerry continued chuckling as Fred made it to the main doors.

"That was some amazing acrobatics, non-doctor," he said, the sarcasm dripping from his verbiage.

Fred glowered, but said nothing and walked inside. It was a stale, long running joke with Jerry. Fred was indeed once a doctor and tenured professor at a prestigious ivy league university. And then, it all fell apart. It had to do with certain nude images of underage children on his work computer, time in prison, being listed as a sexual offender, and the loss of his medical license. Frankly, he was lucky to have gotten this job at Keldo Labs.

He went directly back to his office, which was a set of four cubicles he shared with three other scientists who, in Fred's opinion, were far below his station. He took his jacket off, followed by his shoes and socks. His feet were blue and hurt from the beginning stages of frostbite. He put on a set of cloth lab booties, wrapped himself in his lab coat, and headed for the break room.

There was half of a cup left in the pot. It was brackish tasting, but hot. He drank it down and prepared another pot. He sat down and hugged himself, trying to warm up. He was miserable, but he had to remind himself that it had been worse.

His thoughts drifted back to his first night in prison. His cellmate beat and raped him as soon as the buzzer sounded for lights out. In the ensuing week, he was pimped out in exchange for phone privileges and Ramen noodles. It was a wonder he'd not contracted AIDS.

It was sometime during the first or second week, Fred couldn't remember, when a three-hundred-pound behemoth by the name of Jartain Summerly took a liking to him. He walked into the cell one afternoon, picked up Fred's pimp by the neck, and proclaimed Fred to be solely Jartain's property.

Jartain liked for Fred to call him daddy, even though Fred was at least ten years older than him, and his pet nickname for Fred was Mushy-Butt. Otherwise, Jartain doted on Fred and protected him from the other predators. So, Fred adapted.

Fred served five years before he was paroled. Both he and Jartain hugged and cried on his final day, and a lot of promises were made, but as soon as Fred exited the gate he vowed to never be dependent on an ogre like Jartain Summerly again.

Fred was living in a halfway house and working at a free clinic in the inner city when he was approached by a man who asked him if he would be interested in a job in research which would utilize his wisdom and knowledge. A meeting was eventually arranged with the big man himself, Victor Keldo.

Victor was a living legend in the bio-tech industry. He had over a hundred patents to his name and had a net worth that was somewhere in the billions.

The sales pitch was almost too good to be true. They told him he'd have access to state-of-the-art facilities and a decent salary. How could he say no? He had no other offers on the horizon, and to be honest, if he had to deal with one more angry welfare mother and her brat children with stinky diapers, he was going to jump off a bridge.

The contract seemed odd. It included a detailed confidentiality clause and non-disclosure agreement, but he readily signed it after only scanning it over. When they gave him the grand tour of the labs is when he got the big surprise. Victor Keldo explained the real reason for Keldo Laboratories.

"A few years ago, a glacier in western China melted to the point where the land underneath it could be studied," he said. "A forest was found underneath, creating a litany of speculation in the global warming community."

"I seem to remember that," Fred had said.

Victor continued. "Yes, there was a lot of publicity about it. It's not common knowledge, but several dinosaur eggs were also discovered. The Smithsonian tried to convince China to donate them, but they don't have the resources and money I do." He said it with a smug grin. Fred grinned in return. And then he led Fred into the first lab.

"This is what we did with the eggs."

Fred gazed in wonder. There were a dozen incubation chambers, and each had what was obviously a baby dinosaur. They had elongated snouts and a tail, and even though they were little, he could already see teeth growing. After a long two minutes of befuddled silence, Fred looked at Victor.

"Cloning," he said, in answer to Fred's unasked question. "We extracted DNA from the eggs and here is the result. We call them the Keldos."

"Tyrannosaurus Rex?" Fred asked.

"Good eye," Victor Keldo replied. "But these are a smaller version of the T-Rex. They're commonly called Tyrannosaurus Dilong, a smaller relative of T-Rex. When fully grown, they would reach a length of somewhere around six to seven feet and perhaps four feet tall. And, they'd be covered with feathers."

"Carnivorous," Fred remarked, looking at the teeth.

"Of course."

"For what purpose?" Fred finally managed to ask.

"Think about it, Doctor Menske. Think of all of the possibilities. We've already identified certain unique antigens and high levels of telomerase. Do you know what that is?"

Fred fought down the urge to scoff. "Terminal transferase. It is a ribonucleoprotein…"

Victor Keldo cut him off before he could impress him with his knowledge.

"Indeed. It is believed eternal life can be derived from it. We're at the genesis of groundbreaking biotechnology. And, you'll be part of it."

Fred couldn't stop staring at them. Victor Keldo stepped closer.

"Your job is to make me millions," he said.

Fred was broken from his reverie when Jerry walked into the break room. He spotted the fresh pot of coffee and began filling his extra-large Yeti.

"Hey, save some for me," Fred said.

"I tell you what," Jerry said, turning to him. "If you can whip my ass, I'll fix your coffee for the rest of the time either of us are employed here."

Fred fumed, but refused to make eye contact. Jerry was easily six inches taller than Fred and had a lot more muscle. He was almost as big as Jartain, but nowhere as mean. After all, Jartain was serving four consecutive life sentences for butchering a family. Still, Jerry was nobody to trifle with.

"You're a bully, Jerry Turner," Fred squeaked.

Jerry walked over close and stood before Fred. Fred continued staring at his feet. He then bent over until his mouth was less than an inch from Fred's left ear.

"And you are a pedophile. There is no lower life form on earth than a pedo," he said. He emphasized his statement with a smack to the back of the head. Not hard, but hard enough.

Fred did not respond. How could he, without risking injury?

Eventually, Jerry straightened and walked out of the break room. Fred stood and prepared another pot of coffee.

"I'll get you," he whispered, but only after Jerry had exited the room and was out of sight.

Once he had sufficiently warmed up, he walked down to lab 2. When the magnetic lock clicked, the creatures started stirring. When they saw it was Fred, they actually started emitting excited yips.

"Hi, kids," Fred exclaimed gleefully.

Who would've known dinosaurs could act just like dogs, he thought. He pushed in the cart of raw meat, which excited them even more. He squatted down, got comfortable on the floor, and waited. The creatures were all pent-up energy for several seconds before backing against the cage and sitting, their tails sticking through the designated slot.

Fred went to each of them and drew three vials of blood from the tail of each one. Fred was the only scientist who had successfully trained them to do this. Before, they had a dilemma when it came to drawing blood. The Dilongs had been known to bite.

Only after assuring each vial was labeled and sorted in the trays correctly did he begin feeding them. They resumed yipping in anticipation as Fred started pushing pieces of the meat through the slots in the cage. He was careful though; just last week, Keldo Seven had bit off two fingers from one of the other scientists.

Keldos, that's what they were called. Named after Victor Keldo, of course. Currently, there were seven Keldos. A tag had been pierced through their little ears, each emblazoned with a singular number.

"Hi, Seven," Fred said.

To his surprise, Seven looked at him, as if he knew his name. The little creature walked over and stuck his snout against the cage. On impulse, Fred reached out, stuck his fingers through the cage, and softly stroked his nose. Number Seven emitted a soft, contented growl. The others crowded Seven, vying for Fred's attention, when he saw the light blinking on the phone. There were eleven individual diodes, but he knew this light meant the main line was ringing. Reluctantly, he picked up the receiver and punched the proper button.

"Keldo Research," Jerry answered.

"This is Victor Keldo, who am I speaking with?"

Fred's stomach did a sudden somersault. "It's Fred, Mister Keldo."

"Fred?"

"Uh, Fred Menske," Fred said, wondering how and why Mister Keldo did not recognize his name.

"Ah, yes, Fred. How are the kids?"

"They're doing well, I'm with them now," Fred said.

"Who else is there?"

"It's just me. Oh, well, there is a security guard here, but that's it. It's my understanding everyone else was sent home on account of the bad weather."

"Yes, but someone needs to stay there and watch the Keldos, wouldn't you agree?"

"Absolutely, sir," Fred replied.

"Good man. This bad weather does not look like it is going to abate anytime soon. So, I'm counting on you to stay there and take care of things."

The big man, Victor Keldo, hung up without waiting for Fred to reply. Fred slowly put the phone back on the cradle. This was how Mister Keldo acted toward Fred now, as if he were nobody.

"I'll be back later, kids," Fred said to the Keldos, as he carried the vials to the lab across the hallway, and began cataloging the vials. Once he was finished, he took a break. He'd conduct the testing after a fresh cup of coffee.

The first thing Fred noticed when he entered the employee's lounge was the missing coffeepot.

"Jerry," Fred muttered.

He searched the lounge to see if Jerry had simply hidden it, but it was nowhere to be found. Fred muttered some more invectives before coming up with a thought. He happened to know that in Mister Keldo's conference room there was an expensive coffee urn and even an espresso machine. He crept down the hallway and peeked out into the lobby. Jerry was lying on the couch, seemingly sound asleep. And, his security card was sitting on the receptionist's desk.

Fred was terrified, but as quietly as he could, crept into the lobby, picked up the card, and reversed his steps down the hallway. He nervously looked back down the hall when the door's security lock emitted a distinctive click. He quickly stepped into the conference room and shut the door.

Fred grinned at what he saw. There were trays of donuts, scones, and a fruit platter. All uneaten. When everyone went home early, they left it. When he found the urn full of coffee, he giggled in glee. Fred poured himself a cup and sat in the head chair. He was on his third donut when he realized there was a laptop sitting there. The screen saver was the company logo dancing across the screen. On impulse, Fred reached for the mouse and jiggled it. The screen for the password prompt opened. Fred thought a moment before typing K-E-L-D-O. To his surprise, it worked.

"What an arrogant ass," Fred muttered.

Fred did not even hesitate. He started looking in every file he could. After ten minutes, he stumbled onto the HR files. Human Resources. Fred opened it. There was a sub file of every employee, including him. He opened that one too.

There was the usual stuff, and then he noticed a word document titled performance evaluation. The date showed it was his latest evaluation, which had not yet been submitted. Fred clicked on it.

Everything became numb from the neck down as he read.

There was a singular mention of how he had befriended and conducted the rudimentary training on the Keldos. It then went on to say once the telomerase proteins were successfully isolated, Fred was going to be summarily dismissed and his employment records were to be purged. He would never be associated with the groundbreaking work.

He could imagine the press conference Mister Keldo would give. He'd take credit for everything, of course. That one rookie reporter in the back would then raise her hand.

"Mister Keldo, isn't it true there is a convicted pedophile working for Keldo Laboratories and involved in the research?"

The big man would give a condescending smile and answer that he had no idea what she was talking about. Yeah, that's how it would be. He thought he'd get redemption, he thought he'd be once again recognized by his peers and one of their own.

In a sudden fit of anger, Fred threw the coffee cup at the computer screen, breaking both.

He fumed in silence, his features dark. Fred had battled with depression since the arrest, and if he'd had the means, he would have killed himself after that first night in prison. His self-esteem had been systematically stripped away. Keldo Labs was his redemption.

And, now, that little sliver of hope that life was going to be okay was going to be taken from him. He stood, left the conference room, and slowly walked back to the lab.

The kids, that's how Fred thought of them after spending the last two years with them, rushed the cages when he walked in.

"Are you guys still hungry?" Fred asked.

Number Seven responded with a yip. Fred walked over to the cages and began opening them. They watched him in confusion as Fred took his lab coat off before sitting on the floor. He worked it all out while he walked down the hall.

The Keldos. It was going to end with the Keldos. If he was going to go out, he was going out with a bang. He was going to let the Keldos eat him alive. Victor Keldo could not deny his existence then. He'd have to acknowledge that not only did Doctor Fred Menske work at the facility, he was also actively involved in the research.

"Alright, come on then," Fred said as he lay back and closed his eyes.

He waited. After a few seconds, he felt one of them nudge his hand. He held it out, waiting for the first, painful bite. He felt another one jump on his chest and then nudge his face. He opened his eyes and stared at the face of Seven. Seven nudged him again. Fred instinctively reached up and began stroking him.

"You can do it, boy," he cooed. "Rip my throat out and make it fast."

Seven stared at him with reptilian eyes. Fred was about to slap Seven in order to anger him, but before he could do so, he heard the click of the electronic lock and the door burst open.

It was Jerry. He spotted Fred immediately, ran forward and kicked Fred in the groin. Fred emitted a groan and curled up in a ball.

"You took my card, you fucking pedo!" he shouted.

Fred's eyes were shut tightly. All he wanted was for the pain to go away. He waited for the beating. It was coming, he knew it was. Bullies like to beat on weak, little guys. He kept waiting, but nothing happened. He opened his eyes to see Jerry backed into a corner.

"What the hell have you done with these things?" Jerry accused.

Keldo One and Two lunged forward, biting Jerry on both legs. Jerry howled in pain and ran for the door, dragging One and Two with him. Fred sat there, watching the door shut, the other Keldos began banging up against the door.

The epiphany hit him like a lightning bolt. He got to his feet as quickly as his flabby bulk allowed and opened the door.

"Get him, kids!" he shouted.

They responded without hesitation. Fred clapped in childish glee as Keldo Seven caught up with Jerry and clamped down on his left thigh. Jerry screamed in hysteric pain. The rest of them joined in and after a moment, one of Jerry's legs was torn off below the knee. It only took a minute before Jerry was shredded into several pieces. After a few minutes of feasting, they looked up at Fred with bloody snouts and pieces of meat hanging from their teeth, as if asking, what now?

Fred smiled. "Come on kids, I have so much to show you."

They followed like obedient children as Fred led them out of the main doors.

The End

APEX

By Jeff Brackett

Patty Huber-Beth peered through binoculars at the building in the clearing ahead of them. It looked so large down here, yet the jungle canopy was easily dense enough to hide them from aerial surveillance. If not for a tangled trail of receipts and deliveries, SAD would likely never have known there was anything amiss this deep in the Bolivian jungle.

But you don't order things like restriction enzymes and genetic sequencers without someone finally noticing. And while the delivery routes were misleading to the point of being labyrinthine, someone had finally traced it all to northern Bolivia. It had taken nearly two years, but Homeland had finally done it.

They, in turn, had turned the situation over to the CIA's Special Activities Division, who put together a Special Operations Group. Highly-trained, unknown, single, they carried non-standard, unmarked equipment. There was nothing that could tie the team back to the US. Officially, they didn't exist.

But with three doctorates in various medical specialties, an emphasis on biological weapons, fluency in five languages, and combat experience with a counter-terrorism team in the Middle-East, Patty was exactly what SAD was looking for.

Lucky me.

She managed not to jump when Luke suddenly appeared beside her, but only because she had grown accustomed to him moving almost silently through the jungle. *That* was what had gotten *him* the job on this operation.

Luke Koster was their expert in jungle survival and warfare. He'd guided the team past obstacles with deceptive ease. Here, a pool of electric eels... there, small eyes atop the water that were the only sign of the caimans beneath.

She shuddered at the memory of him tossing a slab of canned meat into the river just before they hit the landing near their target. The sudden, frantically churning water gave testament to the piranha that awaited the unwary.

But he'd gotten the team to their destination without incident - led them to the edge of the tree line surrounding the target site, then turned the mission over to her.

"I don't mess with that biological shit," he'd said. "It scares the hell out of me."

She scoffed. The idea of his being scared of *anything* seemed ludicrous to her.

"Totally serious," he said. "I've seen the training videos. There's shit that can eat you from the inside out if you so much as breathe it. I'll stick with things I can see and avoid, any day."

That was half an hour ago. Now she knelt in the jungle, examining a suspected terrorist bio-weapons facility the size of a department store... with no hint of movement inside. It made her nervous.

"How's it look?" Luke asked.

"Something's off." She shook her head and they went back to the rest of the team. She pulled her knife and drew a quick sketch in the dirt. "Koster and I are Alpha. We'll take the front entrance here on the west side."

She pointed to JR Handley and Stephen Hunt. "You two are Bravo. Take the emergency door we spotted on the south side."

"Charlie Team"—she pointed to Robert Tillsley and Christopher "Stretch" Michael—"goes in through that open delivery door on the north side."

She checked her watch. "Get in position and suit up."

Everyone groaned, and Patty couldn't blame them. While their chem suits were better than standard military issue, they were still uncomfortable—especially in the heat of the jungle. But she wasn't about to go into a suspected biohazard location without one, either. Especially one with no signs of life. She'd seen worse than the training videos.

Bravo and Charlie teams faded into the jungle as Patty stripped off her tactical vest and weapons. She pulled her chem suit from its carry bag and slipped it on over her clothes before strapping her gear in place over it. Immediately, the cloying heat gathered around her like a sauna. It got worse when she put on her mask and hood.

She keyed her mic. "Alpha actual here. Status and com check."

Beside her, Luke keyed his mic. "Koster here. Ready for go."

Her earpiece crackled. "Tillsley here. Ready."

One by one, the rest reported in. She squared her shoulders. "All right. Hit those doors, gentlemen. Minimal casualties."

Patty aimed a hand-held, high powered laser pointer at the security camera on the outer wall in front of her, temporarily blinding it. Koster ran up and smeared mud on the lens before signaling her to join him. Together, the two of them crouched below the windows and ran for the door without a word.

Koster went in first, automatically going low and right. Patty followed, high and left. She preferred him leading in situations like this. He had far more combat experience than she had. She'd usually been the consultant brought in to clean up *after* most of the action was over. Sure, she'd seen her fair share, but nothing like Koster.

They moved past the lobby, checking hallways, open doors, and behind counters. The place appeared empty. Patty keyed her mic.

"Alpha reporting. Front lobby secured. No hostiles encountered."

"Charlie here. Warehouse secured. No hostiles."

"Bravo here. Still clearing offices, but so far, no hostiles."

Something was very wrong here.

"All right. Secure your position and start testing for contaminants."

***

Once they confirmed clean air, Patty gave everyone leave to remove their masks. She advised them to keep the suits on, though. Easier to put a mask on quickly than the whole suit. The AC on her face was cool and crisp though, a welcome relief from the humid jungle outside.

Ten minutes into clearing the building, Tillsley called in. "Charlie actual for Alpha."

"Alpha actual," Patty replied.

"Alpha, we're back in the warehouse area, north side. We found something you should probably see."

"Can it wait? We're still sweeping for hostiles here."

Tillsley hesitated. "I don't think we're going to find any."

Something in the way he said it caused Patty to stop, for the first time paying less attention to the area around her, and more to the com.

"Say again?"

"You really need to see this. North warehouse area."

"On our way." Patty turned to Koster. "Let's go."

With the size of the place, the walk took a few minutes. She was still tense as she and Koster scanned open doors on their way there, only relaxing slightly when Stretch met them at the warehouse entrance.

He led them through the warehouse, past several large, stainless cylinders. She counted fifteen, each one labeled in small, Arabic script. They were a bit taller than she was, and their presence sent chills up her spine. She'd never seen anything quite like them, and she considered how much weaponized anthrax or ricin could be stored in units that large.

"You scanned for contaminants?"

"Yes, ma'am. Everything came up clean."

13

Patty tried to think of what they could have been making here, to need such large storage canisters. She noted the low hum of electric motors, and wondered how much fuel was left in the generator out back.

Tillsley waited beside a closed door. Patty immediately noted the smears of dried blood on the wall and floor.

"That's a bit disturbing," she said.

"Then you'd better brace yourself." He opened the door. "It gets worse."

The stench of freshly dead bodies hit her hard, and she put her hand to her face. A few feet inside was a large cage, similar to what she'd seen when visiting the zoo back home. The floor was covered with straw... and blood. Inside, just on the other side of the door, was part of an arm. Bloody... mangled... skin hanging in strips, it was still easily identified as what was left of a human arm, from elbow to hand.

She swallowed and forced herself to examine the rest of the enclosure. The cage was large, about forty feet square, surrounded by a walkway. The whole area was enclosed by sturdy steel walls.

"What the hell? Were they keeping a tiger or something in there?" Blood was splattered all over the floor and walls from the cage door to nearly every surface. Ripped, bloody clothing and bones lay in a pile in the corner. "Is that the owner of the arm?" she asked.

"Plus several more people. Looks like this was some kind of den or nest. The bodies have been chewed."

"What?"

He simply nodded confirmation.

Their musing over the remains was interrupted by the chirp of her com. "Bravo for Alpha."

"Go for Alpha."

"We have indications here that someone barricaded themselves in a room. Doors blocked, blood splatters inside. Something definitely went down here."

"Where?"

"Last corridor along the south wall. You'll see us."

"On our way."

She gave quick orders to Tillsley. "Secure this area. No one but our people in or out."

Starting to turn, she remembered her earlier concern. "And check the fuel levels in the generators. I don't want us to lose power to the storage equipment. Last thing we need is for these canisters to lose containment."

"Will do."

Patty signaled Koster to follow and they hurried off to find Bravo Team.

***

They stood in the corridor on either side of a pair of double doors and barely glanced up when Patty and Koster approached.

"What've you got?" Patty asked.

"Doors are barricaded from the inside, but it seems pretty makeshift."

She stepped forward and pulled one of the handles. The doors moved a few inches, then stopped. Peeking through the gap she saw scattered tables and chairs.

"Break room," she muttered.

White walls and cheap white linoleum, except where splatters and pools of crimson marred them. She looked down to see what held the doors closed.

"Looks like some kind of white tablecloth or something tying the handles together," she said, pulling her knife from its sheath. "You pull while I cut."

Handley and Hunt pulled lightly, applying pressure to the cloth as she stuck her blade into the crack in the doors and began to saw.

Koster put a hand on her shoulder. "I can't cover you if you're in my line of fire."

She nodded and knelt as she continued sawing. As the cloth began to give way, the doors spread more and more. Finally, the last of the cloth ripped and the doors swung open. Everyone stopped, scanning the room for danger. Nothing moved.

There was another set of doors on the easternmost wall, and a crimson trail showed where something—*someone?*—had been dragged. A high-pitched electronic alarm wailed from beyond them. It was accompanied by another noise she couldn't immediately identify... a familiar, yet not quite identifiable susurration.

"What the hell is going on here?" Handley muttered.

The four of them approached the doors cautiously. Using his rifle barrel, Handley pushed against the right door. Patty was surprised when it moved easily inward a few inches. She tightened her grip on her own rifle and pushed against the left door. It too moved without trouble. She knelt, signaling Handley to do the same. Koster and Hunt raised their own rifles to the ready.

Patty nodded at Handley and they shoved the doors open. The beeping grew louder and the trail of dried blood continued down the hallway through the shattered glass door at the far end. The blood looked even blacker under the strobing red emergency lights.

She'd seen enough decontamination rooms in her time to recognize the setup. Glass doors and walls made everything inside visible to the outside observer. Bright, blueish UV lights shone in flickering counterpoint to the red strobe, and the previously faint whooshing resolved itself into the hissing of decontamination vents running at full blast. Racks to one side held hazmat suits, similar to the ones she and her team wore.

Patty led them past, into the hall on the other side where another familiar sight awaited—a large room with glass walls and doors. Rows of counters with various instruments and computers extending back to the far side of the room showed a standard clean room setup.

A handset dangled from a phone on the metal doorframe. The room was designed to allow techs inside to work on sensitive experiments without fear of outside contamination. In this case, though, the setup was compromised. *Very* compromised. The glass walls and doors were reduced to cubes of safety glass covering the floor. And that same trail of dried blood led across the room, and through the partially opened door on the far wall.

"Just so you know," Handley hissed, "this shit is really starting to weird me out."

"You and me, both." Patty took a deep, calming breath before jutting her chin at the door. "Let's go."

She led them over the smashed glass and into the room. The klaxon and whooshing fans faded behind them as they followed the trail of blood.

"What about the computers?" Koster asked from behind her.

She glanced at the glowing monitors around the room. Two of them lay on the floor, screens cracked and ruined. There was no way of knowing whether or not the actual computers had been damaged without examining them. But there were several others around the room, screens still lit and functional.

Patty shook her head. "After." She wasn't about to split them up at the moment.

Koster nodded and the four of them stalked cautiously through broken glass and blood. When they reached the door, Patty looked at her group to make sure everyone was ready. Seeing everyone in place, she once more knelt and slowly pushed the door open.

The room beyond was dark, lit only by whatever light streamed in from the clean room behind them.

"Let's get some ligh..." Her words trailed off as she heard the clacking of something skittering across the linoleum in the darkness to her left. As one, they flicked on the LEDs attached to their rifles.

More skittering to the right, and the lights moved as one. A shadow flitted across, dodging deeper into the blackness. It disappeared before she could make heads or tails of it. Then that same noise came again, from at least two other places in the room.

Growing up, she'd had a German Shepherd. This was the sound she remembered from when Max had come running across the kitchen—claws scrabbling for purchase on smooth tile.

The four of them kept swinging their lights around wherever they heard the claws and within seconds the room was a disorienting kaleidoscope of flitting beams of light in inky darkness.

Then a bass thrum came from deeper back in the room—a hollow rumbling grunt, almost like the deep growl of a lion echoing inside a metal drum.

To her right, the fore grip of his rifle creaked as Handley squeezed it tighter. "I think I'm gonna need some new shorts."

Under other circumstances, she might have smiled. As it was, she was just trying to keep her heart rate down.

"Just find the damned lights," she hissed.

Handley moved to the right.

Koster slipped past her and began searching along the wall to her left. He kicked something and Patty jerked her light down to see a beaker go spinning across the floor.

"Sorry." Koster kept his light on the wall behind him, still searching for a switch.

Patty watched him for a few seconds, until a blood-curdling scream caused her to spin back toward Handley. Her attention caught on the light attached to his rifle as the weapon bounced on the floor. Farther to her right, screams took on a liquidy, choking quality in the darkness.

She aimed her light at it and what she saw would haunt her for the rest of her life.

Just ten feet away, four... *somethings* worried away at the screeching Handley as they dragged him across the floor—nightmares of downy fur, slashing claws, and ripping teeth. The instant her light hit them they jerked their heads like a terrier with a rat, removing final bits of meat before they scampered off into the inky black of the room. Handley continued to scream, eyes sightlessly staring into the blackness, mouth spraying blood and saliva.

Patty ran to him. Intestines and blood poured out of bloody slashes and holes in his ravaged suit where the things had forced toothy maws into it... into him. She grabbed Handley's own first aid kit from his vest while yelling orders. "Koster, find that goddamned light! Hunt, you cover us. Shoot anything that moves!"

She drew her knife and sliced away the ribbons of Handley's suit that were in the way. When she saw the damage, she nearly vomited. The things had ripped softball-sized holes into the man's abdomen from which entrails hung in dripping strings. Worse was the other hole where his groin had been.

Patty had been a doctor for too long to have any delusions about Handley's chances of survival. Not here in the field with nothing but a first aid kit to work with. He was already dead. His brain just hadn't realized it yet. But she could take away his pain.

She grabbed a syringe from his kit and plunged it into his neck. Within seconds, his shrieks turned to bloody, sputtering coughs. Finally, he looked at her with recognition. He tried to speak, but nothing but fetid air and a final mist of blood came out. Then the life went out of his eyes.

Koster found the lights just then, and they flickered as they powered on. Another deep growl sounded and she caught flashes of movement as green and brown shapes darted across the back of the room.

Hunt fired a short burst, but the creatures moved too quickly. She saw at least four of them as they zipped between laboratory counters to the north side of the large lab. Patty saw the open door on that wall just in time to see it bounce slightly as the things escaped the lab.

"Where does that door go?" she yelled while mentally retracing her path through the building. The warehouse, maybe?

Shouts and staccato bursts of gunfire told her it was.

The three of them ran toward the clamor.

***

Patty keyed her mic. "Charlie Team, friendlies coming in behind the…" *Behind the what?* "Behind the hostiles. Repeat, we are coming in from behind the hostiles. Do you copy?"

"Copy, Alpha. Be advised, Stretch is down. Hostiles have left through the open bay door."

"Can you close it?" Patty asked as she followed Koster at a dead run past another trashed decontamination room. The gunfire had gone silent.

"I-I think so."

Koster slammed his shoulder into the partly opened door at the end of the short hallway. He immediately stepped out and to the left as Patty took a knee to the right of the door. Hunt took a position just inside, behind Koster. The three of them jerked their rifles back and forth, scanning the room.

Patty and Koster had already seen the warehouse, though not from this angle. They ran between two rows of the cylinders Patty had thought of as storage tanks and found Tillsley staring at a panel to the side of the door. He pressed something and the big bay door jerked and moved upward. He cursed, pressed another button and it stopped. He jammed his thumb on yet another button and the door began to rumble down.

A wet trail of fresh blood caught Patty's eye, and she followed it with her eyes to see a booted foot sticking out from behind one of the cylinders.

Be advised, Stretch is down.

She ran toward Tillsley's teammate, though she was pretty sure she knew what she would find. She'd already seen it with Handley.

Sure enough, the sight was every bit as horrific.

The rumbling of the bay door stopped and she heard the quaver in Tillsley's voice as he asked what they were all wondering.

"What the actual fuck *were* those?"

***

Christopher Michael's finger was still crooked around the trigger of his rifle. He'd gone down fighting, but the mangled mess of his throat precluded any thought of survival. He had to have known, and still he'd fought.

Rather than dwelling on the loss of another teammate, Patty scanned the area, alert for any sign of the creatures that had done this. That was when she saw the furry lump across the aisle lying in a spreading pool of blood.

"Good on you, Stretch," Patty said. "Took one with you."

She crossed the aisle to examine it as Tillsley asked again, "I'm serious. What the—"

"Over here," Patty yelled, interrupting him before he could work himself into a full-blown panic.

Keeping the barrel of her own rifle riveted on the body, she heard the others join her. Patty poked with her rifle, ready to pull the trigger if the thing showed any sign of life.

"What the hell is it?" Hunt asked the obvious.

"Not sure yet." It was a bit larger than a large dog or wolf, and she turned its head to get a good look at its eyes. They were lifeless, and she finally relaxed the tiniest bit. Slinging her rifle behind her back, she reached down to touch the carcass. What she had taken for fur felt different, stiffer... like a cross between fur and porcupine quills. She noted the mouth was full of serrated teeth designed for quickly ripping into prey. The feathered forelimbs looked similar to the wings of a bird, but ended in long, sickle-like claws. Whatever the thing was, it was made to kill.

"Is the area secure?" she snapped.

"The immediate area is," Koster said. "The lobby doors were glass, though."

"Good enough for now. Help me carry this thing back into the lab area. I want to get a better look at it." She turned to Tillsley. "You and Hunt bring Stretch."

To her team's credit, no one questioned or argued. They all grabbed their appointed burdens and carried them into the lab they had only recently abandoned.

The analytical part of her brain estimated the weight of the creature at around a hundred pounds as she and Koster hefted it onto one of the counters. The others did the same with their fallen teammate.

"Where's JR?" Tillsley asked.

"Over there." Patty nodded where she'd left the man.

Tillsley and Hunt went to retrieve Handley's body, while Patty tried to get her shaking hands under control.

After they'd laid Handley on another counter, Koster tapped Tillsley's shoulder.

"We'll secure the front," he told Patty.

She nodded, and turned to Hunt. "How's your Arabic?"

"Fair."

She pointed to a nearby computer. "See if you can find out what the hell they were working on here."

"Wouldn't you be better for that? I mean, bio-chemistry isn't exactly my strength."

"I need to examine the thing Stretch killed. I want to see what we're up against. Just see what you can find. If you run up against something you don't know, call me."

He sat before the computer and began cursing immediately.

"What?" Patty asked.

"Password protected." He reached into a pouch on his vest and pulled out a clamshell case. He withdrew a thumb drive and plugged it into a port on the computer. "Give me a minute."

They all had similar password crackers and decryption tools. He would be in the computer shortly.

She turned to the thing on the counter. At nearly seven feet long from snout to tail tip, almost half its length was tail. Its body was covered with a combination of feathers and thin, quill-like structures. The mostly brown and green coloring was accented by a pair of bright blue bands down either side. Patty pulled the mouth open, careful of the serrated teeth lining its beak. The large eyes suggested it might be nocturnal, and she recalled how they had flinched away when she'd shone her light at them.

She pulled the feathered forelimb up, examining it closely. It wasn't a wing, despite the feathers, and the claws at the end of the limb were more like the spurs of a fighting rooster than anything else she could think of. The same went for the feet, though they were larger and stronger, with deadlier spurs on them.

Feathers, beak, spurs… it seemed to be some sort of bird, but like nothing she'd ever seen before. The tail was wrong. And those teeth?

She shuddered. Bird or not, it was built for killing. Digging through several of the cabinet drawers, Patty found one with surgical instruments. She turned on her digital recorder, gloved up and picked up a scalpel.

"Making first incision…"

***

Koster and Tillsley returned quickly.

"Impossible to really secure the front," Koster said. "Too much glass. We shut every door between here and there, and set squealers in the lobby." He held up a small receiver and placed it on his belt. "If they get in, we'll know."

"Good." Patty barely looked up, concentrating more on the carcass before her. "Why don't you and Tillsley pick a station? Help Hunt dig through the servers here."

"Will do."

He left her to her grisly task.

Koster yelled a few minutes later. "Got something."

Patty turned off her recorder and looked up.

"It's a—" his brows wrinkled as he read, "—Troodon. Says here they found enough DNA in fossils found in Canada and were able to replicate it."

Removing her gloves, Patty went to read over his shoulder. "Pack hunters, most intelligent of the dinosaurs…" Her voice trailed off. *Dinosaurs? This wasn't a new species?* "Holy crap. They managed to recreate dinosaurs?"

Shaking off the mix of anger and admiration for the people who'd managed such a feat, she read farther down the screen. Her Arabic was better than Koster's and she quickly read the description. It definitely fit with what she'd seen when she'd done her necropsy.

After a few minutes, she stopped reading and took off her vest. Setting it aside, she began stripping out of her chem suit.

"Alpha?" Tillsley asked.

She didn't pause. "It's not biochemical they were working on here. No need being any more uncomfortable than we have to."

After a second, she heard the rest of her team following her lead.

Later, Hunt called out, "Got something here, too."

Patty went to his station. On the screen, a chart with a mix of text and numbers appeared. It only took a few minutes of translating for her to realize the implications.

"Shit!" Patty pushed off from Hunt's chair and ran back to the warehouse.

"What is it?" Hunt hurried after her. The others quickly followed.

Patty ignored the blood on the floor as she came to the first container. She read the tag and a chill went up her spine.

"What's going on?"

She ignored Tillsley and ran to the next container. She read that one. Then a third, and a fourth. Each label confirmed her dread.

"What's going on?"

Patty took a deep breath. She pointed at the first container. "Boston."

Pointing at another, "San Francisco."

Pointing at various containers, she went on. "Houston, D.C., Florida, Louisiana. They're all slated for delivery to various cities all over the US."

"So?" Hunt shrugged. "They'll get caught in customs."

"Doesn't matter. They've researched the shipping times. The day after the containers hit customs they're programmed to decant the contents."

"Which is?"

"More fucking Tro-whatsises," Tillsley finished.

Patty ran a hand through her hair. "Each unit contains a male and three females on IV sedatives and nutrients. They're programmed with timers. The timer shuts off the power, which stops the sedatives and releases the magnetics on the door."

"And the Troodons wake up hungry," Hunt finished.

"And that's not even the worst of it."

Koster raised an eyebrow. "It gets worse?"

"When I did the necropsy in the lab," Patty blew a breath out, "The damned thing was gravid."

Tillsley shrugged. "Ah, what's that?"

"Wait a sec," Hunt's voice was nearly frantic. "You think they're all pregnant?"

"The term is gravid, and yes. I think these bastards found a way to create dinosaurs from the fossil record, grow them in a cage, impregnate them, knock them out, and put them in containers for special delivery to the Great Satan."

Koster paled. "Three females per container, twenty eggs each is... sixty eggs per container, times fifteen containers. That's..."

Patty finished the math for him. "Nine hundred."

"Shee-it!" Tillsley paled.

"Yeah," Patty agreed.

"No, not that. I mean, yeah, it's bad. But everything happened so fast. I never got—"

The receiver on Koster's vest suddenly emitted a high-pitched squeal.

"They're in the lobby." His voice was grim as he thumbed it silent.

Patty swung her rifle off her back. "And two of them are full of eggs."

"This day just gets better and better." Koster shook his head and led the way.

***

There were seven closed doors between the warehouse and the lobby. The four went through the last one like the well-trained team they were. Patty and Koster flanked right, Tillsley and Hunt went left.

The glass of the lobby door was scattered across the floor. It crunched beneath their boots as they crept across the room.

Patty whispered into her mic. "Hunt, Tillsley, cover the front. And watch your asses."

"Roger that."

"Koster, let's check the back offices."

No one wasted breath with further discussion. Koster led her around the front counter with a quick glance behind it. He signaled and she covered him as they rushed down hallways, clearing rooms and flipping lights on in any open offices. They were nearly to the end of the fourth hallway when gunfire and screams erupted behind them.

Patty and Koster raced back, sliding to a halt when they reached the lobby. A Troodon stood just outside, watching them. Hunt lay face down in the middle of the floor, the pool of blood beneath him spreading quickly. Tillsley held a hand to the side of his neck, trying to staunch the blood leaking steadily from beneath his fingers.

The Troodon outside whirled, even as Patty and Koster both raised and fired, but they were too late.

So fast!

She looked back at Tillsley. He was still alive, right hand still gripping his rifle as he swung it wildly around the room.

"Tillsley, it's okay," she tried to reassure the wide-eyed man. She needed to see to that neck wound. "It's gone, buddy. Let me take a look—"

Eyes wide, he pointed the barrel in her direction and Patty dove to the floor, knowing she was too slow even as he fired. Inhuman screeches from behind warned her, and she rolled onto her back, instinct tightening her finger on the trigger as the creature fell beside her. It was a mangled mess when it hit; Tillsley, herself, and Koster, all having hit it at nearly point-blank range.

Pack hunters! Patty cursed herself for forgetting what she'd read. *And smart. The one out front was a decoy. If not for Tillsley...*

She pulled her eyes away from the creature on the floor and scrambled to Tillsley's side. Blood seeped down his chin as he tried to speak.

"Don't talk," she ordered, ripping his med-kit off his vest.

But Tillsley slapped the kit away and grabbed her arm. She looked at him and he tried once more to speak.

"Ta...too... late. Ja... jenna... jenner..."

The effort proved to be too much though, and his hand had dropped from the gash in his throat as the last of the life leaked out of him.

"Damn it!"

Koster knelt beside her. "What did he say?"

"I don't know. It didn't make sense. Jenner? Jenna?" As she said it, her heart skipped a beat. "Oh shit."

She stood, checking her rifle as she spoke rapidly. "The generator. I told him earlier to check the fuel level." She swapped the mostly spent magazine for a full one.

"So, did he?" Koster was doing the same, scanning the room and the clearing out front at the same time.

"I doubt it." She forced herself to pull the extra mags from Tillsley's vest. "It was only a few minutes later when everything started going south on us. That's what he was trying to tell me when the squealer went off."

Koster went to Hunt's body, still talking as he stripped the ammo from it. "Then how long do we have?"

"The blood and bodies were at least a day or so old. I would guess these things just got out of their cage yesterday. A generator big enough to run this facility has got to be huge, but I bet it also sucks fuel like a frat boy at a kegger."

"So not long is what you're saying?"

"I'm saying I don't know. Assume it could run out at any time."

They both did a final inspection of their rifles, securing the extra magazines.

"We have two objectives now," Patty said. "First, we top off that generator. Last thing we need is the rest of those things waking up."

"That's for damn sure."

"And second—"

Koster finished for her. "We kill the last of those fuckers and blow this place to hell and gone."

Patty looked outside. "By my count, there's two left. Two of them, two of us."

"Maybe," Koster agreed. "But I also can't help but remember that they've already taken out four of us, so those odds aren't exactly reassuring."

She gave a bitter laugh. "That's why we get the big bucks." One last, calming breath, and she looked at him. "Ready?"

"Close enough."

***

They retraced their steps to the warehouse. The bay door just happened to be the closest access to the generator. Patty knelt in position on one side, as Koster moved to the control panel. "Ready?"

She nodded, and he pressed the button and knelt. They both watched for movement as the rising door revealed increasingly more of the rear of the facility. When it was high enough for them to stand, Koster stopped it.

"Any movement?"

Patty scanned the area. "Nothing."

"You got eyes on the generator housing?"

She slowly peeked her head past the door, almost expecting teeth or claws to come ripping out of nowhere. Nothing happened though, as she got a good view of the outbuilding to the left. "Looks clear."

The two of them exchanged a look.

Patty blew out her cheeks. "Shall we?"

He nodded, and they moved deliberately into the open. Patty took point and Koster walked backward, watching their six. Each of them constantly scanned the area as they moved.

The closer they got to the generator shed, the louder the roar of the motor was. They were just over halfway there when Patty spotted a flicker of a shadow just inside the overgrowth ahead.

"Got something at my two o'clock."

"What?" Koster said.

Patty pressed her mic, almost feeling silly for using the com unit when Koster was close enough to touch. "I said I spotted one at my two."

"Got another behind us." His reply came over her headset.

They kept moving.

"Why are they out now?" Koster asked. "I thought you said they were nocturnal."

"They're light sensitive." She kept her rifle and light scanning through the brush ahead. "That doesn't mean it completely blinds them. And I would imagine we've pissed them off pretty well."

They fell silent, intent on getting to the generator in one piece. Patty fired and missed as she saw the head pop out of the foliage. "Must be the male."

"How can you tell?"

"Brighter colors, and it has a feathered crest. The other two we've seen didn't."

Koster was silent.

They were within thirty yards of the shed, and the roar of the generator was deafening. She had to yell to be heard now, even with the communication gear. "Almost there."

Koster cursed. "I lost sight of my target. How about you?"

She scanned the tree line, looking again for any hint of the male's presence. "I got nothing."

"Damn it. I'd rather we could see where they were."

Patty had to agree, but she was more intent on getting to the shed. To her, that small structure represented shelter. Walking out in the open like this, she felt entirely too exposed.

"Almost there," she said into her mic. "We get in, fuel her up, and—"

A flash of movement was the only warning she had. She looked up just as the thing jumped off the roof of the shed. "Down!" she shouted.

Taking her own advice, she dropped to the ground and raised her rifle. The Troodon hit her shoulder as it went over her, and she gasped at the line of pain it left. Those claws were sharp!

Rolling desperately, she pushed to her knees and saw it zip past her downed partner. *It got him!* Ignoring the pain in her shoulder, she raised her rifle. Then she recalled the lobby.

Pack hunters!

Spinning instinctively, she caught the brightly crested male rushing from behind. She squeezed off a quick burst before it hit her like a linebacker, knocking the breath from her lungs as she dropped again.

Terrified and screaming, Patty shoved her rifle up, trying to keep it between her and her attacker.

Only it wasn't attacking. She felt the warmth of its lifeblood soaking through her shirt, and pushed it aside as she rolled to her knees once more. Her body shook as she scanned all around her, looking for the last of the things. When she was sure it wasn't about to jump her, she scrambled to where Koster lay still on the ground.

Pain in her shoulder and abdomen reminded her she hadn't escaped her attackers either, but adrenaline and fear kept her moving. On hands and knees, she checked her friend.

The deep slashes on his lower back looked bad, but his eyes flicked open suddenly and he screamed when she patted his face. His expression went from surprise, to fear, finally settling on wide-eyed agony as he tried to roll onto his back.

"Hold on, Luke. Let me help."

She reached for him, but he shook his head. "Wait. Just... let me be for a second." He calmed quickly and looked at her. "What the hell happened?"

"The male got you. Looks like those spurs cut you up pretty good."

He started to roll over and groaned. "Worse than you think. I can't feel my legs."

Patty went cold at his words. She didn't know if it was the cuts or the impact, but it was obvious that he had a serious spinal injury. She sat back on her haunches, thinking. Her choices were simple. Move him and risk permanent spinal damage, or leave him where the Troodon would kill him as soon as she was gone. That was a no-brainer.

"All right, we have to get you into the shed." She stood, grabbing his hands. "I need you to watch behind me while I get you up into a fireman's carry."

She pulled up on his shoulders. "Use your arms to..." She stopped, watching in horror as she realized the cuts on his back weren't his only wounds. Warm, sickening weight landed on her boots as her friend's intestines slid out of his abdomen.

Koster paled as he began to lose consciousness. "Aw, fu..." he said, and his eyes glazed over. He was dead in seconds.

Patty screamed her fury at the sky. A flicker of movement to her right gave her something to focus her anger onto. She jumped to her feet, wincing at the wound in her side, but unwilling to let it stop her. It was the last one. It had killed her friend. She would see it dead, or die trying.

***

Patty staggered through the trees, alert for movement. She'd been trying to track the creature for a good fifteen minutes, but Koster was the jungle specialist, not her. At this point, she didn't know if she was hunting it, or it was hunting her. Truth be told, she really didn't care.

But she was slowing. She knew she had to find it soon, or she wouldn't have enough strength to fight back. She stopped to listen once more. The other animals of the jungle were silent, wary of the scents and sounds of her and the Troodon. That suited her just fine. It made it easier for her to hear the monster she sought.

She saw movement, and fired once more into the foliage as she ran after it. But this time, the rifle fired a few rounds, then clicked. She'd left Koster's ammo with him when she chased after the object of her fury and now her rifle was useless. She drew her sidearm with a feeling of despair. Her wound was wearing her down, and she wasn't thinking straight. She had to change the rules.

She was pretty sure she knew where she was, and turned toward the river, hoping her prey would follow. She listened again. Sure enough, a rustle from behind told her it was still stalking her. She fired two shots to keep its interest and jogged toward the river.

Let it think it's herding me. Let it think it's trapped me.

She hoped it would let her get to the riverbank. That would give her a fighting chance. She would at least be able to see it as it came out of the trees. Her pistol seemed unlikely to do enough damage, but it was all she had now. That, and her plan.

Let's see which of us is the real apex predator, bitch!

With that thought, she stumbled out of the dense foliage, the mighty Amazon a mere twenty yards ahead. Putting on a burst of speed, Patty ran toward the water. Leaves and branches broke behind her as her pursuer rushed to catch up.

Pulling up short at the water's edge, Patty knelt and aimed toward the sound. As the snout of the ancient hunter emerged, she fired several rounds. She surprised herself when she actually hit her target twice, and it ducked back into the undergrowth.

Patty could hear it racing through the jungle and she followed its path with her pistol, wincing as the wound in her side flared once more. Then it rushed out at her, and Patty fired again. She couldn't tell if she hit it this time, but it didn't turn away. Her pistol clicked, empty, and Patty drew her knife, waving it defiantly.

"Come on, bitch!"

The Troodon launched itself into the air, and Patty was momentarily taken aback by the odd nature of its attack. It jumped into the air, extending long legs before her. Agonizing spurs pierced Patty's chest even as her knife plunged into its neck.

Joined in combat, bloody, screaming, still slashing at one another, the two of them fell into the Amazon.

***

When the roiling water finally settled, there was nothing left to indicate anything had disturbed the tranquil surface. The piranha were sated with more of a feast than they'd had in quite some time. The sounds of the jungle settled into place once more, disturbed only by the distant motor of the generator that kept power to the lab in the clearing.

Then the generator sputtered and died... and power to the shipping modules shut off. Inside the open warehouse, fifteen tiny clicks announced the beginning of a new era of terrorism.

The End

CULT OF THE CRETACEOUS

By Hunter Shea

Branson Island, just off the coast of Washington State

Adam Wright knew these Seven Seals sons of bitches were crazy, but he hadn't been prepared for this. Five men dead, three more wounded, with one guy from the ATF looking like he wouldn't make it through the night. Not with the left side of his head splattered all over the grass.

We should have moved in sooner, he thought. *Stopped Branson before he had a chance to amass these people and all those weapons.* Shit, he had a friend in The Company who could have gone in, buried a bullet in Jacob Branson's brain under cover of night and slipped away, no one the wiser, a year ago. He knew the bullshit line that the FBI handled matters within the US and the CIA took care of the rest, but sometimes a little cooperation and rule bending were in order. Sometimes people, dangerous people, needed to be "taken care of" with extreme prejudice.

Following the rules, waiting for Branson and his Cult of the Seven Seals to make their move, had cost, by last count, one-hundred and eighty lives. Branson's zombie-eyed followers had left the island four days earlier, planting homemade bombs from San Diego all the way to Seattle. At 3:33 PM (which was half of 666), the bombs had detonated. One was in a busy shopping mall. Another in a packed movie theater. Two had been secured under seats in popular fast food restaurants, while the worst of them all went off under the slide of an elementary school playground. For that alone, Adam wanted Jacob Branson and the murdering pissants who'd planted the bombs not just dead, but to suffer long and hard.

"You can't think about it," he muttered under his breath.

"What's that?" his partner, Jill Cavanaugh said. They were hunkered down behind a bullet-riddled black SUV.

"Just talking myself out of running in there so I can do terrible things to Branson," he said.

Cavanaugh had tied her sandy hair in a ponytail, her face smeared with dirt from when the cult had opened fire on them and they had to hit the deck fast. Her bulky bulletproof vest made her look stocky when she in fact was petite, yet strong. Adam had once lost to her in an arm wrestling match at their favorite watering hole. He didn't use the alcohol as an excuse. She'd nearly torn his arm off by the elbow that night.

"You can run, but you won't get far. You saw what happened to Brooks," Cavanaugh said.

They all had. Agent Adrian Brooks, a fifteen year FBI veteran, had stepped on a land mine. Bits of him could be found everywhere, including the brim of Adam's hat. Cavanaugh had pointed it out, but neither of them had the stomach to brush it off.

Branford Island had been in Jacob Branford's family for four generations. Cut off from the rest of the world, the seven-acre island was accessible only by boat. The FBI had commandeered a ferry to bring the personnel and material to the shore. Now he wished they'd brought some tanks.

It was quiet for the moment, both sides in a ceasefire, the clatter of gunfire still ringing in Adam's ears. Through the whine of tinnitus, he heard birds chirping, oblivious to the horror and stupidity of man in their midst. The sun was out with very little clouds in an azure sky. It was the kind of day custom made to celebrate life, not dance with death.

"We need backup," Cavanaugh said.

"Hell, we need air support. I'll take whatever I can get, so long as this doesn't turn into another Waco."

He'd put a call in for more support right after the first man had been riddled with bullets, dead immediately, but the pouring of gunfire making him twitch and dance for several gruesome seconds. Adam was told it would be a while, considering how difficult it was to get to the island. Until then, his orders were to hold his position and not storm the compound, no matter what.

The silver lining, if you could call it that, was that there was no chance of being swarmed by asshole news crews. Surrounded by the Pacific Ocean, they were far from prying eyes.

Sooner or later, word would get out, though. Which is why Adam had to make sure they did everything by the book.

"I don't hear a thing," Cavanaugh said. She waved a parabolic microphone over the SUV's hood, a headset over her ears. "I mean nothing. Maybe we got lucky and they Jim Jones'd themselves."

Adam massaged his temples, the hot barrel of his gun inches from his tender flesh. "Christ I hope not. Mass suicide is not going to work in our favor. They'll blame us for not saving the kids. We'll be eviscerated for letting it happen."

The last intel report stated that there were at least fourteen children under the age of twelve in the Seven Seals compound. Killing Judas Branson and saving the children ran neck and neck for top priority.

The one order he looked forward to carrying out was to make sure Branson was brought out dead. Charles Manson was finally taking an eternal dirt nap. No one wanted another crazy cult leader hanging around for decades, becoming a minor celebrity, his twisted face on T-shirts and bumper stickers.

He looked forward to putting a bullet deep in Branson's brain, but with the way things were developing, his overriding fear was that there was little chance they could save the children.

For now, all he and everyone else could do was remain behind cover and wait.

And hope the Seven Seals weren't serving up Kool-Aid for lunch.

The absence of a coffee shop or store meant it was a long, hungry night. Cavanaugh's stomach grumbled as the first pink rays of dawn settled over what had become a battlefield. That got Adam's stomach barking in sympathy.

Everyone took turns sleeping in their vehicles, half of the assembled keeping watch in case the Seven Seals loonies wanted to try something under cover of night. It was late spring, but it had been cold as late fall when the sun went down.

"I'd kill for a bacon, egg and cheese," Adam said. His back was stiff, his muscles sore. He'd never understood what the term 'bone weary' meant until now.

Cavanaugh's nose crinkled. "I'd trade in my vegetarian card to have three of them along with a side of hash browns."

Adam had been talking to some of the ATF guys. They'd been told the same as him. Stand down until reinforcements arrived. The question they were all asking was, *When the fuck were they getting here?* The ferry had left with the dead and wounded yesterday. They were essentially trapped out here, handcuffed by their orders. If Jacob Branson knew that, he and his psychos would mow them down like tall weeds.

"You hear that?" Cavanaugh said.

"Yes, you're hungry. We all are."

"No. Listen." She nodded toward the shore that was hidden behind a sea of tall trees.

Riding just under the current of the salty breeze was a low, distant humming. Adam looked around to see a host of heads turning in the same direction.

"Wait here," he said, heading for the shore in a crouch. He was joined by Fred Tavares, the head of the ATF detachment. Fred was long and lean and having an awkward time keeping his head low.

"Hope that's the cavalry," Fred said.

"For us and not them," Adam replied, remembering the data sheet on the cult mentioning that there may have been other Seven Seals cells throughout the Pacific Northwest.

Once they broke through the tree line, it was safe to lift their heads. There was no way a cultist could pop a shot at them all the way on the rocky beach.

"What the hell is that?" Fred said, squinting at the approaching ship, the sun's early rays glinting off the agitated water.

"It's too small to be a battleship," Adam joked. "Never thought they'd send in the Navy."

Fred shook his head. "Nah. That's not Navy. I served for six years."

The vessel steaming its way toward Branson Island was enormous. It looked as wide as an aircraft carrier, though nowhere near as tall. The ocean churned furiously as it plowed across the expanse.

"What are they going to do, blow the crap out of the whole island?" Fred said.

"It would make the problem go away. They could blame it on a freak storm."

Adam knew they weren't going to bomb the island.

At least he thought he knew.

As the ship got closer, Adam could feel the thunder of its engines in his chest. It sounded like….

Crap.

It sounded like the end of the world.

Just what Jacob Branson was hoping to bring about.

Inside the compound, Jacob Branson felt the floor vibrate. He'd fallen asleep in his chair overlooking the great front lawn, an MK-47 on his lap. He'd dreamt of running for the ice cream man when he was a kid in Appleton, Wisconsin. Ice cream. A bowl of strawberry ice cream would make a splendid breakfast.

Eddie Feck, Branson's head of security, came rushing into the room.

"We're sending some people out to see what it is, Father."

Branson closed his eyes, leaned back in his chair and smiled. Oh, he could hope it was the galloping of the horsemen of the Apocalypse, coming to set things right in the world.

If that were the case, he'd best get that ice cream now. Yes, that would make a fine last meal.

The massive ship came as close to the island as it could. Adam and Fred shielded their eyes from the sun, trying to make heads or tails of their new arrival. There were no markings on the gunmetal gray ship, but it was obviously military. No one was on deck that they could see, and sun glare prevented them from peering through the glass in the wheelhouse. The mystery ship did little to alleviate the pall of anxiety that had settled into Adam's bones ever since they'd set foot on this cursed spit of land.

They heard a splash, and a squat aquatic transport vehicle circled out from behind the stationary craft. It rode the waves and came up onto the shore. Adam saw it had wheels so it could easily drive on land.

"Like one of those old duck tour boats," he said.

"Yeah, but newer. Not like those rusty old tubs."

Fred was right. It looked like a mega-Hummer crossed with a speedboat, something unstoppable and fast.

It pulled up beside them, salt water raining off the sides and wheel wells. Adam realized his mouth was open wide enough to swallow a bird, but he didn't care. This was just getting more and more bizarre.

Three men were in the aquatic vehicle, all dressed in black fatigues, all wearing reflective sunglasses, heads shaved so the sun shone off their domes.

They parked the strange multi-purpose craft and hopped over the rail.

The largest of the three, a man with a deep cleft in his chin and a slight dent in the crown of his head, said, "Who's in charge?"

Fred and Adam looked to one another, taken aback by the peculiar grand entrance.

The man shook his head. "That was rhetorical. Gentlemen, you can refer to me as The Wrangler and I'm now in charge of this operation."

The Wrangler? What the hell is this guy on? Adam thought.

"I'll need you to gather your men and move them to the safety of the beach so I can deploy my team."

The two men on either side of him said nothing. They just stared at Adam and Fred, or so it felt like without the benefit of seeing their eyes.

Fred was the first to find his voice, "Look Mr., ah, Wrangler, we don't know who the hell you are…"

"Nor will you know by the time our mission is through," The Wrangler said, cutting him off. "In fact, it will be in your best interest to forget everything you're about to see."

Adam's temper rose. "If you think we'll sit idly by while you kill anyone in that compound that gets in your way, you're crazy. Believe it or not, there are innocent lives in there."

The Wrangler smiled. "That's why we're here. To preserve the innocent and make the guilty pay for their crimes."

Something rumbled within the big ship. The front end lowered itself like a drawbridge. It came to rest in the water, twenty feet or so from the shore. A stiff breeze came in from the ocean, bringing with it a smell so alien, Adam's senses reeled.

"You've heard of shock and awe?" The Wrangler said.

There were shapes, enormous shapes, moving within the shadows of the ship.

"Prepare to meet shock and aw-shit-we're-gonna-die."

Kenny Sikinksi had been with the Seven Seals almost from the beginning. Father Jacob trusted him. He'd climbed a tall evergreen, binoculars to his eyes, watching the bizarre scene unfold. What kind of a ship was that? He hadn't been nervous – not even when he was setting those bombs or shooting at the Feds – until now.

Their actions were meant to bring about the end of man. By killing those society cherished most, hate would harden men's hearts. And when there was nothing left but hate, their Holy Redeemer would cleanse the Earth to start anew with the chosen in Heaven.

What he saw rocked him to his core, whipping his brain into a state of confusion that threatened to rip his mind in two.

The abominations coming out of that boat couldn't be. Not if they were in league with the sinners. He scrabbled down the tree, heart thudding, running as fast as he could to the main house.

Cavanaugh had left her post along with a couple of ATF men, leaving plenty behind to keep an eye on things.

"What the hell's going on?" she said, sidling up next to Adam. He didn't answer. He just pointed. Cavanaugh's jaw dropped and she took a step back. "Holy Christ."

Adam was beyond words.

Five monsters ambled out of the ship, splashing into the water. Adam didn't know whether to run, scream, or start shooting. Or just plain old shit himself.

The squat bipeds were almost as large as elephants, though low to the ground and wearing what looked like an armored turtle shell. The shells were dotted with huge lumps. They had near triangular heads with ridges of more bumps and tails like clubs. At varying shades of amber and gray, they looked strangely familiar.

The Wrangler watched a team of men lead each of the beasts to the shore, his hands on his hips, smiling.

"What the hell are those things?" Adam asked.

"Hell is where I'm hoping our little holy roller will think they came from. What you're looking at there are five living, breathing tanks. You liked dinosaurs as a kid, didn't you?"

Adam was too stunned to answer.

"Of course you did. Those are ankylosauria, some of the last dinos to roam the Earth. They're built like brick shit houses dipped in titanium and can move incredibly fast." He pointed at a tan dinosaur, the largest of them all. "That there is my personal ride. I call him Andy, but I don't think he likes it."

What fresh lunacy had Adam stepped into? Dinosaurs? A man who called himself The Wrangler looking as happy as a kid on his birthday, saying he called one of those things Andy? Adam wondered if he'd been shot in yesterday's firefight and was hallucinating in some hospital. In fact, he hoped that was the case.

"Those can't be dinosaurs," Cavanaugh said.

The Wrangler snorted. "They can, and they are."

"That's impossible," Fred said, looking to Adam for confirmation. "Right?"

Adam would have agreed if the mind-bending proof wasn't headed their way, the stench of them ripe and wild enough to make his eyes water. He vaguely recalled drawings of ankylosauria from books in school. At the time, they were nowhere near as cool as a T-rex or triceratops, so they hadn't held his interest.

Well, he was interested now.

He noticed each lumbering dinosaur wore a metal collar around its incredibly thick neck. Their dark, hooded eyes had the look of disinterested cows, though it didn't make them seem any less threatening.

Cavanaugh, who had never been speechless before, had gone mute. Adam saw her hand reaching for his, not out of affection but he assumed to ground her to something real and assuring.

"Why?" Fred asked.

The Wrangler pushed his glasses up the bridge of his nose. "Because we can. Because my Anky Squad will change the face of warfare. Bullets can't penetrate their hides. These puppies are armor plated all around. Not that they'll take on much flak. Once people see us riding herd on them, they'll drop their weapons, crap their pants and either faint away dead or head for the hills. No matter what, problem solved."

Adam bit the edge of his tongue just to shock himself, clear his head. "Who the hell sent you?"

"That's for me to know and you not to find out. Now, you want us to clean up your mess? Like I said earlier, clear a path."

Adam, Cavanaugh, Fred and his men wisely scampered when the behemoths stomped toward the trees. Adam and Fred got on their walkies, alerting everyone to clear the hell out and ask no questions. Trees cracked like tiny toothpicks as the ankylosauria lumbered through them.

"Is any of this for real?" Cavanaugh said, her voice soft and thin.

Adam stared at the marching Anky Squad. "I honestly don't know."

The Wrangler had been waiting for this day for two years, ever since the resurrected ankylosauria had come to maturity. Two years of intense training and prep work, losing many men in the process due to the irritable nature of the beasts. The steel rings around their necks were the granddaddy of all shock collars, and two years of conditioning had gotten his ankies under his control.

Ankylosauria, when they had roamed the planet during the Cretaceous period, were docile herbivores. When their DNA had been rescued and tinkered with for this project, their nature had been deliberately altered. You can't have war machines that just want to graze on plants. These ankylosauria loved meat – the rawer the better. Their newfound aggression made them tougher to break than a wild bronco, but The Wrangler had persevered. He had that dent in his skull and a metal plate to thank them for. He didn't begrudge them his injuries. They were just animals, after all.

His very special animals.

If all went well here, they were on to the Middle East next, then North Korea. The cat would be out of the bag and the world would tremble.

"Hand me the bullhorn," he said to one of his men. He'd mounted Andy, sitting in a custom made saddle behind one of the armored lumps. Wearing his own bullet-proof armor, rider and beast could ram the compound with zero fear. The bullhorn came to life with a sharp whine. "Attention morons of the Seven Seals, especially Jacob Branson! You have one minute to put down your weapons and leave the compound. Failure to comply will result in, well, you seriously don't want to go there."

He hoped the cult idiots couldn't see his ankylosauria lined up and ready to roll. He'd kept them behind the tree line on purpose. The dinosaurs had crushed a few of the SUVs by accident, making a hell of a racket. The casualties of war. Jacob and his band of spaced out freaks couldn't have missed the deafening crunching of metal and glass. They had to be wondering what was going on.

The Wrangler stared at his watch.

Thirty seconds to go.

Jacob Branson gathered his family into the walled-in courtyard. Everyone was accounted for, all two hundred and five souls. Many looked frightened, but there were a lot of smiling faces as well. The entire family was armed, including the children. This is the day they'd been waiting for.

Taking a deep breath, his eyes twinkling with purpose and anticipation, he addressed the crowd. "Brother Kenny has reported to me that the beasts from the pits of hell have been conjured up to test us. These demons have been sent to put our faith on trial. They want you to bow before Satan's lapdogs, to denounce all you believe in, to give up your right to eternity in Heaven. Now, are you going to let that happen?"

Half the family gave a soft, "No, Father."

Branson wagged a finger, his eyes cast to the sky. "I'm afraid that's not good enough. I want you to say it so Jesus himself can't ignore the choir of the chosen. Now, are you going to let a few simple demons frighten you into abandoning your rightful place in paradise?"

This time, they all heartily shouted, "Never, Father!"

Now he smiled. "That's what I want to hear. We all know that the man upstairs loves a martyr above all others. You think Joan of Arc is treated the same as Joan, the pious little biddy who went to church every day of the week? No sir. Joan of Arc can pick up the phone and Jesus will answer no matter what time of day or night. Joan of Arc may have been burned to ashes on Earth, but in Heaven, those ashes rise above all others. After today, not only are you going to be safe and warm and happy beyond all measure in the Kingdom of God. No! You are also going to be in that special place, basking in the close comfort of He who has given and shall taketh away."

"Amen, Father," several women in the front chanted, their eyes closed and guns raised to the sky.

"You hear the voice of man's destruction on that bullhorn, asking us to lay down our arms? What say you to that?"

"No!"

"What say you?"

"No!"

"Okay then. Let's show those demons the misfortune of their ways."

A round of cheers exploded in the courtyard. Even the young ones were gleeful to defy the demons and claim their reward.

Jacob Branson licked his lips, tasting the remains of strawberry ice cream that had crusted there. He couldn't wait to taste Heaven's own strawberry ice cream. He bet it was better than even Ben & Jerry's.

The chorus of happy voices and chanting gave The Wrangler pause. These fucks were really more than a sandwich shy of a picnic basket.

On the other hand, he understood the palpable glee that preceded battle. Those moments before a fight always brought a tingle to his groin. He was humming so hard at the moment, he had to adjust the crotch of his pants.

He turned to the other riders of his Arky Squad. "Looks like they've chosen the hard way."

Four heads nodded. The Wrangler hated small talk or bravado speeches. Today, they would let the ankylosauria do all the talking. The beasts had grown restless from the echo of shouting across the meadow. One of them had to be shocked several times to keep it from breaking cover. The Wrangler spotted a section of what looked to be raw meat in the tall grass. He assumed it had been part of one of the men that had stepped on a land mine.

"Sir."

The Wrangler tore his attention from the ragged slab of beef and looked down at Simpson, his personal assistant. Simpson lifted his bullet-proof helmet up to him. "Come back safe."

Reaching out for Simpson, The Wrangler pulled him close and kissed him long and hard. "Get ready to celebrate."

Simpson hopped down from Andy and scooted to get his camera. They were going to capture every moment of this wonderful victory as proof that the Arky Squad was ready for worldwide deployment.

Looking over at the other riders, The Wrangler simply shouted, "Mow 'em down!"

Pushing a button embedded in the saddles' pommels, the ankylosauria roared, thundering forward.

Adam and Cavanaugh couldn't just idly sit by and not see what the hell was going on. When the dinosaurs cried out, his heart had stopped. The ground shook so much, he thought there was an earthquake.

"Let's go," he said to Cavanaugh.

Everyone else seemed content to stay back. There was a fear of seeing and knowing too much. Out here, in the middle of nowhere, it was easy to be made to disappear. A full-grown man wouldn't be more than one bite for one of those ankylosauria.

Adam sprinted through the trees, Cavanaugh on his heels. He gave a start when he saw the flattened SUVs. The dinosaurs were galloping toward the compound, kicking up clods of dirt the size of baseball infields. The first land mine went off under one of them but didn't harm it or slow it down one bit.

"They're going to kill all of them," Adam said. "This isn't about tactics. It's about showing how unstoppable they are."

A team of men had set up high-powered cameras, recording everything.

Cavanaugh had taken her gun out, but they both knew there was nothing she could do. "Jesus Christ, Adam, the kids."

When Jacob Branson saw the creatures powering toward them, he nearly wept with joy. Proof that his family had succeeded was right before him. Yes, faith was a wonderful thing to have, but validation was ecstasy.

Great and powerful explosions sent plumes of flame and fury into the air as Hell's creatures marched onward, unscathed by the meager weapons of man. The men he'd sent to the outer perimeter fired at will. Bullets did nothing but create shiny sparks when they hit the demons. Atop each one was a rider clothed in black, equally impervious to their firepower.

Revelation foretold that there would be four horsemen of the Apocalypse.

Today, at the edge of a new world, Jacob counted five.

He wondered if the devil himself had decided to go for a ride.

Oh, to face the devil like old Daniel Webster. What an exquisite moment that would be. He bet Jesus would share a bunk bed with him for doing such a thing. Grabbing as much ammunition as he could, Jacob Branson left the dwindling safety of his house and rushed to meet his destiny.

The Wrangler whooped with rage and bloodlust. The concussion of tripped landmines hammered his eardrums. Bullets zipped everywhere. One pinged off the side of his helmet, stunning him for a brief moment.

These Seven Seals ass hats weren't running away, but no matter. It was more fun watching his ankylosauria mow them down…and then some.

He could feel the bellows of Andy's lungs between his legs. The dinosaur rolled on like a force of nature. They came upon the first group of men, firing from a narrow trench. The ankylosauria first stomped them into paste, and then paused to feed. Eating the remains didn't take more than a few seconds. The Wrangler hit the button and urged Andy onward.

A rocket propelled grenade exploded above the head of the ankylosauria to his right. Its rider, the quiet and brooding Graymoor, shattered into a pink mist. A riderless ankylosauria was going to be a problem, but one they could deal with later.

The Wrangler hunkered down, taking cover behind the armored lump on Andy's back as they got closer to the compound. His bullet-proof material had its limits. It was up to Andy now.

A stream of cultists popped out from behind bales of hay that weren't fooling anyone. The ankylosauria went straight for them. The one that was on its own stopped in the midst of a crowd of a dozen men and women, all firing point blank at it. The ankylosaurus swung its club-like tail in a wide circle, crushing chests and heads. It bent its head to munch on the bodies, the survivors having run out of bullets, bashing it with the stocks of their guns.

These people were fucking crazier than The Wrangler thought. He didn't see an ounce of fear in their eyes.

Spurring Andy on, he took the lead. He wanted to be the first to break down the walls of the compound. The cult leader had to be in there somewhere. It would be fun to watch Andy reduce him to crimson tapioca.

Bullets rained down on the Arky Squad. The cultists had taken to the rooftops and windows, saving their most high-powered weapons for last. The Wrangler felt the impact on his shoulder, almost knocking him out of his saddle. All around him, ankylosauria were seeking the source of the annoying gunfire out and squishing people, replenishing their stores of energy with blood and bone and meat.

The wall, about six feet high and made of white-painted brick, was coming up fast. The Wrangler braced himself. Andy lowered his head and surged through the obstacle as if it weren't there. Brick and mortar blasted in every direction, creating a smoke screen of dust. The Wrangler heard the other ankylosauria tear down the rest of the wall.

Andy stopped.

"What the hell are you doing?" The Wrangler shouted, his voice echoing within the helmet. He hit the button. The ankylosaurus didn't move.

They had done countless drills in smoke-filled fields before and there had never been a problem. He touched the comm mic on the side of his helmet.

"Status!"

"She's refusing to move."

"Goddammit, I'm taking –"

The ankylosauria may have stopped, but the gunfire hadn't. From the sound of things, they now had two rogue dinosaurs.

What was going on?

The thud of bullets thwacking his armor brought flares of pain to multiple parts of The Wrangler's body. Daring to look over the armored lump, he saw the dust swirl, clearing.

Sweet baby Jesus.

Adam and Cavanaugh had commandeered one of the remaining SUVs. He did his best to follow the rutted path of the dinosaurs, hoping they had tripped most of the landmines. The strange men who were filming the debacle didn't even try to stop them.

Cavanaugh said, "I guess we make for compelling viewing."

The SUV's shocks cried out as Adam drove straight into a cavity created by the ankylosauria.

"I hope they get this," he said, thrusting his arm out and giving them the finger.

They saw the compound's wall shatter like brittle plaster. It was a fucking nightmare. They rattled past bloodstains in the torn up soil that had once been human beings.

He started to wonder just what he was hoping to accomplish. They couldn't stop those beasts, and they couldn't save anyone in that compound.

But he needed to do something. Sitting back and watching – or filming – was inhumane.

This time, Cavanaugh did grab his arm. The pain shocked him out of his troubled thoughts.

They were almost there.

Standing before The Wrangler and Andy was a line of children. None of them could be older than twelve. They pointed weapons at the dinosaur, utterly unafraid.

The ankylosauria remained stock-still, refusing to touch the children.

Yes, the dinosaurs had been bred to be vicious killing machines, a guarantee that America would be the mightiest military power on Earth, bar none. But their creators had also been hyper aware of public relations. Civilian casualties had always been a by-product of war. However, if they could train the ancient dinosaurs not to harm children, well, that was one less cry in the crowds of liberal sissies that would inevitably protest the program. Save the children, save the future. A future where Uncle Sam controlled all.

The only problem was, children were supposed to run from the savage beasts. Not these cult crazies. They were more curious than frightened.

And they stood between The Wrangler and the remaining Seven Seals.

The Wrangler pressed the button over and over, trying to shock Andy into at least barreling forward, the pain making the dinosaur forget that there were non-targets in its path. So what if there were some squished kids? With the way they were looking at pure death, they were lost anyway.

Andy, nor any of the other ankylosauria, moved.

The shooting had stopped.

The children stared the dinosaurs down.

This couldn't be happening.

One of the children pointed at the house and the others stepped to make way for Jacob Branson. The Wrangler knew the man's face well from his dossier.

"And the meek shall inherit the Earth!" Jacob Branson proclaimed. He had several military grade guns slung over his shoulders and a belt of grenades at his waist. He touched the top of each child's head as he walked among them. "Mighty Goliath was no match for David. I should have known. Amen, I should have known."

The Wrangler dug his heels into Andy's side but he knew the ankylosaurus couldn't even feel it. If Andy wouldn't move forward, at least he could retreat until they formed a new plan.

A new plan.

It was always about brute force and fear.

When there was no fear and brute force had come to a standstill, what was left?

A little girl, no more than five, approached Andy, her palm up to touch his lowered muzzle.

She was petting it!

Jacob Branson grinned. "It seems you've lost, Old Scratch. The day of righteousness is here."

With a wave of his arms, the armed cultists on the roof opened fire.

"No!" The Wrangler shouted, though Jacob Branson would not be able to hear him.

Out in the open, The Wrangler was a sitting duck. His body was pounded by round after round, until his armor finally gave way.

When the black riders were dead, Jacob signaled for a ceasefire.

He looked to the children. "You've done a wonderful job, my sweet children. God has truly blessed you. I promise, you will be the first to be taken into his Kingdom."

Little Randy smiled, his top front teeth missing.

"Now run along while I send these vile beasts back to Hell."

The children dropped their weapons and scattered, hopping over dead people and picking their way through the rubble of the wall. They'd been taught to wait in the field for the divine light of Heaven to claim them. They were excited to finally be taking their trip.

Jacob Branson felt powerful. Almost as powerful as Jesus himself.

And now he would look the demons in the eye and cast them out. They were unclean filth and it was apparent there was no place in this new world for them.

"You have lost!" he shouted, arms upraised. "Back to the fires of Hell with you!"

The demeanor of the beasts suddenly changed. The one before Jacob blew out a great gust of foul smelling air through its wide nostrils. It glowered at him with eyes black as the pits of damnation.

With a flick of its head, a head that was harder than steel, Jacob's chest was caved in, his body flying through the air. He smashed into the exterior of the house, broken ribs rupturing his lungs.

The demons charged as one, bringing down the compound. Jacob felt and heard the carnage, but he couldn't look. His family screamed in agony. Some prayed to God. Others seemed to take great delight in their deaths.

Crumpled against one of the remaining upright walls, Jacob Branson did not want to die. Not this way. Where was the light of Heaven? Where was Jesus?

There was only madness and death here.

He opened an eye, stinging with dust, and saw a demon hovering over him.

He didn't feel a thing as it consumed him whole.

Cavanaugh had gathered the children, taking as many as she could in the SUV and heading back, away from the insanity in the compound. Adam stayed with two boys and a girl, waiting for Cavanaugh to return. He didn't dare try to walk with them across the field for fear of tripping more landmines.

One of the ankylosauria was visible in the haze of smoke and fire and dust. It reared its head and bleated. He thought he saw someone's leg in its mouth.

"They're so nice," the little girl said.

Adam knelt down so he was eye-to-eye with her. She had beautiful blonde curls and wide, green eyes.

"Who's nice, honey?"

"The demons. They're taking mommy and daddy to Heaven."

Andy shivered.

The End

NO TEARS LEFT IN THE FLIPSIDE

By Jake Bible

"More tracks here," Fish and Wildlife Service Officer Jennifer Loch called out as she stared at the prints in the mud. "Morgan? I have more here."

Jennifer paused, listening to the strange calls of animals she didn't recognize. Her job had been to help track down a long list of tourists that had gone missing in what should have been the western edge of Yellowstone National Park. The military, the Forest Service, FBI, state and local law enforcement, everyone was out trying to figure out what had happened to the one hundred square mile area.

Because it certainly wasn't Wyoming anymore.

Wyoming didn't have giant ferns or trees with thirty foot circumferences. The state also didn't have creatures straight out of the Natural History Museum. Prehistoric creatures that resembled dinosaurs.

Dinosaurs. Dino. Saurs.

But that mission, the rescue mission, was long gone. All Jennifer wanted to do was get out of the prehistoric Hell and back to normal Wyoming. And getting out was proving harder to do than it should have been. The radios weren't working and compasses were more than slightly off.

The only saving grace was the boot prints left by the military squads that had cut through the area. Rangers or SEALs, she didn't know. All she cared about was the fact there were boot prints. And she knew how to follow boot prints.

Jennifer prayed those prints would lead out of the nightmare and not farther in.

National Park Service Ranger, Morgan Herschel, jogged up to Jennifer's side, his eyes cast down at where she was pointing.

"Boot prints. Thank God," Morgan said. "Finally more tracks."

"Which means we may be close to getting out of here," Jennifer said as she crouched and put the tips of her fingers to one of the prints. Still soft. "We're maybe a couple hours behind."

"They're going the wrong way," Morgan said. "Why are they going in? They should be going out."

"You sure?" Jennifer asked.

"Yeah," Morgan replied. He pointed. "They came from there and that's out. I'm sure of it."

Jennifer stood back up and glanced the way they'd come. She was visualizing the strange dome that encompassed the one hundred square miles they'd been tasked with searching. Air, light, people, vehicles could easily pass through the dome. It was like a shimmer of light more than an actual physical dome.

"They're not looking for us," Jennifer said. "They have a mission."

"Who cares?" Morgan replied. "We're following the tracks out, not in. They can have whatever mission they want."

A crash and crunch from their right made them freeze and duck down low. Morgan was older than Jennifer, in his mid-forties as opposed to her mid-thirties, but he clutched at her arm like he was a young child afraid of the dark.

The earth shuddered and Jennifer put a finger to her lips. Not that Morgan needed to be told to be quiet. His lips were sealed and he was trying to breathe as quietly as possible.

The earth shuddered again and Jennifer closed her eyes, trying to visualize what could possibly be large enough to make the ground shake. Her mind, her memory, her ability to extrapolate data from images, was why the FWS paid her to do what she did.

Track.

Every small bit of information helped her track down large predators: bears, wolves, mountain lions. But as the ground continued to shake, Jennifer had no illusions as to who was being tracked. They were. And the predator tracking her and Morgan was much, much larger than a bear or wolf or mountain lion.

Much larger.

Morgan's eyes were huge in his head. Jennifer studied his face, worried he was having an embolism or stroke. Then his huge eyes met hers and all she saw was pure terror. He was more afraid than she'd ever seen any living creature before. Then the look in his eyes shifted and she tried to grab at him before he could do what she feared he would do.

"Hey!" Morgan shouted, jumping up and out of Jennifer's reach, his arms waving over his head. "Hey! Over here!"

Every instinct in Jennifer's body told her to stop him, to get up and grab him. But since entering the strange world that had appeared in the middle of the real world, Jennifer had learned to tell her instincts to take a flying leap. Her instincts were honed in a world without ten-ton predators.

Like the one that crashed through the foliage and came to a grunting stop only a few feet from Morgan.

Jennifer wasn't a paleontologist. She couldn't identify the creature with any certainty. Maybe a T-Rex? Maybe something like a T-Rex? It certainly was close to the images she'd grown up seeing. But with more color and…life. So much more life.

The game of trying to figure out the species was a coping mechanism Jennifer had developed over the past few days. Focus on the creature, not on the victim.

Morgan was snatched up in the beast's mouth with a loud *whomp* then *crunch*.

There were no tears from Jennifer. Morgan had been the sixth member of her search party to die at the teeth of one of the anomaly's carnivorous monsters. That meant only she and Hackson still lived. She assumed. Jennifer had no idea where Hackson was anymore.

Crunch. Crunch. Crunch.

Jennifer remained as quiet as the little mouse she basically was compared to the beast only a few feet away, her breathing slow and silent. If she cried, let loose with even a small sob, the monster would whittle the party down to only Hackson. So she sucked back the tears and waited as the beast chewed, chewed, chewed, then swallowed Morgan down. Then she waited another five minutes after the dinosaur lumbered past, its tongue licking its lips, content with the meal that had offered itself up.

With trembling hands, Jennifer pushed back the long sleeve of her shirt and checked her watch. It had stopped. She had to guess that maybe twelve hours had passed since she abandoned the campsite her party had set up. She had no idea how long was left to find her way out before the military came in with all guns blazing.

The Army already had their hands full keeping the prehistoric creatures from escaping out into the real world. Jennifer had been told in no uncertain terms that once they were given the go ahead, it was going to be a scorched earth situation. Any survivors left would be wiped out along with the massive creatures that were constantly testing the perimeter the Army had set up around the shimmering dome.

Eyes averted to the bits of Morgan that lay scattered in the dirt and mud, Jennifer focused on the boot prints, took several deep breaths, then pushed on, determined to find the way out.

Having her 30/30 rifle on her would have helped with the climbing anxiety that threatened to overtake her, but she'd run out of ammo for the weapon a few days back. She hadn't expected to use up so many rounds when she'd first been trucked inside the dome. But she also hadn't expected pretty much anything that had happened so far.

There was a loud trumpeting from off to her right, exactly the direction the boot prints had come from, and where Jennifer was headed. Jennifer paused, listened hard, then stopped herself from jumping when the trumpeting echoed through the forest once more.

She'd learned enough to know that the trumpeting was not from a carnivore, but that didn't mean she was safe. The herbivores were almost as aggressive. They weren't looking to eat her, but a good mortal trampling wasn't out of the question. So far, every creature she'd come in contact with was viciously territorial. Emphasis on the vicious part.

More trumpeting, closer.

Jennifer stepped off the path the owners of the boots had made and ducked down behind what she guessed might be a palm. Or banana plant. Or something that couldn't be defined.

The ground shook with heavy footfalls then stilled. A small trumpeting. More footfalls. Another small trumpeting. Then a loud trumpeting from a long way off to Jennifer's right.

Footfalls, pause, footfalls, pause, small trumpeting.

Jennifer knew that pattern. It was pretty much the exact pattern that all young used no matter the species.

Her guess was confirmed as a snout appeared, shoving a huge fern to the side on the opposite side of the boot print path. It snorted and sniffed then revealed itself, pushing past the massive fern and out onto the makeshift path.

The creature was in the ankylosaurus family, or something close to it. Maybe three feet high at the shoulder and ten feet long from nose to tail, the creature turned to the side, revealing its armored back and horned head. It put its beak to the ground and sniffed long then bleated like an angry goat, took several steps back, bleated again, spun in a circle, which destroyed much of the foliage around it as its mace-tipped tail shredded half the plants.

Jennifer was barely able to scramble backwards as the tail came within inches of taking her head off. She gasped at the shock then clamped a hand over her mouth.

The young ankylosaurus froze in place, its nostrils wide, scenting the area.

Then it turned its head and locked eyes with Jennifer.

She screamed, got to her feet, and ran. The young ankylosaurus did the same, heading in the opposite direction.

But Jennifer didn't know that. All she knew was a creature that weighed as much as a bull elephant had spotted her. That meant she needed to run before the much larger mother of that huge creature arrived. And Jennifer moved.

She ran and ran, her legs pumping and lungs burning, as branches and fronds whipped against her face. She held her arms up to protect herself, but it was close to futile considering the density of the forest she was in.

On she ran.

Until she ran out of ground.

Jennifer screamed as her legs kicked against nothing but air and her arms pinwheeled. A sound she hadn't noticed before was suddenly quite clear as she went tumbling straight down, only an arm's length away from a waterfall that should not have existed.

The water was ice cold and all air was forced from Jennifer's lungs as she hit the frothing, foaming pool below.

She fought against the weight of the waterfall and managed to get clear of the pressure beating down at her from above.

Then she nearly froze.

She saw shapes. Definitely shapes. Swimming towards her, mouths open, teeth bared.

Close to drowning, Jennifer unfroze and scrambled to the surface, her arms reaching, her legs kicking, her lungs burning.

Sweet air hit her face and something very wrong hit her legs. Pain shot up from her right calf, almost blinding her in its intensity. Pain from her left calf joined the horror show. Jennifer kicked hard, trying to knock away whatever had attacked her. She felt her legs move, but didn't feel anything connect.

The river's current was taking her away from the pool and the waters around Jennifer were turning red with her blood as she desperately tried to paddle to the shore.

She screamed as she felt her right knee collapse under the weight and force of a jaw that had to be as long as she was tall.

"Here!" a voice shouted and Jennifer was briefly distracted from her agony by the end of a rope smacking her right between the eyes.

She focused on the rope and grabbed it with her left hand. Her shoulder was almost pulled from its socket as the rope was yanked tight and she was quickly dragged through the water to the shore.

"Jesus! Look at that thing!" a second voice shouted.

"Do not move," a man said close to Jennifer's ear as she was dragged up onto shore.

Jennifer couldn't have moved if she wanted to. Her body was an icicle, shivering uncontrollably. Her arms were dead tired and her legs were…maybe not there.

Gunfire erupted around her and the pain in her knee grew worse, if that was even possible. Then the weight and pressure were gone. The gunfire stopped and several hands lifted her away from the river and carried her to the cover of a copse of trees close to a low berm of grass and dirt.

"What's your name?" a man asked, his face coming into Jennifer's blurry view. "Lady? You got a name?"

"FWS Officer Jennifer Loch," she replied.

The man smiled. "Hello, FWS Officer Jennifer Loch. Officer? Not Special Agent?"

"I don't do investigations," Jennifer replied just before a scream burst from her lips.

She thrashed and looked down to see another man tending to her legs. Most of which were no longer attached to her body except by thin strands of bloody sinew and tendon.

"Oh God…" she gasped.

"Sorry," the first man said.

He pushed on her shoulders and held her down. Two more men appeared and grabbed her arms then another pressed on her hips.

"Go ahead and scream," the first man said. "The dinos already know we're here."

Then the man at the ends of her legs lifted a machete and brought it down swift and sure.

Jennifer lost consciousness after the second whack.

***

The sun had set and it was full dark when Jennifer came to. Her first instinct was to scream. The hand clamped over her mouth stopped that immediately. The face of one of the operators came into view with a finger to his lips. Jennifer nodded. It hurt to nod. It hurt a lot.

That pain brought back a memory and she almost did start screaming, but the man's eyes locked onto hers and she knew that if she screamed, she'd get them all killed.

The ground shook slightly. Whatever was lumbering by wasn't too close. But close enough that the operators were all taking defensive positions, their rifles to their shoulders.

As soon as the unseen beast was for sure gone, the operator removed his hand from Jennifer's mouth.

"Castor," the operator said, nodding at her. "Jennifer, right?"

"Yes," Jennifer said, her voice a shaky squeak. She glanced in the direction of her legs, but didn't dare take a real look. "How bad?"

"Down to business. Good," Castor said. "You've probably saved a few campers in your day and know that panic is one way to hurry up and die."

"Hunter," Jennifer said. "I hunt predators."

"So do we," one of the other operators said. "Garfield."

"Nimm."

"Stackhouse."

"It's hard to see. Four of you?" Jennifer asked, her voice giving out on the last word.

"Here," Castro said and tipped a canteen to her lips.

Jennifer drank enough water to quench her thirst, but not too much to make her sick despite still being unbelievably thirsty.

"Four, yeah," Castor replied.

"What branch?"

"No branch."

"Private military contractors?"

"Private, yes. Military? At one time. Contractors? No. We have full time jobs and you're looking at it."

"Who do you work for?" Jennifer asked, confused.

"Someone that has enough money to send us in here without batting an eye. And enough tech to keep us connected."

Castor pointed to his ear and smiled.

"We have a rendezvous we need to get to in twelve hours. You up for being carried? It's going to be more painful than probably anything you've ever experienced and we can't risk you screaming. Understood?"

"Yes," Jennifer replied. "I can take pain."

"Morphine will help," Stackhouse said from his position. "We have plenty."

"I can take pain," Jennifer said more firmly, then fixed her attention on Castor. "You never answered my question."

"Right leg is gone from mid-thigh down and left leg is gone below the knee," Castor answered matter of factly. "Stackhouse is our medic and he has you fixed up as well as anyone can be fixed up in a place like this."

"Thank you," Jennifer said to Stackhouse.

"You bet," Stackhouse replied.

"You ready for the bad news?" Castor asked.

"Jesus..." Jennifer responded and squeezed her eyes closed tight. "Hit me."

"No stretcher," Castor said. "We have a collapsible one, but it's way too bulky to use and still navigate this damn forest. You're gonna be a sack of potatoes for the next eleven clicks. With no screaming. Can you take that kind of pain?"

"You said there's morphine, right?" Jennifer asked.

"Plenty," Stackhouse replied.

"Then I can take it," Jennifer said to Castor. Her brows knitted together. "Wait...eleven clicks? The perimeter is farther than eleven clicks."

"Not going to the perimeter," Castor said. "We're going to our rendezvous point. A landing zone for a very fast helo."

"A chopper? But all of our vehicles broke down in less than a day when we came inside this dome," Jennifer argued. "And you have comms too? Radios stopped working just as fast as the vehicles. No tech is working."

"Let's just say our employer is very tech savvy and heard about what was happening before sending us in," Castor said. "We have access to equipment that hasn't seen the light of day yet. Which is why our employer sent us in. Test the equipment and gather intel."

"And also so you can help with the rescue effort, too, right?" Jennifer said.

"Yeah, not so much," Castor said. "Mostly because there is no one to rescue."

"Except her," Nimm said with a chuckle. "Sorry. Don't know why that was funny."

"There are campers and tourists still inside this dome," Jennifer said. "We couldn't find them, but they have to be–"

"Not a dome," Castor said. "A bubble. Our employer has a theory we're on the bottom half of the bubble and the top half, where all the tourists and campers really are, is below us. Our job is to test the theory in twelve hours when this bubble rolls over."

Jennifer was silent.

"She blinking a lot and doing that stare thing?" Garfield asked.

"Yeah," Castor replied. "Just like we all did when Mr. Thompson proposed his theory to us."

"I'm sorry, but you think we're in a bubble and the bubble will flip over to do...what? Reveal where everyone has been hiding all this time?" Jennifer asked. "Because that's crazy. Certifiable crazy."

"Not going to argue with you there, but yes, that's what we believe," Castor said.

There were a couple of throats cleared.

"Or what we are paid to believe," Castor amended.

"How can your boss know any of this?" Jennifer asked.

"The magic of private satellites. He saw what happened when this bubble first arrived," Castor said then shook his head. "We need to move. Now. Ready?"

"Hell no, I'm not ready," Jennifer replied. "But don't have much of a choice, do I?"

"Here," Stackhouse said as he put an injector pen to her neck and pressed the button. "This will help the trip."

Jennifer winced at the sharp pain from the quick needle prick then laughed.

"What's funny?" Castor asked as he slowly, carefully, and with Stackhouse's help, lifted Jennifer up over his shoulder.

"I used to hate needles," Jennifer said. "Don't really give a good goddamn about them now."

"And that's funny?" Castor asked as he eased her body into a better carry position.

"Better than crying," Jennifer replied as pain shot through her body and she bit her lip to keep from doing just that– cry.

***

The stump of Jennifer's still bleeding left leg slammed into the tree root and there was no holding that scream back. It ripped at her vocal cords, tearing at her throat as every ounce of her being screeched into the night's darkness.

Darkness that was punctuated by the bright flashes of muzzle fire.

Once her screams had died, her voice shredded, Jennifer realized that her screaming was far from the loudest noise in the night. While the rifle fire was suppressed enough that her vocal straining had overpowered the gunshots, the screeching of unseen predators that surrounded the group was easily a few notches above Jennifer's range.

"Three o'clock! Four on our three, dammit!"

Someone spun in that direction and squeezed off six controlled shots. Creatures cried out in pain, large bodies fell.

"Eight! On our eight!"

Something large leapt from the ferns and slammed into one of the operators. It was too dark for Jennifer to see who it was, but she heard the tearing and ripping of flesh as the man shouted for help then went silent with a squelch and slow gurgle.

"Five to our ten!"

Muzzle fire concentrated in that direction as Jennifer shoved up on her hands and dragged herself to the trunk of the massive tree belonging to the roots she'd landed on. She spun about and put her back to the tree. She wanted to tuck her knees up to her chest, but one leg no longer had a knee and the other didn't have anything below it to support the knee even if she had the strength to tuck. Which she didn't. Crawling had taken everything out of her.

Three shapes converged on an operator, but he rolled out of the way, his action illuminated by the strobing of the rifle fire against the pitch blackness. His rifle barked over and over as the three shapes whipped about and went in for another attack. Two of the shapes fell fast, parts of their heads gone in a split second. The third made it to the operator just as his rifle clicked empty.

"Eat shit, dino bitch!"

The dino struck. The operator struck. Both roared in pain as the dino bit down on the operator's shoulder while the operator stabbed the dino over and over again in the belly. Then there was one last roar from the beast as it collapsed onto the man.

Silence.

"Clear," someone said quietly.

Bright dots filled Jennifer's vision, the after effects of the muzzle fire, and it was hard to focus on anything unless she turned her head to the side. Movement to her left. She swiveled her head in that direction.

"Jennifer?"

"Here," Jennifer replied.

The movement to her left became more defined and Castor crouched close to her side.

"Are you injured?" he asked.

"You mean besides my legs?" Jennifer replied.

"Yes, that's exactly what I mean," Castor said, his voice nothing but business.

Jennifer couldn't see his eyes, but she'd met military operators like him before. Those eyes would be cold as steel, trying to penetrate into her soul to get all of her answers with one look.

"Castor? We gotta move, man," someone said.

"Help me get her up, Nimm," Castor responded.

A soldier approached from the shadows and helped Castor get Jennifer back up onto his shoulder.

"Jesus Christ. The bastard pretty much tore my arm off," Stackhouse said from the spot where he lay, a dino corpse collapsed across his legs. "Gonna need some help here."

"Take care of Stackhouse, Nimm," Castor said. "Stop the bleeding and get him up. We can't stay."

"How much time do we have?" Jennifer asked, struggling not to cry out with every jostle. The morphine was long gone from her system and pain consumed her reality.

"Not much," Castor said, sounding more exhausted than she felt. "Four hours to get to the LZ."

Castor carried her over to where what was left of Garfield was strewn about the small clearing where they'd taken their stand. The remains could only be identified as human because of the scraps of fatigues and chunks of equipment intermixed with the blood and offal.

"Dammit," Castor said.

"What were they?" Jennifer asked.

"You're the Fish and Wildlife predator lady," Nimm said as he worked on Stackhouse's shoulder. "You tell us."

"I don't know these types of animals," Jennifer replied, as Castor carefully knelt and picked through Garfield's remains until he found a set of dog tags.

"Raptors," Stackhouse grunted. "Like the Jurassic Park ones. But way different."

"That clears it up," Nimm said.

"They're dead. That's what matters. We let the eggheads figure out what they were later," Castor said as he walked over to Nimm and Stackhouse. He was careful not to bounce Jennifer too much and she was very thankful for that.

"That's as good as it gets, Stack," Nimm said as he stood up and offered Stackhouse a hand.

Stackhouse stared at the hand then looked down at the dino that was sprawled across his legs, the creature's intestines spilling out into the dirt.

"Oh, right," Nimm said.

It took the man ten minutes to get the body off Stackhouse. It was like trying to move a cow corpse, nothing but dead weight and awkward limbs.

Once Stackhouse was up on his feet, the three remaining operators pulled out a plastic coated map and a red-tinted flashlight.

"We should be here," Castor said.

Jennifer couldn't see where here was since she was facing backwards.

"We need to go here," Castor continued.

"You can set me down while you plan," Jennifer said.

"Yeah, but getting you back up would be a lot harder," Castor said. "We're all running on fumes here."

"So we have four hours to get from here to there?" Nimm asked. "Gonna be close."

"How can you know where you're going?" Jennifer asked. "This land is nothing like what it should be. If you have a map of Wyoming then you are looking at the wrong map."

"Satellite," Castor replied in a tone that suggested she should have known that.

"Oh, right," Jennifer said. "Your employer."

"Here to there in four hours," Nimm said. "We need to book ass now."

"There'll be more of those assholes out there," Stackhouse said, his voice weak and thin.

"There is more of everything out there," Castor countered. "It's why Thompson sent us in and not the bottom of the barrel."

"Guys, we got to go," Nimm said.

"Yeah," Castor agreed. "Jennifer? You want some morphine?"

"I don't know," Jennifer replied. "Yes, I would love some. But I don't want to wake up from a doze like I did before, in the middle of Hell and disoriented as guns are firing and goddamn dinosaurs are attacking. Maybe give some to Stackhouse so he's not–"

"Pain gives me an edge," Stackhouse replied with false bravado.

"He's gotta stay sharp," Castor said. "But you can sleep."

"I'm good," Jennifer said.

"You sure?"

"I'm sure."

"Alright. Then we move."

"I'll take over and carry her in thirty," Nimm said. "We can trade back and forth."

"Works for me," Castor said as the group left the small clearing, cutting back into the dense foliage of ferns and palms.

***

Jennifer struggled through the first hour. The pain was excruciating, but she knew it would be harder for the men to carry her if she was passed out and dead weight. But as the second hour began, and the sun rose, Jennifer could no longer take it.

"I need a shot," she said through gritted teeth.

"No problem," Castor said. "Hold up, guys."

"In my pack. Third pocket," Stackhouse said as he dropped to the ground and rested his back against a tree, taking his pack off and tossing it to Nimm. "Red cap, white cylinder."

"I know what morphine looks like," Nimm said as he picked up the pack and opened the third pocket. He hunted through the pocket then growled low. "Or not. You sure it's the third pocket?"

Nimm froze as he looked towards Stackhouse.

"Do not move," he whispered.

"What is it?" Castor asked.

Jennifer was able to swivel her head and see where Nimm stood, blocking her view of Stackhouse. But Nimm's still form couldn't block Jennifer's view of the almost camouflaged creature that clung upside down to the tree trunk that Stackhouse was sitting against.

"Nimm, stay still," Castor ordered.

"Doing that," Nimm replied.

"Stack? Do not move a muscle," Castor said.

"What we dealing with?" Stackhouse asked quietly.

"You have a bogey about a meter above you," Castor said as he crouched and carefully slid Jennifer off his shoulder. "It's very interested in the top of your head."

"How big?" Stackhouse asked.

"Rottweiler," Castor said. "With feathers and lots of teeth in its beak."

"Great," Stackhouse replied.

"Nimm? I want you to jump to your left on my go," Castor said.

"Copy that," Nimm replied.

"Go!"

Nimm jumped to his left and Castor whipped his rifle around and fired five shots. Bark kicked up from the tree's trunk, but the creature had already moved, retreating back up into the limbs and leaves, hidden from sight.

"There!" Stackhouse yelled and pointed behind them all.

Nimm spun about as another of the creatures leapt from a different tree. The man couldn't get his rifle up in time to stop the dino. It collided with his head and chest, rear claws ripping and shredding Nimm's belly wide open before the man had stumbled back more than two steps.

Nimm screamed.

"My three!" Stackhouse yelled.

Castor turned and fired, dropping two more of the creatures as they came whipping down out of their perches. A third and fourth leapt at him from a different tree and Castor put those down.

"Go!" Stackhouse yelled as he struggled up onto his feet. He pulled a pistol, aimed, and fired once. Nimm's screaming stopped.

The creature that had been tearing the man apart, squawked and hissed then whipped about to face Stackhouse, its beak coated in Nimm's blood.

"Go, dammit!" Stackhouse yelled at Castor. "Get your asses out of here!"

"Not leaving you, man!" Castor said as he fired five more times, knocking back two more creatures. He ejected his magazine then slapped in a fresh one.

"Get her on your shoulder and run!" Stackhouse yelled between trigger pulls of his pistol. "I'll try to follow!"

"Stack!" Castor yelled.

He glanced over his shoulder and saw what Jennifer had already observed. Stackhouse's fatigues were soaked in blood from his shoulder down to his knees. His wound had opened wide and he was bleeding out fast.

Stackhouse fired over Castor's head until his pistol clicked empty. Three dinos fell from the trees they were climbing down from. Ejecting his spent magazine, Stackhouse struggled to get a fresh one free from his belt.

"Go!" he yelled as he dropped the magazine and bent to pick it up.

Castor started to argue again, but one of the creatures jumped onto Stackhouse's back and clamped its beak across the back of Stackhouse's neck. With one bite and a twist, Stackhouse collapsed, his head bent at a very wrong angle.

"Castor," Jennifer pleaded.

"No," Castor growled.

But he slung his rifle and grabbed Jennifer up in his arms, not bothering to throw her over his shoulder. He took off running and Jennifer cried as the jostling sparked fresh waves of agony through her entire body.

She cried until her eyes dried, her ducts empty of liquid. She had no tears left. None for her, for the fallen men, for any of the insanity that had plagued the land she once knew by heart.

The sun rose as Castor ran with her in his arms. He'd settled into a steady jog, but Jennifer could feel his arms shaking underneath her.

"Put me back on your shoulder," Jennifer said.

"Can't stop," Castor gasped. "We're barely gonna make it to the LZ."

"If something comes at us, you can't fire with me in your arms," Jennifer said, looking up into his beet red face. Sweat poured from his pores in rivers of salty liquid. "Castor? You're going to drop me soon."

Castor glanced down at her, his eyes meeting hers for a brief second. Then he was looking back up, focusing on the path ahead. After a few more minutes, he slowed, slowed, then stopped and set her down on the ground. He fell to his hands and knees and retched. Slapping at his waist, he found his canteen and took two quick sips then handed it over to Jennifer.

"That's all we have," he said as he unslung his rifle and checked the magazine. He snarled at the very few rounds inside then slapped it back home. "And this is all I have. Shit."

"Pistol?" Jennifer asked after taking two swallows of water and handing the canteen back.

Castor took the canteen, clipped it to his belt, then patted three magazines on his belt.

"Yeah. It'll have to do," Castor said as he left his rifle in the dirt.

Jennifer didn't ask him why. The rifle was extra weight and hard to use while running with a woman over his shoulder. That was obvious.

"Let's have a look at you," Castor said and crawled over to Jennifer's legs. He studied them without touching or moving either stump. "They're bleeding a lot, but not enough for you to bleed out. I think."

There was a loud screech from a way behind them. It was answered by four other screeches, each coming from different directions.

"Get me back up," Jennifer said. "We're being tracked."

"No shit," Castor said. He lifted her up onto his shoulder. "Doesn't sound like they're in front of us yet."

Jennifer whimpered as Castor adjusted her position. He didn't apologize. They were both in full on survival mode and apologies were a waste of energy.

Castor drew his pistol, pulled back on the slide, then holstered the weapon.

Again, Jennifer didn't ask why. He had put a round in the chamber, but he wasn't about to go running through a prehistoric forest with his sidearm drawn. Not with her weight threatening his balance every second of the way. She figured he was probably trained well enough he could draw and fire when the time came.

They started off again.

***

The screeches and calls became more frequent and closer in as Castor jogged with Jennifer on his shoulder. The creatures were herding them in a specific direction. That direction happened to be the same way they needed to go. Or Jennifer hoped.

"Thank God!" Castor cried out suddenly, bringing Jennifer out of a semi-stupor. "Yes, sir. We're maybe a quarter click from the LZ!"

Castor's body tensed and Jennifer realized he was listening to a voice over comms.

"No. I'm it. I have a Fish and Wildlife Officer with me. She's severely wounded, both legs pretty much gone," Castor replied to a voice Jennifer couldn't hear. "Ambushed by dinos. They're everywhere and most are hungrier than shit... No... Yes, sir... We'll be coming in hot... We've got company dogging us... If they're the same as the ones that killed Nimm and Stack then a meter and a half and maybe a hundred pounds. Long beaks with very sharp teeth and claws from Hell..."

Castor continued to listen as he jogged.

"No, Garfield was taken out by some raptor looking bastards," Castor continued. "Yep, just like the movie. Sort of. Two and a half meters and at least five hundred pounds... I hope they aren't what's dogging us or we're dead as soon as we hit the LZ... Open ground is a scary thought..."

A screech came from their right, maybe only a few meters away in the brush. Castor drew his pistol and held it down next to his leg as he continued to jog.

Jennifer lifted her head for a better look and spotted movement behind them. More than a couple of large creatures were ducking and dodging through the foliage, staying hidden enough that she couldn't get too good of a look. But by the way the ferns were being shoved around, the creatures weren't the smaller dinos that had killed Stackhouse and Nimm.

"Castor," Jennifer said.

"Hold on," Castor said. "What? You see something?"

"They're on us," Jennifer said. "They know where we're going. You're right. As soon as we're in the open, they'll strike."

"Shit," Castor said, then relayed over comms what she'd said.

"Roger that," Castor said after a few seconds. "How many? Not enough!"

Castor took a few deep breaths. Jennifer could hear his lungs struggling to fill with air as he continued moving forward.

"You need at least a dozen to secure the LZ," Castor said. "I know, sir, but... I do copy that... Of course. You can only send who you have. They need to be ready, though. These bitches are smart and fast."

Castor said nothing for a long while and Jennifer thought the conversation was over.

"I do, sir. Samples are in my pack... No, sir... Yes, sir... Let's goddamn hope so, sir..."

A head poked out from between two very thorny bushes and eyed Jennifer and Castor. Jennifer gasped as it blinked a couple of times then ducked away, lost from sight.

"They're here," Jennifer said. "Castor! They are right here! They aren't going to–!"

Her words were drowned out by gunfire as Castor drew his pistol and started shooting at two large dinos that had come out of the forest in front of them. One had half its head taken off by two rounds while the other fell onto its side, shattered bone sticking out in splinters from its left haunch.

"Hold on!" Castor yelled and he picked up speed. Jennifer was amazed he had any energy reserves left.

They broke from the tree cover and out into an open area. It was half the size of a football field, but filled with small pines and other conifers, none taller than a couple of feet. The earth was scorched for as far as Jennifer could see, which wasn't far considering her position.

"Fire," she said.

"I am!" Castor shouted as he squeezed the trigger until the pistol clicked empty then ejected the magazine.

"No, I mean… Never mind," Jennifer muttered as Castor managed to slap a fresh magazine into his pistol and resume firing at the encroaching dinos.

Two more dinos fell then the pistol clicked empty again.

Dinos were closing in from all sides. Jennifer could see them clearly as Castor spun in a slow circle while he reloaded his pistol for the last time.

"This is it," Castor said.

The dinos moved in, their eyes locked onto Castor's pistol. They'd figured out what the real danger was. Castor swung his arm to the side and the dinos in that direction leapt back, ducking their bodies low to the ground once they'd landed.

"That's right, you sons of bitches," Castor snarled. "Now you're learning."

"Coming from behind!" Jennifer shouted.

Castor turned and fired twice, wounding only one dino, but sending the two others scrambling backwards.

"Turn again!" Jennifer yelled as she realized what hunting pattern the dinos were using. They were a classic pack, very much like wolves. "Two this way!"

Castor turned again and fired, sending those dinos scrambling.

"Four rounds left," Castor said. "Four of them."

"They're making you waste your ammunition," Jennifer said.

"They're what?" Castor replied. "Bullshit!"

"Here they come!" Jennifer yelled.

Castor turned, fired twice, but didn't hit either of the dinos.

"Again!" Jennifer shouted.

Castor spun about once more and fired his pistol empty. Those two dinos jumped to the side, avoiding the bullets. Castor threw the empty pistol at them and they froze, looked down at the weapon, then one let out a triumphant squawk.

"We tried," Castor said.

The dinos moved fast then all skidded to a halt as a helicopter roared overhead, turned in a tight arc, then settled above the clearing. Heavy caliber rounds ripped into the earth and three of the dinos, obliterating them. The last dino screeched then was gone back into the forest.

Castor looked up and waved. He got him and Jennifer clear of the landing helicopter then rushed towards the open doors as heavily armed men jumped out of the main fuselage to secure the landing zone. Hands grabbed at Jennifer and she screamed as her legs were bumped against the edge of the helicopter's fuselage. Castor scrambled in right behind her.

Jennifer was secured to one of the bench seats next to Castor and she started crying again. But only a single tear came out. Castor hesitated then wrapped his arms about her as the men securing the area climbed back in and the helicopter took off.

"All done," Castor said into her ear over the roar of the helicopter's rotors. "We're safe."

"Look at that!" someone shouted, loud enough to be heard even without headphones.

Castor leaned towards the open doors and Jenifer followed his gaze.

The land below was turning. It was literally turning on its side as the helicopter rose higher and higher. There was a brief shimmer as the vehicle got above the bubble.

Inside the bubble it was as if two different worlds lay on opposite sides of a very thick disc of earth. One side was the prehistoric hellscape that Jennifer and Castor had just escaped. The other side was a scene that Jennifer knew well. Wyoming. Her Wyoming.

Everyone was shouting and talking, but Jennifer couldn't hear them. All of her attention was on the ground below as it turned and turned until the prehistoric world was lost from sight and the lost part of Wyoming was fully back, seated as if it had never been gone.

But the shimmer of the bubble remained as the helicopter banked left and flew off to the staging area the government had set up.

"It'll happen again," Jennifer said.

"What?" Castor shouted then snapped his fingers. Two headsets were handed to him and he put one over his ears then seated a set on Jennifer's head. "What did you say?"

"It'll happen again," Jennifer said. "That turning or whatever. It'll happen again."

"How can you know for sure?" Castor asked.

"The dome or bubble or whatever," Jennifer replied. "It's still there."

"Maybe it was a one and done situation," Castor suggested, but the look on his face said he didn't believe that.

"Yeah, sure, maybe," Jennifer replied and gave him a sad smile.

They both stared out at the bubble and the land far below.

"We'll be at the staging area in twenty-five minutes," the pilot announced.

"Thanks," Castor replied then focused on Jennifer. "They're going to debrief you once you're up for it."

"You saw what I saw," Jennifer said.

"I know, but…" He shrugged.

"I know," Jennifer replied. She'd been a government employee long enough to know exactly how it worked.

She turned away from the open doors and settled her head against the back of the seats. There was chatter over the headsets, but it didn't take much for Jennifer to block it out.

She only hoped one day maybe she could block out what had happened down below, down in that world that shouldn't have existed and was now gone. Her tears may have been dried up, but they'd be back. And they'd be accompanied by nightmares. That was confirmed by the looks that the operators around her were trying not to send her way.

Jennifer smiled as a man leaned forward, holding up an injector. She nodded and he put it to her neck then depressed the button. The pain eased and she closed her eyes.

Time for tears and nightmares later. For the moment, it would be well-earned oblivion.

The End

NORSE SEA HUNTERS

By Brad Harmer-Barnes

The waters had been calm for two days now, and the initial novelty - not to mention the initial excitement - of the raiding party to England was beginning to wear off. Olaf and Gunbjorn were old hands at this, well past their mid-twenties, and both feeling that this might have to be their last journey. Once broken bones were aching more than ever, eyesight was dulling, and reactions were slowing. Neither would ever admit that they were growing tired of it - that was a weakness that no true Norseman would ever show.

The *Skalla* had originally belonged to Olaf Sigmærsson's father, yet was showing very little sign of aging. The figurehead carved in the shape of a snarling red dragon was beginning to fade a little, the once vibrant red turning pink at the edges, worn by wind and salt over many years, but besides from this it bore the weathering well. Right now, it nestled under a pile of blankets and skins in the bottom of the boat. It would be attached once the village they intended to raid was in sight.

There were fourteen of them, all younger than Olaf and Gunbjorn, with the exception of Unnulf, the godi. Unnulf was older than anyone else in the village, and he smelt like it, too. Thankfully he was in the stern of the ship, downwind. He was a cantankerous, foul man, though he was said to be blessed with second sight, which could prove to be a boon on any journey.

Olaf cracked his knuckles and looked ahead, hoping to see land on the horizon before long. "Is it just me or does this pissing journey get longer every bloody time?"

Gunbjorn, broad shouldered and red headed, harrumphed a short laugh. "Aye. You'd think it would speed up as we got older, but it just feels colder and longer. Still, I'll never tire of it, whatever Herkja wants me to do."

Olaf looked over his shoulder. Besides himself, Gunbjorn and the godi, there were eleven more men working the oars - though to call them 'men' was a little bit of a stretch. Some were not yet capable of growing so much as a wisp of facial hair, and the youngest - Øpir - still had the high pitched voice of a young boy. This proved to be the source of much teasing for the lad, though his many tormentors quickly learned that he could throw a punch with the strongest of them.

The splash and roar of the waves on the prow became a soothing white noise, and Olaf fell once more to staring out across the sea. Gunbjorn pulled a small piece of wood from his cloak and begin whittling it with a small knife. Olaf watched for a moment before asking, "What is that you're making?"

"Won't know until it's finished."

"You never were one for planning things out, old friend."

Gunbjorn shrugged. "Makes life more interesting. Who wants every step of every stinking day mapped out ahead of you? That'd make me feel even older than I do now."

Olaf realised that Unnulf had shifted position and was taking a shit over the side of the ship. He quickly averted his eyes, not through any sense of modesty, but simply because he didn't want to see the godi's straining face, or his geriatric penis flapping in the breeze.

"Ah, I'm getting to be an older man now, Gunbjorn. Life will hold very few surprises for me, anymore. Look at this, for example. How many times have we done this now? The first time I came on a raid, when I was no bigger than Øpir and maybe even younger, I made water in my pants as soon as the ship made land. Then again when we came in sight of the village. By the time we were actually upon them, swords waving, I was shaking every step of the way."

"Aye, I think all of us have a similar story, my friend."

"Perhaps, but these recent times I haven't felt so much as a tingle of fear. It's as though I've lost any sense of adventure, any sense of excitement to be had. It feels like I might as well be farming or weaving back home with the women and children for all the thrill it gives me. It saddens me, my friend. I wish I could have that excitement back."

Gunbjorn continued whittling. Olaf thought for a moment that he was carving a badger, but then it was gone. It was like trying to make out faces in clouds that were constantly stirring and shifting. After a second's pause, the red haired man answered him. "You've gotten too good at it, that's your problem. You're a good warrior, Olaf Sigmærsson, and maybe you're just not getting enough of a challenge sticking farmers and beheading monks. You need a war, or something of the like."

"Perhaps."

Gunbjorn stopped whittling for a second and gestured at the rowing warriors with his knife. "Failing that, why don't you try and see it through their eyes? This voyage may be no grand deal to you, but Øpir there has made water at least three times in the last hour already. You have two children, aye?"

"Aye."

"Then you know how good it feels when you see them walking, or talking, or even just able to sit up and clap for the first time. It shows you that you're being a good father, that you're able to prepare them for all the things that the real world is going to throw at them. Look out there. You should feel the same about this. As leader, you're a father figure to all those lads out there."

"He's off again."

"What?"

Olaf gestured to where Øpir stood up and made his way awkwardly to the side of the boat before urinating into the sea.

Gunbjorn led out a deep roar of a laugh, and Olaf could not help but chuckle along with him. Gunbjorn's laugh and smile were infectious, and even on your darkest days he could make you feel happy that he was around. He looked out at the crew and realised that his friend's words had made a difference. He was the leader of the crew, and captain of the *Skalla*, and they looked up to him, as he had looked up to his father on his first raids. It was a responsibility, for sure, but it was also life affirming.

His attention was suddenly called back to Øpir. The young man let out a strangled screaming noise, and stumbled backwards, tripped over the oarsman behind him, and fallen half on and half off of the bench, a stream of hot urine fountaining up into the air. Gunbjorn's laughter grew even louder at the farcical display, but there was something about Øpir's panicked expression that did not sit easily with him. His back letting out a strained popping sound, he pushed himself away from the prow and strode down the centre of the ship. The vertical stream of piss was tapering off and soon stopped completely.

Øpir looked up at his leader, and paled a little further. "Olaf...over the side..."

Olaf reached down and pulled the young boy up by his bicep. "All right, lad. What's all this about? If you want to be invited along on the next raiding party, you can't go pissing over all your fellow warriors. You know what the first rule about being in a shield wall is? It's 'try not to piss all over everyone'. Do we understand one another, lad?"

The young man nervously extended a finger towards the side where he had been standing. "There. Alongside us. I saw a monster!"

Olaf couldn't help but raise an eyebrow. "A monster?"

"A sea monster."

Olaf gestured to Gunbjorn, who quickly joined them. "Øpir here says he saw a sea monster swimming alongside the ship."

Gunbjorn shrugged. "Maybe he did. There are sea monsters in these parts. My uncle saw one once. Great big thing with a long neck and rows of teeth. Three eyes he said, but he said that about lots of things."

"He exaggerated about lots of things?"

"No, he said lots of things had three eyes. He was a bit strange."

Olaf decided to leave that thread of the conversation for another time and cocked an eyebrow at Øpir. "What did it look like?"

"It... It was white, I think. Or a very, very pale grey, at least. It looked washed out or sun bleached or something. Faded, I suppose. It swam past us, heading in the other direction when I was taking a piss. It was huge, though, Olaf. Bigger than any fish I ever saw. I stood staring at it for a second, then I saw its fin cut up through the water, about twenty feet out from us. It was like a shark's fin; you know the one that sticks straight up out of the back? It was like that only, well, it was taller than I was, and I'm not a small man."

"A six foot shark fin?" Gunbjorn asked. "If he's right, then that'd have to make the whole thing...well...I don't know, but it'd have to be..."

"Longer than the *Skalla*..." hissed a voice behind Olaf, accompanied by the smell of curdled milk and rotten teeth. He turned to see Unnulf way too close to him. The crud on his yellowed incisors looked thick enough to take a thrown spear.

"Could be," Olaf agreed. "If there *are* sea monsters then who can say how large they might be."

"There are many tales of the giant shark that haunts these waters," continued the godi, his thin, grey hair rippling in the breeze. "My grandfather saw it once, long ago, and said it was larger than his entire longship, and when its jaw opened it could have swallowed five men whole. It is said to be old as this sea itself, and there are very few who have seen it...and lived."

Gunbjorn shared a look with Olaf. "Well, you said you wanted to do something more interesting."

Unnulf coughed, and grabbed Olaf's cloak. "If what Øpir saw is true, then this is no ordinary shark. This shark is the living embodiment of Rán, the God of the Sea. He is here to make certain that only the strongest and worthiest warriors are able to sail past and continue on their journey. Those that do not measure up, he takes in his belly, before shitting them out on the bottom of the ocean, to rot for all time, never to see Valhalla."

Olaf batted the older man's hand away from him. "You think that Rán has nothing better to do with his time than to swim around the sea as a fat shark, eating random fishermen? You had a strange perception of things, godi."

Unnulf tapped his right eye socket with a finger. This eyeball was murky and covered with a film of grey. "The gods took this eye from me, Olaf Sigmærsson, but I still see further than most. If the great shark of this ocean is not Rán himself, then he is at least his servant. You would do well to remember this in the days to come, Olaf Sigmærsson. I warned you."

Gunbjorn bit his bottom lip and watched Unnulf scurry back to his position in the stern of the ship. "I don't like the godi any more than you do, but he does have the gift. If this is the work of the gods, then he would be better placed to understand their reasons than either you or I."

"I don't think that there's any real reason to believe that the gods would be testing us, do you, Gunbjorn? Even if they did, why would they do it through a simple waste of spunk like Øpir?"

Gunbjorn tilted his head and coughed awkwardly. Olaf realised that Øpir was still standing there. "Don't you have an oar to man, lad? If this shark is as big as you say it is, then I think we ought to be out of here as soon as possible, don't you?"

Øpir nodded and squeezed back to his position.

"Probably just his imagination," muttered Olaf. "First time out on the water. First time out for this distance, anyway. It was probably just a dolphin. They like to race alongside the ship, sometimes. Maybe they find us as entertaining as we find them."

"I hope for their sakes they find us more entertaining. Dreary little creatures."

"You're all sunshine and light today, you know that?"

Gunbjorn shrugged and the two of them stepped back to the prow, straining their eyes for any sight of land.

Olaf heard the sound out in the water to their port side, and wasn't quite able to process it at first. At first he thought that a large stone had been thrown into deep water, only in reverse. Spinning to face the noise, his cloak snapping in the wind, he heard Gunbjorn gasp in shock - a sound he never expected to hear in all his life.

The cries of the men came then, accompanied by the jingle of mail and swords and the clatter of oars falling to the deck as hands fell limp. There, fifty yards from the *Skalla*, Olaf got his first sight of the shark. Its flesh was a faded grey, almost white in patches, and one dead, black eye regarded them coldly. Its maw opened wide, revealing a mottled grey and pink mouth riddled with a hundred razor sharp teeth. The jaws smashed down together and the shark submerged from its brief jump above the ocean. Another cascade of salt water fountained high around it, and then it disappeared from view.

"Gods," breathed Gunbjorn. "I never knew they could get so big. I've never seen one that big. How did it get so large? How is it alive?"

"Questions later," growled Olaf. "We've got something else to worry about first."

He pointed toward where the monster had dived, and Gunbjorn felt his stomach sink. The shark's dorsal fin - six feet above the water if it was an inch - was plowing through the water towards them. A v-shaped foamy wake spread behind it, and it spread wide.

Gunbjorn's eyes widened, and he unhitched his axe from his belt. "I guess we're getting our first battle before we even land. That's rather unexpected."

Olaf had already strung his bow and nocked an arrow. He squinted in concentration and against the glare of the sun on the surface of the North Sea. Several of the crew had had similar ideas and a few arrows struck the water near the beast. Only two hit, and only one sunk in. Seeing how tough the skin and blubber of that thing must be, Olaf applied a little more pressure than usual, his muscles burning. "Smile, you..."

The arrow left the bow, and he thought he could almost hear it scream through the air. He didn't see it strike, however. Whether through luck or judgment, the shark chose that exact second to dive, and the fin slowly faded from view.

"Olaf," Gunbjorn cried, grabbing him by the arm, and gripping the side of the boat with his other hand. "I've seen a shark do this before. Grab a hold!"

"What?"

Gunbjorn raised his voice above the clamour and shouting of the men. "Everyone, grab a hold of something! Your bench, the oar, the side of the craft - anything."

"Gunbjorn, what in Odin's name..."

The rest of his words were lost in his throat as the *Skalla* rocked hard to the side. All the men swore and cursed in fear and indignation as their beloved longship was assaulted by the colossal shark.

With a scream and a splash, Øpir (who apparently had not held on tight enough as commanded), dropped into the ocean. The boat rocked back in the opposite direction again, trying to regain its equilibrium, and Olaf strained to reach out a hand to the boy.

Øpir splashed and cursed and thrashed in the water, and - as the boat slowly rocked back to a standstill - it took three of the crew to fish him out. He sat in the centre of the boat, shivering and trying to get water out of his ear, which many of the men found to be most amusing, especially in the wake of the recent excitement.

"Rán is testing us!" Unnulf cried from his position at the stern. "You see now? It is he, come to test who among us is worthy!" He finished this with a pointed look at Øpir, which Olaf thought was rather unnecessary.

"I told you to pack that talk in, you old goat. That was a little bit of excitement, that's all. The shark - a big shark, to be sure - is gone now. It's taken a swing at us, found that we're not all that tasty, and now it's buggered off again to go and find something that's a bit easier to eat."

"A big shark," muttered Gunbjorn. "That's the biggest bloody shark I've ever seen, and I'll wager you've never seen one bigger neither. That's a sea monster, and you bloody well know it."

Olaf waved him away. "You're sounding like Unnulf. I pray to Odin that you don't bloody start smelling like him and all."

"You think it's gone? Truly?"

"Why wouldn't it be? It's taken one run at us, and probably chipped a tooth or two. One of the lads stuck him with an arrow. He's in no hurry to come back for another bite, don't you worry, Gunbjorn."

Gunbjorn sighed. "My uncle used to say that when he was a lad, he saw his friend's father's fishing boat attacked by a shark. It was a smaller boat than the *Skalla*, mind, but apparently it just chomped and bit away at the timber until the boat was just debris. It must have smelt the fish inside...or the fishermen."

"How many eyes did the shark have?"

"Well, funny thing, actually..."

"Never mind."

The boat rocked again, harder this time, and Olaf swore that it had actually been lifted up off of the surface of the ocean and dropped down hard again. Curses and shouts burst from the crew, accompanied by the ranting of the ancient godi. Olaf gripped the prow to steady himself and his eyes fell on the water beneath the boat. There, carving a path through the dark water, he saw the vast, white shape of the hunter of the North Sea. Already, it was fading into the blackness below, but he felt physically shaken at the sheer size of it.

"It was the monster," he called to his men. "He's going to come around for another pass. Asvald, Olvir, Hæming: ready your arrows. You are the surest shots amongst us and stand the best chance of catching the thing. Aim for the eyes, the base of the fin and the mouth. The rest of you: swords and axes! If we can't kill it, we at least need to make it think twice about eating all of us for dinner. If we can't manage that...well, we can at least give the bastard thing indigestion."

The older amongst them muttered a surly agreement, and the younger amongst them gave a cheer of pride and aggression. They had come on this voyage looking for their first true taste of combat, and although it had taken an unexpected form, they were excited nonetheless. The rasp and ring of steel choroused along the boat, and Gunbjorn and Olaf joined them.

"Eyes peeled lads, this thing could charge us from any side. Eyes peeled...eyes peeled..."

With a yelp, Gunbjorn fell backwards into the boat, jarring his tailbone. Olaf looked to what had caused the man such alarm and there, a mere two feet in front of him, was the shark! It had raised its head up out of the water, and Olaf had never seen a mouth like it. It was large enough to swallow a normal sized shark whole, and at least three rows of pale, white teeth ringed the nightmarish orifice. An arrow was loosed and struck it in the roof of the mouth - from whom, he could not tell - and the shark let out a foul exhalation, stinking like a mountain of fish guts left out in the sun for a month, rancid and steaming.

Olaf flailed wildly at the shark with his sword. A few other blades in the periphery of his vision flashed forward, and all failed to meet their mark. The shock of the beast's arrival, coupled with the rocking of the *Skalla* made melee combat all but impossible.

Time slowed down for just a moment, and Olaf felt as though the glassy, black eye of the shark stared straight into his own, as if in challenge. Then, the moment was passed, and the monster's jaw clamped down straight onto the hull of the *Skalla*. Aged timbers groaned, creaked and were splintered under the leviathan's unstoppable bite.

The men cried and shouted once more around him, two more arrows flew past, sinking into the water around the shark as they were crushed in its jaw and wrenched off and into the water. Olaf staggered back, joining Gunbjorn prone on the deck, and he met the shark's gaze once more. It crunched down hard onto the wood in its mouth and slipped off sideways into the water, its huge body following after it.

Two or three of the crew shouted challenges and insults after it, but the rest just fell silent, watching as its full ninety yards - or more - swam away from them, the tip of the dorsal fin probing above the water like a mocking salute. It moved slowly, unfazed by their presence, and not in the least fearful of them. It ruled these waters, and it feared neither man nor beast.

For a moment the only sound was the cawing of the birds, and the splashing of the water around his ankles.

Around his ankles?

"We're taking in water!" Olaf yelled, kicking his legs and frantically getting to his feet. Gunbjorn caught him under the armpits and yanked him upright.

"Øpir, your axe!" Gunbjorn called.

The young man stood there dumbfounded, still staring after the shark. "Would you look at the size of that thing..."

Gunbjorn stepped over and boxed his ears. "Cut your chatter. Axe. Now."

The weapon fell limply into Gunbjorn's hands, and he brought it down savagely onto the rowing bench that Øpir had just vacated. Five blows later, and he had cut it down to several smaller planks of stout wood. "Olaf!"

Olaf caught the planks as he threw them over to him, and with the help of two of the burliest crew members, they attempted to plug the breach before the boat began to sink too low in the ocean. The pressure of the water was intense, but with the three of them working together, they soon slowed the incoming tide to a trickle. Satisfied that the repair would last at least until they landed in England, Olaf tasked Øpir and another of the skinny boys to bailing out the water with their helmets, while all the strongest took back their position at the oars, determined to reach land as quickly as possible.

"You looked the creature in the eye. I saw you."

Olaf turned to see Unnulf scrutinising him with his one good eye. The godi had obviously decided that he was sick of being up the back of the boat, as he had brought his cloak and staff all the way to the prow with him.

"Aye, I looked the beast in the eye. You know what I saw? Fuck all, godi. A dead, black eye, as dumb and black as any shark I ever saw before."

Unnulf's chuckle sent a chill down his spine. "Who are you trying to fool Olaf Sigmærsson? Are you trying to impress me? You know this is no ordinary shark. I saw you shaken. I saw you question what you saw before you. You know that Rán has come to test you. You are afraid that you will be found wanting."

The breeze picked up, pulling Olaf's cloak tight with a crack and a snap. "I fear neither man nor animal, Unnulf."

"This is a god, Olaf Sigmærsson. This is an avatar of the depths of the ocean itself, old as time and ageless as the wind. The *Skalla* is going to be found unworthy, Olaf Sigmærsson, and then what will you tell your men when they find that you have led them to unworthy of entering Valhalla. Surely you see that your weapons have no effect on it? The arrows merely bounced straight off of it, and your own blade was unable to strike it. There is no escape from..."

Olaf's hand shot up, catching Unnulf by the throat. "Listen here, you scab from a troll's foreskin: that's a big shark all right, but it's gone now. We're going to need to do some repairs when we land in England, but we're going to make it there all right, you trust my word. We've lost some planks of the hull, and Øpir has added another pants pissing to his tally for the day, but there's no chance of me disappointing this crew. Not in this life, nor in the next, do you understand me, you curd from a cow's arse?"

The sea fountained up behind him, and Olaf looked over his shoulder quickly. Gunbjorn let out a cry and drew his sword.

The shark had thrown itself up out of the water and was trying to drag the boat down with its weight!

Tilting sharply to the port side, the shark's mouth gnashed open and shut, blasting the crew with its foul stink. Gunbjorn took a swing at it with his sword, and the blade sunk in an inch, before being stopped by the tough blubber and muscle under its pale grey skin. Thin, watery red blood flowed from the wound, though the shark itself seemed unaffected.

"You see now, Sigmærsson?" Unnulf screamed in Olaf's ear over the cacophony of shouts and splashing water. "Look, how the beast wants to devour us all! The *Skalla* is going to sink, and drag us all down with it to rot in the thing's guts before being shat onto the bed of the ocean!"

Olaf's blood boiled, and with a roar of anger, he grabbed the godi in both hands, lifting him up in the air. The older man kicked and struggled in his grip as he charged past the crew, directly towards the white ghost that had been haunting them.

Stepping up onto one of the benches for extra momentum, Olaf roared a challenge to the shark and threw Unnulf up into the air, and directly into its mouth. The godi's face was locked into an expression of pure terror, and one arm shot out towards the crew of the *Skalla* in a desperate plea for salvation.

The shark felt the godi land in its mouth, and the jaws clamped down hard. A hundred bone knives sank into Unnulf, piercing his chest and crushing his rib cage, nearly separating his arm at the shoulder. Shocked and unsure how to process what they had just seen, the crew of the *Skalla* backed off a pace and the shark bit down again, causing Unnulf's shrieking to increase in both pitch and volume. One hand groped desperately for some sort of purchase to pull himself free from the maw of the leviathan, but found none.

The shark shook its head from side to side and mashed its jaws twice more. Unnulf slipped further and further down the thing's throat. When nothing below his shoulders was visible, the megalodon slid back down into the water, and the boat righted itself violently. Gunbjorn hurried over to Olaf's side and the two of them watched the giant shark swim down and away from them.

"That should keep it happy for a while," Olaf muttered, before smirking at Gunbjorn and then turning to the rest of the crew. "Come on, lads! Øpir, you and that skinny friend of yours get to bailing this water out. I want to be able to dry my feet in the next five minutes, you hear me? Asvald, how about you tell us one of your stories to keep us entertained. If you all put your backs into it we might be in England by supper."

The crew cheered and set to their work straight away. Their leader had taken care of the problem and - more importantly - there was still more work to be done before they could rest. Gunbjorn followed behind Olaf, and they sloshed their way through the ankle deep water back to the prow of the ship. "What in Odin's name was that thing? I've never seen a shark that size. Never seen one act like that, either. It was...well, it's all very strange."

Olaf shrugged his shoulders. "There's strange things in the world, and I think we're lucky to see even as few as we do. How many of your friends and family back home can say they've seen a true sea monster?"

"Just my uncle. One time, he was fishing for crab out in..."

"I'm sure this is a very entertaining story, but let's not tempt the hand of Loki, and instead save it for when we're on dry land, eh?"

Gunbjorn nodded his agreement. "Aye, that is fair enough. You know, I'm glad to see the back of Unnulf, but...well...It's bad luck to sail without a godi."

Olaf looked at him, strangely. "Yes. I agree. Imagine the mess we'd be in if we hadn't had one with us."

The End

OPERATION: SEVERN

By William Meikle

"Give over, cap," Wiggins said. "That's never a dinosaur? It's far too wee for starters. It's a bloody bird of some kind, that's all."

Captain John Banks stood on a rocky shoreline beneath high cliffs, looking at the dead thing that had been trying to peck a hole in the side of their dinghy when he shot it. Wiggins had a point, in that the thin body had a coat of fine, almost downy, blue-green feathers, and a long hard snout that was almost a beak. The eyes, already clouding, had been large and pale, almost shining, like an eagle watching for prey. But the thing was three feet long, not counting an obviously reptilian tail, there were teeth in the beaked snout, and sharp talons on what passed for both hands and feet.

Besides, Banks had been briefed, where Private Wiggins and the rest of them had not, as yet.

The thing at his feet looked exactly like a smaller version of the one the colonel had shown him in a photograph that morning back in the barracks in Lossiemouth.

"This washed up in Bideford harbor yesterday after a storm. The boffins already know where it came from, as the island's been off limits for a century and has been closed to both shipping and curious public ever since," the officer said. "Some kind of experiment gone tits-up and given the hush-hush treatment, you know how that dance goes."

Banks had nodded, and tapped a finger on the photograph. He didn't like the look of the rows of teeth that showed up bright in the harsh lighting, or the curved talons that protruded on both fingers and toes. Something had pecked out one of the beast's eyes, but somehow that only made it look all the more menacing and dangerous. But he didn't speak of any of that – the colonel was a pragmatist, dealing in bullets and numbers, men and missions. Banks kept it short.

"But something has survived?"

"Looks like it, doesn't it? Head over, have a shufti and report back with recommendations."

Twenty minutes later they'd been on a flight south, then via a Devon airfield to the island in the Severn Estuary, at the head of Bristol Channel, in a dinghy, now not quite as pristine as it had been a minute earlier.

There wasn't a hole in the rubber, but if he hadn't shot the beast, there would have been in short order. Now the four-man squad had hauled the dinghy up onto the shore, and stood around looking at the dead thing.

The mission was not off to a good start.

Banks nodded toward where an overgrown track wound up the side of the cliffs.

"There's a facility of a sort up top, supposedly not in use. And as far as I know, we're the first people here in a hundred years. Back then they were experimenting on something that looked like this," he kicked at the dead thing. "They were all supposed to be long gone. Now we know they're not. And now you know as much as I do, so let's move out and see what there is to see."

***

What there was to see looked, at first glance, to be a lot of not much. The rough track proved to be a tough climb through tumbled rock, scree, gorse and matted grasses. The view at the top was hardly worth the trip, being of a mile-long flat plateau punctuated by half a dozen ruined buildings amid more of the rough grass and gorse. Narrow tracks, like deer runs, ran off in all directions through the vegetation, but everything lay still and quiet, even the clouds overhead seemed to loom menacingly as the wind dropped. No birds sang; there wasn't even the drone of an insect to cut through the silence.

"Very nice," Wiggins said sarcastically. "Well worth the trip."

"Quiet, man," Sergeant Hynd said. "Yon thing on the beach didn't just appear out of thin air."

"Maybe there was only one of them," Wiggins replied.

"Aye, sure," Hynd replied. "And when has our luck ever been that good?"

Banks called for silence, and led the squad toward the closest of the tumbled ruins.

***

The first building that they reached had been a storage hut of some kind; red brick walls, now crumbling and holed, and an iron roof, corroded down to little more than paper-thin rust that came apart in their hands. They found nothing of note in the rubble beyond two empty tins of paint nearly as rusted as the roof, and the haft of a broken shovel.

They had more luck in the second, larger, ruin, where the ceiling had partially fallen in, but had survived over almost quarter of the structure, and had preserved what lay under it. Banks had Wiggins and McCally hold up the roof while he and Hynd rummaged underneath in a pile of tumbled brickwork, cabinetry and rubble. Hynd came up with a rolled up map, and a battered leather satchel. They backed out to let the other two lower the roof; Banks got rust and dirt in his hair, but by then he was already unrolling the map. He wasn't sure what it was going to portray, but he wasn't expecting what he saw. The paper was old, yellowing in places, and gray-black with mold in others, but the once-vivid colors had survived enough to be able to be deciphered.

"That's South America isn't it?" Hynd said as Banks traced a river with his finger.

"Yep. Amazon basin. Someone has marked out a route from the Atlantic coast to a high plateau in the jungle. But I'm buggered what it means to us here."

Actually that wasn't quite true, for something was stirring at the back of his mind, but it wasn't given a chance to come forward; the silence around them was broken for the first time.

Trills and whistles came from the long grass on the path they had come in on, high and echoing, like birdsong in the morning air. They were answered by return calls from both their left and their right. The grass moved, as if something crawled through it, making its way closer to the squad, although nothing came into view.

Banks looked at Wiggins.

"Still think it's just wee birds, Wiggo?"

A head came up out of the grass, large pale eyes behind a toothed snout, and a bunch of red feathers at the back of the skull that made it look like a punk's mohawk. The head cocked to the left, then right, and the trill it let out sounded like a question. The eyes blinked, and then it disappeared back down into the grass. More trills and whistles sounded, a whole chorus of them.

"Well, they know we're here," Wiggins said. "But what the hell are they? And, please God, cap, don't say dinosaurs."

"They're dinosaurs," Banks replied with a smile. "At least, they're supposed to be. Some kind of black-ops experiment around the time of the First World War is what I was told. But somebody screwed up."

"Aye, very nice," Wiggins replied. "So now we've seen them, can we go?"

"I think we're going to have to ask nicely," Hynd said. He motioned to their left. Six pairs of large pale eyes watched them from the long grass, eyes on heads that were the size of rugby balls, and on long-necked bodies a good five feet high.

"Not so wee birdies," McCally said. "What now, cap?"

"Back off, slowly," Banks said, keeping his voice low.

He stepped backwards, and the squad followed his move, but he was acutely aware that they were going the wrong way; their dinghy was down the path that was now being blocked by the beasts. More heads came up in the grass to look at them.

Scores of them.

***

Banks stuffed the battered leather satchel inside his flak vest and unslung his rifle. The squad followed his example, but Banks wanted to avoid a firefight, at least until he had more info at hand on the situation here.

"Easy, lads," he said, still backing off. "They're curious about us, that's all."

Wiggins laughed softly.

"Aye. They're wondering whether we're tasty."

As one, the creatures' heads cocked to one side, listening.

"Look at them. They don't understand your accent, Wiggo," McCally said, and laughed. At that, three of the largest of the beasts barked back in reply.

"It wasn't that funny," Wiggo said, then Banks hushed them all to silence again as they retreated along the spine of the island.

The beasts came on, following them but not getting any closer.

"Cap?" Hynd said after they'd traveled a hundred yards in this manner. "We're going to fall off the top end if we go too far. Do you have a plan here?"

Banks had been eyeing a squat building some twenty yards behind them that looked to be in better condition than any of the others, being made of old stone, with a timber and slate roof that he guessed pre-dated the other, government-built structures that hadn't fared so well.

"Into this one," he said, heading toward the building doorway where an old wooden door hung by a single hinge, creaking in the wind. "We need to make some quiet time."

***

Once they were all inside, McCally pulled the old door closed behind them. It didn't fit very well in the frame, and couldn't be locked.

"This isn't going to keep anything out, cap," the corporal said.

"That's all right, lad," Banks replied. "I don't mean to be hanging about for long. I just need a wee think."

Wiggins stood by a window that, miraculously, still had glass in the frame, looking out over the length of the island.

"They're still there, just standing about, watching us, cap," he said.

"Keep an eye on them, Wiggo, and shout if anything changes."

Banks had a look around the shed's interior. It might predate the experiments, but it had obviously been in use at the same time; the far end of the building was caged off, iron bars like a prison cell. A row of what appeared to be horse bridles hung on hooks on the wall, along with riding crops, small whips and assorted whistles on leather thongs for hanging around your neck. A large placard on the wall had been crudely painted in large red lettering.

"One = HUNT. Two = STOP. Three = HOME."

"What's all this bollocks now?" McCally said.

Banks understood the meaning of the words straight away.

"They were trying to train them," he said softly.

"Train what? Those things outside?" Hynd replied.

Banks nodded.

"I'm guessing here, but you saw how curious, almost smart they appeared? Now imagine a whole flock of them in the fields of France, running at speed, across a minefield and into an open trench. Imagine the mayhem."

Even as he said it, he could see it in his mind's eye, could almost hear the screams, see the slashing talons rip into and through muddy uniforms, smell the blood as it sprayed from torn throats to fill the wet pools in the trenches.

"They wanted a new weapon," he whispered.

"And, not for the first time, got more than they bargained for," Hynd replied. "Aye, I can see that, cap. But where did they find beasties like this? Aren't these buggers supposed to be long extinct?"

Banks was about to reply, then saw that Corporal McCally had walked over to the whistles and taken one off the hook. He already had it at his mouth.

"Don't..."

McCally blew a single, long, note.

"...blow that."

"We've got incoming," Wiggins shouted, just two seconds before the shed door was thrown open and three of the beasts came in at speed.

***

Banks had no time to react; the first beast looked him in the eye, barked once, and launched itself into the air, feet and hands both outstretched, reaching for him, screeching as it came. Instinct and training kicked in; he rolled left and had his weapon up and aimed, pulled the trigger and put two quick rounds into the thing. It fell out of the air and landed, still twitching, at his feet.

Wiggins hadn't been so quick. The second beast went for him, and hit him, hard, in the chest before he got his gun up. He went down under a flurry of slashing talons and shrieking beak. The private managed to shove the barrel of his rifle sideways into the thing's mouth, stopping it from getting at him, but that only sent it into a greater frenzy. Its taloned hands tore sharp scratches in his flak vest, and there was blood at Wiggins' thighs where the equally taloned toes dug through the material of his trousers.

Banks kept rolling, stood and in one fluid movement kicked the creature full in the belly, launching it against the wall where it landed with a thud that shook dust out of the shed roof. It scrambled, looking for footing, but even as it prepared to launch itself again, Banks, with Wiggins beside him, shot most of its head off with a burst of fire.

There was one more shot, on the other side of the shed, then two loud, shrill blasts of sound. Banks looked over to see Hynd standing over another dead beast, with a tin whistle at his mouth.

Everything fell quiet.

"I guess two really does mean STOP," Hynd said laconically.

McCally went to the door and looked out.

"They're still there, cap. But they've gone back to just watching us again."

"For now," Banks said. "Just don't go blowing any more whistles unless I say so."

He looked over at Wiggins.

"You okay, lad?"

The Glaswegian patted himself down.

"I've still got my baws, but I'll need a new pair of trousers, cap," he said, and smiled. "And I'd like to bugger off out of here, if that's okay by you?"

"We're on the same wavelength on that, at least," Banks said, and fished the satellite phone from his belt.

He got put straight through to the colonel. It only took a few minutes for him to make his report, and much less time for the colonel to reply.

"Wildfire in one hour, on this mark," the officer said.

"Wildfire. Aye, aye, sir," Banks said, switched off the phone and turned to the squad.

"You all heard. Let's get the flock out of here. Double time."

They made for the door, stepping gingerly over the dead bodies of the three beasts. Banks took one of the whistles off a hook on the wall and dropped the thong around his neck. He had a feeling he might need it.

***

The beasts outside had only retreated as far as the long grass and stood, partially hidden, heads raised, watching the squad closely as they left the shed. Banks saw the red mohawk at the front of the group, and wondered if this one might be the leader. He kept his gaze fixed on the individual, and it met his stare, unblinking.

"Will they let us pass, cap?" Hynd said.

All the heads cocked simultaneously, listening. In other circumstances it might be almost comical. Banks took a step towards the red mohawk. It didn't flinch and stood its ground. He took another step, and this time the beast moved, not backward, but sideways. All of the rest of the animals moved in the same direction at the same time, as if defending the patch of ground to Banks' right.

"There's something over there they don't want us to get close to," Hynd said.

"Aye," Banks replied, as all the heads cocked to one side again, listening. "I wonder what it is?"

"Cap? We should head straight for the dinghy," Wiggins said. "My cock's hanging out of my trousers here."

McCally laughed, and four of the creatures barked in response, then they all went quiet as Banks took two steps to his right. On his third step, they all moved as one in the same direction. The one with the red mohawk kept its stare on him as it too moved.

"Follow me," Banks said. "We came here to see what's what. If what they're protecting is important to them, I want to see what it is."

Wiggins knew better than to disobey, and when Banks took another step to the right, his squad, and then the whole flock of beasts, moved in the same direction.

***

After ten more steps Banks was on the edge of one of the thin tracks, with the whole flock of beasts on the path ahead of him, blocking his way, the red mohawk at the head of them, only ten feet away now. Now that it had come all the way out of the long grass he saw that this one was larger still than the others he'd seen close up, thicker around chest and legs, the downy feathers on its flanks shimmering like a rainbow aurora in the sun. Its tail, long and leathery, swished behind it, and its snout opened and closed with a clack as it stared at him. Behind it the rest of the beasts were arranged in a wedge. Banks knew that one wrong move now would mean they'd have the whole flock swooping down on them at once; he thought they had enough firepower to handle it, but he didn't want to put it to the test.

Besides, I might have a better idea.

He lifted the whistle to his lips.

"I hope you've got a spare pair of trousers, cap," Wiggins said.

"That's the least of my worries," Banks replied, and blew hard on the whistle, not one, but three piercing notes.

As he'd hoped, all the beasts responded as one and, led by the red mohawk, trotted away in that strange bounding run, and stood in a circle around the shed with the wonky door.

HOME.

Two of them started to feed messily on the carcass of the dead one that Banks had shot.

"At least we know what they eat," McCally said softly.

"And while they're about that, they won't be bothering us. Come on. Let's see what they were hoping to hide."

Banks led the squad away along the trail. Behind them the red mohawk cawed, as loud as any rook. Banks looked back; the beast looked nervous, head bobbing and twitching, its gaze still fixed on him. It took two steps forward in his direction, but when he blew, three high tones again on the whistle, it stepped back among the rest of the flock around the shed door.

"How can they be trained?" Hynd asked. "There's been nae buggers here but us for a hundred years."

"My guess?" Banks said. "They teach each other. Smart, and sneaky wee beasties, so watch your back."

He led the squad off down the track. Behind them the red mohawk cawed again, but when Banks looked round, it was still with the others around the door.

***

More of the loud cawing came from behind them, more insistent the further they walked from the hut. They found the cause of the beast's worry not long afterward; a clearing in the grass that looked like it might be used by the creatures as a communal area. Two of the feathered beasts sat, almost hidden in the vegetation. Their heads came up, and pale eyes looked directly at Banks. Wiggins stepped forward, too quickly, and one of the two got up, unsteady at first, then, once it was on its feet, launched

83

itself at the man with a screech.

McCally put it down with three shots that echoed along the spine of the island, to be answered by frantic cawing from the direction of the shed at their back. The second beast trilled and barked, and answering trills sounded loud.

"Maybe we shouldn't have done that," Hynd said, and pointed with the barrel of his rifle to where the beast had been sitting. Six large eggs, bigger than tennis balls and heavier at one end than the other, sat in a circle in a flattened patch of grass.

The still sitting creature lifted its head high and called out loudly, and was answered again. Banks blew three high notes on the whistle, but the answering calls were getting louder, and closer.

"I guess the training only works so far," he said and turned to the men. "Leg it. We've got company coming, and Wiggo isn't dressed for it."

***

They ran full pelt along a track that Banks knew was heading in the right direction but had no idea whether it would actually bring them out on the cliffs above the shore where they'd left the dinghy. The cries, trills and caws of the creatures echoed loudly around them, and now they were coming from all sides.

No attack came, and Banks was wondering why when they reached the end of the track where it reached the cliff top. The beasts stood there in a long row, between them and the way down to the beach. The red mohawk looked at Banks, bobbed its head twice, and cawed loudly.

Banks lowered his weapon, and lifted the whistle to his mouth. The red mohawk never took its eyes off him as he blew, three times.

"Go on then," Wiggins said. "Bugger off home, there's a good dinosaur."

The whole flock cocked their heads to the side, but that was the sum total of any movement.

"I told you," McCally said. "They don't understand Glaswegian."

The red mohawk was still staring at Banks, and showing no signs of moving away.

"How long have we got, cap?" Hynd said.

"Half an hour or so at a guess, maybe less," Banks said, as the red mohawk took a step toward him.

Banks raised his weapon, showed it to the beast, and fired two quick shots, over its head. That got their attention quickly enough and when the red mohawk turned and ran off into the long grass the rest of the flock followed.

Within seconds the squad stood alone, on the cliff top looking down to the dinghy on the shore below.

**

"Well, that was easy," Wiggins said.

"Too easy, lad. Remember, they're smart, and sneaky. Eyes open wide until we're out on the water. Now shag it, people, double time. We've got a shitstorm incoming, and we don't want to be here when it happens."

He let McCally take point, with Wiggins and Hynd following. He brought up the rear, trying to keep one eye on the rough, steep track, and the other on the cliff top above them, expecting at any moment to see a row of bobbing heads pop up on the skyline.

It was slow going, having to watch every step to avoid losing footing and get sent to the rocks waiting below, made slower still by having to watch their backs. But in any case, Banks was looking in the wrong place for an attack; it came halfway down the cliff, from a thicket of gorse at a bend in the track above a bank of scree, and all he saw at first was the flash of red of the mohawk. Then it was on him, its full weight catching him on the chest and knocking him over. Instinctively he threw out his spare hand, and caught the beast by the neck as the snout headed for his throat. When he lost balance and fell aside, he took the creature with him and they tumbled and rolled, off the track and down a scree slope, accelerating as they fell.

He knew there was a drop somewhere ahead, but had no time to worry about it as the red mohawk tried again for his throat while its taloned hands tore ribbons of material from his flak jacket, trying to reach the soft parts below.

Banks was vaguely aware that shots were being fired, but he hardly heard them above the tumble of falling scree and the screeching of the red mohawk, its teeth only inches from his face, its hot, rancid breath on his cheeks.

Then he was falling through open air, a panicked second where he thought he was about to be dashed, hard on the rocks at the bottom of the cliff. Instead he landed soft, feeling vegetation scrape and tear at his hands and legs. There was a hard tug at his neck, and he thought the beast had got through his defense, then he saw the red mohawk's tail flick as it escaped off into the thick gorse when Hynd, Wiggins and McCally came running to his aid.

He felt around his neck as he stood, and realized what had happened.

"Smart and sneaky right enough," he said as the others arrived at his side. "The wee bugger has made off with the bloody whistle."

"That's the least of our worries, cap," Hynd said. "We're going to need a new taxi."

They were standing on a rocky outcrop above the shore. Banks followed Hynd's gaze and looked down.

There wasn't much left of their dinghy but a mess of ripped rubber strips and torn wiring in the propeller housing.

***

Banks checked his watch.

"No time," he said, "the hit's already incoming. Get into the water. It's all we can do now."

He followed the others down to the shore, had a last, longing look at all that was left of their dinghy. He winced as he strode into the cold waters, feeling the chill bite at his ankles and the tidal surge tug at his legs, threatening to suck him all the way out to sea.

He got out the phone and called in. The colonel wasn't happy at the loss of the dinghy, but promised, curtly, that a chopper would be on its way – if they survived that long.

Then all there was for it was to wait.

He turned back to look at the island, just in time to see the flash of red as the mohawk bobbed down into the gorse after having a look at them. He realized something else; a bombing run on the top of the island wasn't going to kill anything that was down with them close to the shore.

I have to get them back up top.

He turned to the men who stood now, knee deep in the light surf some five yards from the shore.

"You know how to whistle, don't you?" he said. "Then whistle."

He put two fingers at the side of his mouth and sent out a high whistle, three sharp notes. The effect was immediate; the red mohawk head, and ten others behind it, popped up out of the gorse, all cocked to one side, listening.

"Home!" Banks shouted. "Go home."

The other three men joined their whistles with his.

The red mohawk strode out of the gorse, the others following behind, and came almost to the waterline.

"Go home!" Banks shouted, and whistled again.

The red mohawk looked at the ruin of the dinghy, then at the men out in the water, then back at the dinghy.

Banks whistled again. The mohawk cawed back, three times, then turned and ran, full pelt up the track to the cliff top, with his flock following close behind.

Banks didn't get time to celebrate, for at the same time he saw a black speck in the sky to the north, getting larger fast. The napalm blazed all across the cliff above seconds later, before they even heard the sound of the plane, then everything was red and roasting and roaring, so much so that they had to turn their back on it. Even then he felt the heat scorch at the back of his neck.

But it was over in seconds, and when he turned back, the whole top of the island was venting smoke and the last flickers of flame.

He raised his fingers to his lips and whistled, once.

But there was no reply.

***

It was only later, settled in a bar on the quayside in Bideford, that talk turned again to the origin of the beasts. Wiggins asked again, where the dinosaurs had come from. Banks lifted the satchel he'd carried with him since the shed, opened it and took out a battered leather-bound journal.

"We got rid of the boogers from the island," he said. "But I'm rather happy to think that there might be still more of them where they came from, somewhere in the Amazon."

He opened the journal and read.

"Being the journal of Edward Malone, and a telling of his adventures in Maple White Land in the Amazon Basin with Professor Summerlee, Lord John Roxton and Professor Challenger, July 1908."

The End

EXTINCTION

By Rich Restucci

Elmo, Utah. June 8, 2009.

Chloe Richards huffed as she bustled into her professor's tent. It was hot today, and she was out of breath and sweating from hurrying to show him her find. "It's a Tyrannosaur," she breathed, leaning over and putting her hands on her knees.

"I'm not shocked," the older man said, looking over the rim of his glasses. He wagged his head from side to side with an arrogant, almost annoyed shake. "This is Utah."

"Yeah, but—"

Professor Thorn cut her off, "Is this important? I'm quite busy." He shuffled some papers together for emphasis.

She righted herself, standing tall and showing him a photograph on her phone. "Yeah, it is."

He stared at the photo for a moment, squinted, then took the phone from her. "Is this a joke?"

On one of the larger teeth of the theropod fossil were the clear indents of the letters P ME DA.

Garden Park, Colorado. May 31, 2017.

"This… this is too much."

The suited man stared down his nose at Chloe. He looked exactly like her old professor, Doctor Thorn. "Ms. Richards, I assure you, it's possible."

"But *how*?"

"I'm not entirely sure. It has something to do with the separation of gravitational fields. The further you are from a field, the faster time moves. We can manipulate the fields and generate a temporal rift. The important question is: Will you go?"

"You've already sent a team?"

"Yes," the suit answered, "and they've returned. Twice. You'll experience some headaches the first couple of days because of the high oxygen content in the air, but we have a medication that will allow you to breathe normally. The headaches are light, I'm told."

"Of course, I'll go!"

The man smiled and put a sheaf of papers on the desk. A non-disclosure statement sat on top.

In two hours, Chloe stood on the steel and glass catwalk which had been erected across the center of a two-hundred foot, doughnut shaped tube. Nine others were with her. Two scientists she didn't know, and seven armed escorts. A pallet of plastic-wrapped Pelican cases would also be making the trip.

"We're buddies on this one." One of the men told her. He was pretty good looking and was armed to the teeth. "When the Spin is done, we're about four feet above ground level. You're going to fall, so be prepared to land properly. You won't be dizzy or disoriented, but you'll have a very slight headache after ten or so breaths. You ready?"

Chloe nodded. "What's your name?"

"David," the guy said and put his thumb up.

The other four soldiers put their thumbs up and suddenly Chloe was falling.

Garden Park, Colorado. Late Cretaceous Period.

Chloe landed hard on her feet. The impact was a bit jarring, but David held her by the arm so she wouldn't fall over. She looked up at him and smiled. He smiled back. She looked down, the ground black and steaming. A circular burn pattern, two hundred feet in diameter, surrounded the team.

"Watches!" One of the soldiers whispered loudly, and everyone checked their wrists. The return trip would be in five days and four hours exactly. Chloe had learned that the entry point of the Spin was significantly larger than the exit point. If they weren't in a twenty-foot radius of the entry point, they wouldn't be going home on the next Spin. The same soldier began counting down. "One hundred-nineteen hours on my mark… Three, two, one, mark!"

Everyone pressed a button on their identical watches, and four of the soldiers fanned out into the tall grass.

"So, you're the dino-chick."

Chloe turned to size up who had spoken. It had been one of the other two scientists, a man of indeterminate age with close cropped hair and a strong build.

She chortled. "Yeah. Yeah, I'm the *dino-chick*. Who're you?"

The speaker was fiddling with an aluminum case and he closed it gently. Chloe had noticed a foam padded lining and a single aluminum tube before he was able to shut the case.

"Colonel Thaddeus March, Army. Specifically, USAMRIID."

Chloe knew what the acronym meant, but she couldn't figure why an infectious disease consultant was necessary on this jaunt. She began to stick her hand out for an introductory shake, but March spun on his heel and moved toward the lush tropical forest.

The four scouts returned at the same time, each uttering one word to the commander, "Clear."

The soldier in charge nodded, and the group began to unpack the pallet of cases. A guttural roar, long and loud, rent the air. The men all raised their weapons.

"What kind was that?" David asked Chloe. He was aiming down the sight of his combat shotgun, sweeping the barrel from left to right and back.

"Like I know what an animal from sixty-five million years ago sounds like. If it was standing in front of me, we could discuss taxonomy."

"Sorry, of course." David looked nervous.

"Technically we aren't standing in the past." The third scientist smiled at Chloe. "We're standing in one possible present time. Traveling into the past is impossible." This guy did stick his hand out and she shook it. "Anthoney Archambault, Cal-Tech. The Anthoney has an *e* on the end."

"Chloe Richards. The Chloe also has an e on the end." She smiled back at him as they cut the plastic wrap off the pallet of gear.

The team of ten shouldered packs, with two of the military men pulling sleds. As they moved toward the forest, Chloe felt the first bit of discomfort in her skull. She remembered she would have to endure a headache.

She was breathing heavily in twenty steps. "Ugh," she said under her breath as the heat of the day made her begin to sweat.

The beast smelled food. It raised its considerable head higher, breathing in the scent of a meal. This was not the fleeting scent of live prey, it was the deep, powerful smell of decay and the underlying but delicious odor of blood. While the warm flesh and the brief, terrified screams of fresh meat were considerably more pleasing, the beast was not above the pungent taste of carrion.

The beast was the apex predator of its time. Almost no creature dared face her, and everything ran when they saw her or caught her scent. She moved quietly for a creature weighing almost eight tons as she crept up on the odor. Many times before she had surprised other carrion eaters when they had thought they were perfectly safe. On those occasions she had tasted both the warmth of the living and the pervasive bitter of the rotting.

She could hear things eating through the dense forest. The tearing of flesh made an exquisite sound. She breathed deep the scent of what was to come but could not detect anything fresh. The odor of the dead must have overpowered the aroma of the living.

Slowly, ever so slowly, she poked her nose through the bush until she could see her prey. Her eyes focused on the scene in the clearing in front of her. She was immediately confused. Two horn-faces, a club-tail, and several of those egg-eaters were feasting on one of her kind. She watched as one of the smaller egg-eaters ripped off a chunk of tongue and swallowed it down. Her dead kin was the male rival she sometimes consorted with and this filled her with rage. She burst into the glade with a mighty roar, shaking her head and bearing her ample teeth.

The creatures stopped their meal and turned to stare at her. They appeared all wrong, with pieces of them missing and bones protruding here and there. One of the horn-faces had no belly, the jagged tips of broken ribs sticking out of its empty mid-section at mismatched lengths.

The creatures, usually prey animals and terrified of her, should have scattered into the jungle at the very idea of her. Instead, they began to awkwardly stumble in her direction, their last meal dripping from their mostly toothless jaws. Something was terribly wrong here. An odd sensation came over the beast. A forgotten feeling which she had not encountered since she was very young. Until this moment she had had no cause to suffer this emotion and she didn't like it. She turned tail and sprinted into the bush, her vast weight crushing foliage as hunter turned to prey.

"Well, we weren't really told anything," Chloe said to Anthoney. "I only just met everyone today." She looked across the campfire to the three soldiers stringing a series of heavy wires through poles at about three, six, and nine feet from the ground.

"Ditto. You're a paleo-scientist and I'm the quantum guy," he answered her. "I get both of those sciences as necessities on this trip." He lowered his voice to just above a whisper, "But what's a virologist doing here?"

"That's classified," Dr. March said from behind them. He moved out of the darkness with three cups of coffee, handing one to each of the other scientists. He sat on the log next to Dr. Archambault. Something screamed in the night, Chloe and Anthoney whipped their heads around to stare into the dark forest.

Dr. March's face was partly in shadow, but Chloe could still see half of his smile. "Relax. Our escorts are providing a defensible perimeter right now. Those cables will conduct ten thousand volts into anything that touch them." March took a gulp of the steaming liquid and continued. "We're quite safe, I assure you."

"I still can't believe I'm here," blurted Chloe. "This is like a dream."

March raised his eyebrows, "Did you often dream about dinosaurs and visiting the Cretaceous period?"

"Duh, *paleontologist*?"

March and Anthoney laughed. "Touché."

She looked at March "So why me? Any researcher in the world would have jumped at the chance to be here. I'm a nobody. There are hundreds of people more qualified than me to have as your paleo-consultant."

March stared at the fire. He blinked twice and took another huge gulp from his cup. "Because you have no one. No family, few friends, none of whom you speak with on a regular basis. You've been on one date in six years and your coworkers all say you're a workaholic, but you mostly work from your private lab in your garage."

It was her turn to blink. "How… how did…"

March tore his gaze from the orange coals and sighed. "Nobody will miss you. Nobody will miss any of us."

Anthoney harrumphed. "You mean if we get killed."

"Exactly," March nodded.

"All set, Doc," Sampson, the military commander, told March.

"Excellent, thank you." He stood. "We should get some sleep. Long day tomorrow. The animals won't come near the fire, and if they do, they'll get turned away by the cables. Good night."

Chloe and Dr. Archambault stood as well. "Night then," he said to her and they moved off to their tents.

David was standing outside her tent when she arrived. He held the flap open for her. She crossed her arms. "You're not that cute. We just met."

He smiled at her. "My tent is there." He pointed to the one next to hers. "I share it with another guy, but I'm on watch until three."

"Thanks, David." She crawled into her shelter.

"Keep your shoes inside with you and check them before you put them on. If you have to pee, you get me first. I won't peek. And I am cute," he added as he strode off.

Russo stared into the sweltering evening. From twenty feet up on his platform, he had a bird's eye-view of the small camp from forty feet outside the wire. He would get no sleep tonight, but he knew that before he signed up for this mission. Going back millions of years to hang out with dinosaurs while he baby-sat the Doc and his stooges? It was worth losing a night's rack. Holy shit this was cool. He couldn't ever tell anybody, not that they would believe him, but it was still cool. He brought his rifle up, placing the night vision optics to his eye, and scanned the area. He had heard some crashing through the brush an hour ago but hadn't seen anything with the scope.

Something smelled bad though. They had scouted the area then set up the fence, but they must have missed whatever dead thing he was smelling now. One of the rules he had to memorize was that they didn't set camp near dead animals or on a game trail. Too many carrion eaters that would easily switch to live prey. Russo smiled. He was the live prey. That was both exhilarating and terrifying at the same time. His smile didn't fade as he lowered the rifle barrel. Too cool.

The smell of rotting meat suddenly became overpowering. When a stick snapped behind him, he looked over his shoulder and down. Seeing nothing he brought the rifle back up to utilize the night vision. As he slowly swept the rifle barrel left, it impacted something with a wet slap. Russo had a brief glimpse of a huge reptilian mouth before the teeth of the creature closed around his head and left shoulder. He tried to scream, but the disgusting tongue of the thing smothered his entire face in a wet press of foul smelling saliva. The thing bit down, two-inch teeth slicing through Russo's neck, left shoulder, and right forearm. The barrel of his rifle bent almost ninety degrees from the pressure of the Tyrannosaur's bite. Russo's lower body fell off the tree stand, landing with a hushed thud in the bushes. The left side of his upper torso slid down the thing's gullet, through its open abdominal cavity and onto the ground next to the rest of him. Covered in stinking slime, with his eyes blinking rapidly, his mind had three seconds to process that there were now two pieces of him before life mercifully fled.

The creature bent its head down, grasping the rest of Russo's corpse between its jaws. The thing tore at the soldier's remains, swallowing great chunks of the man. Each bit of the ravaged corpse fell from the ragged hole in the animal's abdominal cavity, but it didn't seem to notice.

A small mammal, akin to a ferret, scampered away from the carnage. The massive reptile noticed and gave an unsteady chase, crashing through the brush.

"What the hell was that?" demanded Sampson. "Russo report! What have you got, over?"

Tent flaps opened, and members of the team rushed into the center of the camp.

"That sounded big!" Anthoney whispered to Chloe.

The armed men were sweeping left and right with their weapons, using night vision goggles or weapon optics to search for the source of the sound.

"Russo, come in! Russo!" Sampson scoured the camp but didn't see his man. He knew Russo was outside the wire, so maybe the soldier couldn't respond as hostiles were near. "Sound off!"

Each of the soldiers sounded off with a whisper and each of the designated body guards informed Sampson that their charges were present.

"Riley, Summers, go check Russo. Constant contact with base! Moveout!"

Two of the soldiers peeled away from the group and moved under the wire. March ran to his tent and returned with his aluminum case.

"What the hell is in there?" asked Anthoney, pointing at the briefcase.

"Classifi—" March was interrupted by a human yell from the forest.

Several large thuds and some snapping foliage alerted the group that something large was near. Gunfire erupted from the direction Riley and Summers had gone.

David grabbed Chloe's arm, "We might need to run, are you ready?"

She glanced down at her bare feet, "I need to get—"

A horrible rasping sound caught everyone's attention, eyes and rifles shifting to the right. The group stared at a huge creature standing just outside the electric wire. The firelight illuminated a triceratops staring back.

Chloe gave an audible sigh, "It's only a triceratops. They aren't carnivores, it won't hurt us. It's *beautiful*!"

More rifle fire came from behind them.

"Contact!" screamed through the soldier's headsets so loud that Chloe heard it.

Odd sounds came from the triceratops as it lumbered forward. It struck the electric cables with its plated head and plowed through them. Electricity flowed through the creature, its flesh popping and searing. It didn't slow, which didn't make sense. Even by the light of the fire and the waning moon, Chloe could tell the animal was sick. Dark fluids stained its mouth and nostrils and it swayed as it stumbled on unsteady feet.

One of the soldiers fired a single shot, which struck the animal in the head plate. It took no notice other than to turn toward the shooter. It picked up speed stomping toward the campfire and the man behind it. Through the darkness, Chloe thought she saw the shiny white of bone poking out of the beast's left shoulder. Her eyes widened when the firelight illuminated protruding rib bones and she noticed most of the animal's mid-section and tail flesh were missing.

"How... how can it be alive?" she whispered aloud to herself.

"It isn't!" March yelled.

A scream from the forest was the last straw for Sampson and his three men. They began firing at the triceratops, rifle and shotgun rounds penetrating the left side of the creature. It didn't slow in the least and as it crashed through the fire, Riley came running from the trees. He made it eight steps before a Tyrannosaurus, also missing portions of itself, leaned from the shadows and grabbed him with its jaws.

The triceratops' beak slashed forward and hit the soldier in front of it. He fell to the side, but the massive creature kept moving, making its way to the Tyrannosaur. The immense meat-eater was trying to swallow the unfortunate Riley, but the triceratops moved forward, completely unafraid of the theropod and gored it with its horns. Neither animal seemed to care.

Both animals backed away from each other when the bottom half of Riley fell to the ground. The triceratops got to him first, and its beak crunched down on the dead man's leg.

One of the soldiers began screaming as he fired his rifle at both dinosaurs. Chloe stood stunned until David pulled her away from the slaughter. "Come on!"

They sprinted back toward the other end of the camp, Chloe and David out in front, Anthoney and March following closely behind. Chloe and her group reached the fence on the far side of the camp and carefully skirted under it.

"What the hell was that?" Chloe demanded.

March caught his breath. "*That* is why we're here."

The four of them dashed forward and disappeared into the tall grass.

The blue glow of David's watch illuminated his face. "Only ninety-eight hours to go." He looked toward the eastern sky, the faintest glimmer visible over the dense canopy of the forest. "It will be light in an hour at most." He had tried the radio several times, but none of his team had responded.

Chloe leaned against an ancient tree and inspected her feet. They were battered and bloody. David noticed and began to unlace his boots.

"Stop," she said and he did, glancing up at her. "They won't fit me. I appreciate it, but don't."

"She's right," March added, "If we're going—"

Chloe stabbed a finger at him. "What the hell is going on? Why did that animal look like that? What did you mean it wasn't alive? It was moving around! Why didn't the Tyrannosaur attack the triceratops?"

"Sorry, that's all classified."

She shook her head. "You son of a bitch. Those men died for *you*? It was all *you*?"

"Those men died on a mission," he spat.

"They were my men," David rebuked with venom, "my team and my friends." The soldier brought his shotgun up. He didn't point it at the doctor, but March got the message.

March put the aluminum case on the ground. "Lower your weapon, soldier."

"Shut up, Doc. We have a lot of time left before the Spin brings us back. Do you really think we're going to live long enough to reach the return point if we don't know what's going on?" Now David did aim the weapon at March. "Spill it, or the three of us will swear you were eaten." He jacked the pump on the shotgun once for emphasis.

The doctor took a step back, glancing at his three incensed teammates and sighed. "There's a rare species of plant here, an ancient predecessor of nightshade that has… special properties," March confessed. "When an extract of the plant is combined with some modern chemicals and bombarded with ionizing radiation, the synthesized reactant is, for lack of a better word; *unbelievable*. Imagine the possibilities! We could drop a teaspoon of this stuff," he pointed to the case, "into an enemy water supply, or have an aerosol spray infect an entire regiment! They would be killing each other in minutes. How many lives could we save? This will change warfare, possibly eliminate it!"

"A weapon," Anthoney breathed. "We're here for a biological weapon." He shook his head in disbelief and disgust.

The virologist continued. "We tested it on one animal the second time we were here. We figured if the experiment got out of control, it would be seventy million years in the past. We destroyed the infected animal after the experiment! We burned it until there was nothing left."

The sun peeked over the trees and chased away the shadows as March reached down for his case. "I need more samples of the plant to formulate a vaccine before we can utilize the reactant as a weapon."

As one, the group shifted their gaze across the prairie when something huge began crashing through the brush.

She had to get away. The feeling of fear was all encompassing as the beast ran for her life. She burst from the trees into the grasslands, the foul smelling creatures lumbering after her. They were slower and smaller than she, which usually meant she could kill them easily, but there were dozens, and she had already torn several to shreds. Even when there was barely anything left of one of them, it crawled after her with a hunger which, until now, she believed only she possessed. She had to negotiate the trees and thick foliage in the forest, but the smaller creatures could bypass all of the bush, nipping at her. The things had almost caught her twice.

She thundered through the meadow, the tops of the stalks up to her mid-section. Coming across an open portion of the grass, trampled and black, she noticed one of the two-feet. It also smelled foul and was missing one of its top appendages. She rushed forward, leaning in with her jaws. Once she had it in her mouth she shook it violently and tossed it to the side, torn and broken.

She could smell more of the two-feet, these ones very much alive, and she dashed forward, following the scent. If she were quick, she could sate her gnawing hunger and still be away before the dead things caught her.

In moments she could discern their scent auras through a thin stand of trees on the far side of the grassland. Four orange, vapor-like forms, motionless and ready to be devoured. She dared a quick, furtive rest, catching her breath before the dead things could find her. Only a few exhalations later, the sickly-sweet stench of death assaulted her nostrils. Rustling in the stalks behind her, which on any other day would have meant fresh meat, triggered her fear and got her moving again. The mutilated head of her younger consort lifted above the tall grass and he snapped at her. She deftly sidestepped and raced toward the scent-auras as fast as her strong legs would carry her.

Anthoney strained to see what was coming, "What is that?"

"It's big, whatever it is," David blurted.

"It's a Tyrannosaur!" Chloe had time to yell before it burst from the grass directly behind them. The beast was moving quickly when it reached to the side and snapped at March. He tried to dive to his left, but the animal succeeded in grabbing him by the shoulder. The creature bit down and held him as he screamed. The head of the Tyrannosaurus bobbed up and down as it ran through the grass with March locked firmly between its jaws. Both disappeared into the forest on the far side of the vast clearing.

"Holy shit, it ate him," Anthoney screamed. "It ate him!" He pointed at the wide swath the creature had made in the grass with its massive girth.

David grabbed Anthoney, covering the scientist's mouth with his hand. He pulled Chloe with them and they ducked down behind the small stand of trees they had been resting near. Another Tyrannosaurus, this one a bit smaller, stumbled into view. It lifted its head to peer across the top of the grass canopy, moving its head from side to side. One of the theropod's small arms was missing, a nub of yellow bone protruding from its mauled left side. A large portion of the creature's cheek had been eaten away, exposing the dagger-like teeth all the way back to its neck. The belly of the thing was also missing, shreds of brown flesh dangling into the open air. An Avaceratops stumbled into view weaving between the legs of an animal that it should be terrified of. The small, frilled, plant-eater had no flesh on half of its tail, bone exposed the length of it. The broken spikes of ribs also poked through its side and a portion of its frill was hanging at an odd angle. A toothless, duck-billed animal perhaps thirty feet long, entered the clearing followed by several ornithomimus, two pachycephalosaurs, and the triceratops the group had encountered last night. All sported horrible gashes or missing anatomy that no animal should be able to live without. Vile fluids rained from open wounds coating the yellow, trampled grass in thick puddles of red and black.

A roar from the forest in front of them had them all turn towards the sound. The things lumbered off at different speeds on unsteady legs, more infected creatures faltering through the stalks after them.

When no more rustling came from the grass, David poked his head around the ancient trees.

"It's clear. We should move and get someplace where they can't reach us. I want to check the Spin location first to make sure it's clear, then we head into the jungle. They didn't seem to smell us when they moved past."

"They're dead," Chloe stated flatly.

"They sure looked it," David agreed, shouldering his pack. "But how the hell can they be walking around if they're dead?"

Anthoney pointed at March's case, "It has to be whatever's in that. Whatever is in there is making dead things walk."

"It's more than that," Chloe added with a shiver. "They're eating each other. Not just the carnivores, all of them. The herbivores are eating meat as well, which is impossible because some of them wouldn't be able to digest it." She looked at her bloody feet. "It must be contagious. It's spreading, and probably because of fluid transfer. Also, prey animals and carnivores are moving together in herds. That goes against everything I've ever been taught." David moved to help her, but she gently pushed him away. "Do you have anything I can wrap my feet within that backpack?"

He fished around in his assault pack, finding a gray sweatshirt. He cut the arms off and Chloe put her feet in them as if they were giant socks.

"What do we do?" Anthoney enquired. "How the hell do we live three more days with those things running around?"

David shook his head, "You knew the risks."

"Yeah but there were supposed to be live dinosaurs, not undead ones!"

"What difference does it make?" The soldier demanded, "Live or dead, if they eat you they eat you."

"Because now *everything* wants to eat us! I never thought I would have to run from a dead triceratops!"

David shrugged and turned his attention to Chloe. He crinkled his face up in sympathy, "Can you walk?"

"Damn skippy I can walk. I can damn well run." She leaned on him as she tied the sleeves of the sweatshirt arms closed over her feet.

"What's that?" Anthoney was pointing back through the clearing. A figure stood at the edge of the grass, where the stalks had been trampled by the herd of mix-matched dinosaurs minutes before. It was a man dressed in the same black tactical clothing as David. "Is that Sampson?"

Anthoney put his hands up next to his mouth to focus his shout to their comrade, but David told him to wait. There was something wrong with Sampson. He slowly turned his head in several directions then took two unsteady steps forward before stopping. He looked to be searching for something. A second man appeared through the grass.

Anthoney swallowed hard, "Jesus…"

It was Summers. His right arm and a third of his chest were gone. His head leaned so far to the right it looked as if he would topple over. His left arm stuck partially into the air, his whole body out of whack.

A red streak exploded from the grass behind the men, leaping high into the air and landing on Summers, knocking what was left of him to the ground. The seven-foot creature ripped into the thing that had been Summers, its lower feet running in place shredding the corpse with its savage claws. It reached it partially feathered head down to the soldier and ripped a chunk away from the exposed chest, throwing its head back to swallow its prize.

"It's a Dromeosaurus!" Chloe whispered. "We need to get out of here, now! There will be more of them!"

The Dromeosaurus, a bipedal meat-eater looking like a cross between a dinosaur and a huge, red bird, spun to face Sampson, who was advancing on it. The animal lowered its head and spread its feathered arms. Even from a distance of sixty feet, Chloe could see the lengthy claws the theropod possessed. It sunk even lower on its haunches for a brief moment then launched itself at the oncoming Sampson. Both went to the ground, but the dinosaur was up in an instant, tearing at the flesh of the human.

Sampson latched his hands onto the creature's neck when it leaned down to take a second bite. Surprised, it pulled its head up, Sampson coming with it. The animal shrieked when Sampson sunk his teeth into its shoulder. A second Dromeosaurus burst from the grass, followed by a third, and the animals made short work of the ravaged men.

"Stay low and follow me." David moved into a low crouch and the three survivors made their way toward the forest on the far side of the grassland.

80 Hours Until Next Spin

Crouched in an alcove of rock on the side of a high hill, three people looked down on the dark canopy of a prehistoric forest. They had run and dodged various wildlife, living and dead, and were finally able to take a wary rest.

David propped his MRE heater next to a rock and shook his head, "We can't have a fire."

"But won't it keep the animals away?" pleaded Anthoney.

"Yeah, the living ones. The dead ones don't seem to mind the flames."

"He's right," Chloe agreed. "A fire would just be a big beacon to them. We need to stay hidden until we can make our way back to the exit point." She stared at the stone roof of the rock outcropping they were under. She shivered, even though the evening was torrid. "Although a fire would be nice." She touched the stone, taking some of its warmth for herself.

Anthoney shivered as well, holding his arms across his chest in the heat. "We can catch it."

Chloe and David looked at him expectantly.

"Those two soldiers were clearly dead. Dead but moving around. I didn't put it together right away, but March talked about using whatever this is as a weapon. It was probably designed for humans. We're human. We can catch whatever that horrible condition is."

A bestial roar echoed through the trees. The group wasn't exactly used to the sound, but they weren't as terrified when they now heard these new noises as they had been. Crashing through the trees below them was something immense and it was moving quickly.

David passed the sausage and gravy MRE to Chloe, who took it eagerly.

"Careful, it's hot."

The three of them ate quietly, listening to the sounds of the forest around and below them. The preternatural noises of creatures extinct for millions of years was not lost on the visitors. David sat wary, Anthoney terrified, and Chloe eager to see more of the life the Cretaceous had to offer. She frowned when she realized that life might have been put in danger by humans from the future.

She sat stock still, an idea flowing through her mind. "There have been several mass extinctions throughout history. One of the most common theories for the last great extinction, which occurred at the end of the Cretaceous, is that an asteroid collided with Earth causing worldwide destruction and a nuclear winter from ash and debris thrown into our atmosphere."

"We know that," Anthoney confessed.

"What if it wasn't an asteroid? What if the extinction was caused by whatever this is? What if this infects the whole planet?"

"Then wouldn't everything be dead?" David asked. "Wouldn't there be some evidence of this... this whatever it is in our time? How could humans have evolved if there was no life left?"

Chloe continued, "During the last extinction, seventy-six percent of all species were lost. That's more than three quarters of all life on Earth." She nodded, "That's pretty substantial, but we have no evidence it was a plague. Several species of animal lived through whatever caused the extinction, maybe they aren't susceptible to whatever this is."

Anthoney finished his food and put the container in a plastic bag. "I believe in the theory of divided timelines. That means that you can't go into the past and kill your grandfather because it would create a paradox. You couldn't kill him because then you couldn't be born to go back and kill him. That means if you did go back and kill your grandad, you would create a different timeline where he doesn't exist but you do. So we can do whatever we want back here and our timeline will be unaffected." He shrugged. "I don't know if I believe that the last mass extinction was caused by this plague or not."

"Right," Chloe agreed, "but—"

Anthoney interrupted her with a scream of pain and terror. He tried to move forward, but something wrapped around him like a wide snake. It was amazingly fast, with dozens of spiny legs. The thing bit him in the side with three-inch, horizontal mandibles as the legs of the creature kept poking him all over. He was screaming and gurgling before either David or Chloe could do anything.

"It's a centipede!" Chloe screamed.

David brought his shotgun up, aiming it toward his unfortunate comrade. "I can't get a shot! It keeps moving!" He rushed forward and poked the weapon against the arthropod's center, careful not to have Anthoney on the business end. David pulled the trigger, blowing the centipede in half. The top half let go of its meal and scuttled away. David shot at it again, but it was too fast and crawled up and over the roof of the alcove. The bottom half began to flip over and over until David shot it over the edge of the cliff.

"Where is it?" he yelled, "Where did it go?" David searched, the barrel of his weapon pointing in all directions, while Chloe tended to Anthoney.

Her friend was making coughing noises and crushing his eyes closed in pain. He held his right hand over his left side, the left hand scratching at the rock floor of their half-cave.

"It... was so... strong. So... strong. I couldn't... couldn't..."

"Let me see," Chloe begged, "let me see it!"

He moved his hand and she ripped his shirt away. Thick blood streamed from a deep slice just below his bottom rib. Dozens of smaller holes covered his chest where the creature's legs had poked him. They were beginning to turn red, and some already had small blisters.

"David, trauma kit!"

He was there in an instant, handing Chloe a medium-size red bag. She un-zipped it and fished for a bandage.

"It burns," wheezed the injured man. "It burns all over."

"Some species of Scolpendra have legs that will sting when they crawl on you, and that's in our time." She looked at David, "Centipedes are venomous."

The soldier got down next to her, "Was it dead? Infected?"

"No. It wouldn't have been so fast, and it wouldn't have stopped attacking. Anthoney, can you move?"

"Hurts…"

"Yeah, but can you move your arms and legs?"

He nodded, flexing his fingers and lifting his knees as he lay on his back. "Yeah."

Chloe worked on her friend for a long while, stapling the laceration in his side and administering pain killers. At some point while she was washing the blisters on his chest, he mercifully passed out.

"Christ," bemoaned David, "that thing must have been four feet long."

28 Hours Until Next Spin.

The beast felt sick. She had escaped her relentless pursuers time and again, and she was exhausted. They had nipped at her as she ran but were unable to penetrate her skin with their pathetic beaks and mouths. She took a sniff of her surroundings to ensure the things weren't close before she plunged her jaws into a small river for a drink. More a moving puddle, it was difficult for her to get any liquid, the stream was so shallow. She drank, more mud than water, but the dank substance elicited some refreshment nonetheless. She simply could not rid herself of the taste of those things. She had bitten into many of them in the past day, spitting out their lacerated carcasses as soon as she could. Her last true meal had been one of the two-legs, and it had been small. Bones with little flesh. She was starving.

Her breath ragged, she lay down next to the river, listening to the trickle as it flowed over the rocks. She closed her eyes, secure in the knowledge that she was the queen of this land and none of the things would dare touch her.

She stood some time later, a new and gnawing hunger that was all consuming coursing through her entire being. Gone was the fear and trepidation of the previous day. This hunger would never be sated, it would be her driving motivation until time took her.

14 Minutes Until Next Spin

Anthoney had taken a turn for the worse in the three days since the centipede attack. The paralyzing venom hadn't affected the man too badly, but infection had set in. Many of the blisters left by the arthropod's legs had ruptured, oozing a vile-smelling pink pus. The bite on his side was festering even after repeated broad spectrum oral anti-bacterials. Chloe had removed Anthoney's bandage to apply a topical antiseptic cream, and she could see the wound was putrid.

David had fashioned a crude stretcher out of his tactical webbing and some tree branches. The group of three waited impatiently just inside the tall grass on the edge of the Spin location.

"Is it clear?" Anthoney whispered through agony and fever.

Chloe held his hand, but David answered. "Yeah, there's nothing there. We got this."

"You know, this really sucks," the injured man breathed.

Chloe harrumphed, "This was supposed to be the trip of a lifetime."

"You sound like a travel brochure," David told her then shifted his binoculars. "Holy shit, look." He pointed across the blackened grass to where the larger of the two dead T-Rex stood, unmoving. The creature's back was to the clearing.

David looked at a now unconscious Anthoney. "We have twenty seconds once the Spin starts to get to the center of the vortex." He sighed. "We'll never make it if we carry him and run."

"We can't leave him!"

"No, we can't." The soldier stared at the huge, undead animal, then at the center of the scorched grass a hundred and fifty feet away. He glanced at his watch, "Stay here. Run when the Spin starts. You'll know it when you see it."

He picked up the stretcher and made for the Spin point. He watched the back of the T-Rex as he traipsed over the blackened stalks.

"They made it!" Chloe breathed.

She saw a shimmer in the air above where David and Anthoney waited. The already burned grass began to smoke, then there was a loud whooshing noise, almost like a massive gust of wind.

The Tyrannosaur turned its gaze toward the sound and immediately began to thunder toward the food in front of it. Chloe burst from the grass, sprinting toward her friends as David began to fire at the massive animal with his shotgun. She realized when she was almost halfway to the Spin that the T-Rex would get there before her.

Chloe skidded to a stop in the steaming grass. Suddenly it was very hot. She turned and dashed back toward the tall stalks.

The Tyrannosaur had reached her friends and it stretched its torn and bloody jaws down towards David as he stood between it and Anthoney. The soldier fired one last time before he, Anthoney, and the dinosaur simply disappeared.

Dozens of undead reptiles stumbled into the clearing, searching for the source of the sound they had just heard. Chloe slowly backed further into the grass, running only when she was certain the creatures hadn't seen her.

19 Days Since Last Spin.

It was getting harder and harder for her to evade the undead things. She hadn't seen a living animal in weeks. The only good thing was that the dead ones seemed to rot to the point of immobility after just a few short days. She crept up on one of those things now. It had been the large female Tyrannosaur she had spent the last three weeks trying to avoid. Mostly bones, the thing would never move again. Part of the enormous animal was already covered by sediment from the river it lay next to.

She pulled her knife and knelt next to the theropod. Twenty minutes later she stood, thinking about the end of life on Earth. She glanced back, reviewing her toil on the tooth of the T-Rex. She hoped it would work. Carved into the tooth were the same three simple words she had carved over a hundred times now on dozens of species: HELP ME DAVID.

The End

THE FIRST MAN ON EARTH

By Geoff Jones

Ray saw the first dinosaur an hour after arriving in the past. His jaw hung open as he gawked out the side window at the creature, which looked like a giant turtle with lumpy spikes on its shell. He flipped through the ID cards until he found a match. "Ankle-saurus?" He glanced at the photo of his wife taped to the dashboard. "I'm probably not saying it right." Adeline would have known how to pronounce it.

According to the ID card, a hammer-like club grew on the tail of an *Ankylosaurus*. He needed to be cautious. His land wagon might look like an armored personnel carrier, but it was really little more than a glorified motor home. In fact, it was designed to deteriorate, so that no trace of the mission would be left behind.

Ray nudged the accelerator and the land wagon rolled through the forest. The giant conifers grew far apart, giving him room to stay clear of the turtle dinosaur, which rotated in place, watching him. As long as it faced him, Ray couldn't see the tail, which suited him just fine.

"These guys aren't so bad," Ray told his wife's photo, attempting to channel her optimism. After all, the fate of humanity depended on him.

The vehicle shuddered with the squeal of crunching metal.

Ray spun around. On the other side of the land wagon, a second turtle dinosaur cocked its clubbed tail in the air. It swung, striking again. Ray's head slammed against the side window as the impact shook the five-ton vehicle. Stars flickered in his vision.

He reached up and felt blood in his hair. "Shit." He had to get out of here.

The first dinosaur spun around, pointing its business end in his direction. Ray floored the accelerator. All six wheels whirled in the pine needles.

The creature struck the back of the land wagon as Ray passed by.

"Goddamn it." He peeked at the picture on the dashboard. "Sorry, Addie." Adeline didn't approve of profanity. Not because she was prudish. Hardly. But she thought it made him sound unrefined.

The land wagon's only windows were in the cockpit. Ray switched on the rear viewscreen. The turtle dinosaurs receded in the distance as he drove away from them.

Ray let out a long breath, trying to relax. "I told them I was the wrong guy for the job." He had been here an hour and already damaged his ride. He wove through the tree trunks, watching for more dinosaurs and checking the rear viewscreen to make sure he wasn't followed.

After a kilometer or so, he stopped in a clearing to examine the damage. The only door, centered on the rear of the land wagon, wouldn't open, so he climbed through the ceiling hatch and crossed the roof to the rungs on the back. The door frame crumpled inward where it had been struck by the turtle dinosaur's club. The rooftop hatch was now Ray's only entrance.

Climbing in and out wasn't a problem. Even at fifty-two, Ray was strong and healthy. What would happen when he was old and feeble? He'd worry about that later. For now, he had to focus on saving the world.

Was the world really worth saving? The events of the last month suggested otherwise. A nuclear holocaust had ravaged the planet.

"Adeline is worth saving," he said, knowing he would never see her again.

Ray walked around the land wagon, a six-wheeled cargo vehicle designed to cross any kind of terrain. The tail strikes had cratered the aluminum hull in three places, but other than the door, the damage seemed superficial. Ray used the rungs on the rear to climb back up top. He stood looking at the forest and touched the congealing blood on his scalp. He'd live.

The smells of sharp pine and rotting vegetation reminded him of northern California, where he and Adeline had walked among the sequoias on their tenth anniversary, back before they could afford to travel overseas.

If only she hadn't been overseas when the war started.

Ray climbed inside and sealed the hatch. He'd have time to mourn Adeline after he completed the mission. He had nothing else to do with the rest of his life.

The hatch opened over a short corridor behind the cockpit. Ray turned to the back of the vehicle, which was devoted primarily to storage. As he ate his way through the food supplies, it would hopefully become less claustrophobic.

Several boxes of foodstuffs had fallen to the floor. Ray replaced them on the stacks and then noticed the sleeping compartment. The wall bulged inward right in the middle of his tiny bed, where the turtle dinosaur had hammered it.

"Son of a bitch." He would have to sleep on the floor. Almost as bad as sleeping alone.

Ray returned to the cockpit and continued northeast at a plodding twenty-five kilometers an hour. By mid-afternoon, the forest gave way to open scrubland, dotted by squat palm trees and clumpy bushes with broad, paddle-shaped leaves.

Palms were a good sign. Ray needed to find an inland sea and then continue north along its shore until he reached the area Colorado would occupy in sixty-nine million years.

The team at the White Rock Institute had identified Denver as the best place to leave a time capsule with information inside that could prevent the war. The geology would change little between now and then, and urban development would explode in the early twenty-first century, all but guaranteeing the capsule's discovery. Denver was also an easy enough trip, only five hundred kilometers north of the Institute's home in Los Alamos, New Mexico.

When the sun dropped low on the western horizon, Ray parked the land wagon on a small hillock. Bugs as big as his fist flitted above the ferns, but there weren't any dinosaurs around. It felt like a safe enough place to stop for the night.

He called up the Stargazer software and glanced at the photograph. "Any tips on working this thing?" Adeline was always better with computers. Once night fell, a small camera on the roof would monitor the stars to determine his latitude. Ray looked out the window at the blue and orange sky, his first Cretaceous sunset. "You'd love the view here, Addie."

Adeline had been on her way home from Thailand when the end of the world began. They had been married twenty-six years and never conceived, which had been painful in their thirties, but Ray was thankful now. Losing a wife was hard enough. The photograph taped to the dashboard showed Adeline sailing on the San Francisco Bay. She leaned out over the water with the tiller in one hand and a rope in the other. The muscles twitched around Ray's mouth. He loved looking at the picture, no matter how much it hurt.

He let the software calibrate the camera and went to the back for dinner, settling on a tube of goop labeled "Pork Protein" that tasted like over-salted ham. He drank extra water to compensate, wishing for something stronger. He would need to find fresh water before long. The land wagon carried a three-day supply and water was the one thing Ray was allowed to collect freely. His instructions prohibited him from killing any animals and if he found edible plants, he was directed to limit what he took.

Rat-tat-tat-tat-tat. Rapid pinging filled the land wagon, amplified by the aluminum hull. It sounded like a machine gun.

Ray dropped the Pork Protein, raced up front, and snapped on the exterior lights. A big yellow bird with shiny black talons perched on the hood. Its innermost claws curved like question marks. One of them twitched and tapped the metal. *Rat-tat-tat-tat-tat.*

Ray waved his hand at the windscreen. "Go on. Shoo!" The bird ignored him. It wasn't really a bird, of course. It had a snout full of teeth instead of a beak, and feathered arms instead of wings. Dents covered the hood, like a car after a hailstorm. The bird dinosaur leaned over and sniffed the glass.

Ray still couldn't believe Rebecca had chosen him for this mission. He knew nothing about dinosaurs. She should have sent Charlie. He was the dinosaur nut, even had little plastic ones on his desk.

"Charlie isn't exactly fast on his feet," Rebecca had told Ray. "You're the kind of guy who gets things done. That's what this mission needs. There's no telling what you'll encounter."

Ray smirked. "How's this for fast on my fucking feet?" He reached under the steering wheel and flipped a plastic switch. The wipers swished across the glass.

The bird dinosaur pounced, tearing off one of the wipers with its teeth.

"Shit." Ray thumbed off the switch before it could snatch the other one too.

The dinosaur stepped forward, staring at him, one foot now on the bottom of the windscreen. The hooked talon cocked back, then bulleted down. A crack bolted across the glass.

"Fucker!" The land wagon was getting torn to pieces. Ray punched the steering wheel in anger, triggering the horn. The bird dinosaur jumped. The electronic bleat was loud inside the cabin and had to be deafening outside. Ray held down the horn and the sound blared through the night.

The dinosaur flapped its arms as if shooing away bees and leapt away into the dark. Yellow feathers floated down on the windscreen.

Ray looked over at Adeline's picture, feeling embarrassed and unrefined. "I'm not sure Charlie could have done any worse."

***

Ray set off at first light. As he drove through the scrubland, he saw more of the yellow bird dinosaurs, but none came close to the land wagon. According to the ID cards, they were some sort of dromaeosaur, possibly a *Saurornitholestes*, which Ray didn't even try to pronounce.

"Dinosaurs need common names," he told his wife's photo. "Nobody walks their *Canis lupus familiaris*. You walk your dog." He pictured Adeline smiling at the comment. "From here on, those will be known as Greater Yellow Glasscrackers."

The going was slow on the morning of his second day. He had to weave around the larger clumps of shrubs and rarely got up to twenty-five kilometers an hour.

According to the Stargazer software, he had camped last night somewhere west of Taos, which meant he had gone about a hundred kilometers. The land wagon had a two thousand kilometer range. After the hydrogen cells died, it would become a lodge.

When that happened, Ray was supposed to remove the wheels and disassemble as much of the engine as possible, to help ensure that all of the parts rusted and rotted. Except for the time capsule, everything on the land wagon had been designed to decompose over the millennia, which was one reason Ray had gone so far into the past.

The team had argued about how far back to send the mission. Ray suggested six years, right before the last U.S. election. He thought that would allow plenty of time to stop the war. It also meant he could see Adeline again. He could tell her he was sorry.

"Won't work," Rebecca insisted. She'd explained that the time machine was imprecise. She could target a specific millennium, but not a particular year or even a century with any certainty.

Charlie was adamant that Ray go back before the appearance of *Homo sapiens* or any recent human ancestors. If Ray did anything to alter the course of human evolution, the mission would be for naught.

In the end, Rebecca had settled on the late Cretaceous, right before the last great mass extinction. It would give the land wagon plenty of time to decompose, but more importantly, any impact Ray might have would be less likely to ripple forward. Seventy-five percent of all species were going to become extinct anyway.

Not unlike what was happening in modern times.

As the sun reached its zenith, Ray came to a wide river blocking his progress north. A herd of four-legged dinosaurs grazed on the far bank, their knife-like tails undulating in the air behind them. Long fleshy growths hung from their faces and they walked with their heads low to the ground. They were huge, bigger than elephants.

The closest match on the ID cards was a type known as ornithopods, but most of those had duckbills. None of the pictures showed that fleshy crap growing on their faces. "Of course not." Ray nodded. The ID cards were based on the fossil record. There weren't any bones in those hanging growths. It occurred to him that anyone studying an elephant skeleton wouldn't know it had a trunk unless they saw a live specimen.

The junk hanging from the dinosaurs' faces wriggled like squid tentacles. They looked grotesque, but Adeline would have thought they were cute. She was a champion of the underdog. It was one reason Ray loved her so much, and might also explain why she had loved him back.

Every so often, one of the Squid-Chins stood on its hind legs and looked over at the land wagon, as if daring him to cross the river.

"Well, what now?" Ray asked Adeline's photo. The water here was too swift and deep for the land wagon. Somewhere to the right, the river had to empty into the sea. If he went that way, he'd be blocked by the estuary. That meant he had to go left until he could find a shallow place to cross.

Ray cranked the wheel and started west. Foothills rose above the scrub in the distance and beyond that, a low mountain range. He couldn't let the river stop him. If Ray failed to complete the mission, there would be no one else to try. Los Alamos was gone.

The team's phones had chirped simultaneously with the dreaded warning:

BALLISTIC MISSILE THREAT INBOUND
SEEK IMMEDIATE SHELTER
THIS IS NOT A DRILL

The mission commander had been training with her backup in the Sangre de Cristo Mountains when the alert came through. There wasn't time for her to return to the lab. In a snap decision, Rebecca had ordered Ray, a glorified project manager, to go instead. She had activated the time machine five minutes before the missiles hit Los Alamos.

Ray was humanity's only hope.

***

Late in the afternoon, he found a place to cross. He parked the land wagon next to a wide pool and climbed to the rooftop. On the slope ahead, basketball-sized boulders covered the river. The water cascaded noisily underneath the rocks until it reached the pool, where the terrain flattened out. The rocks on the slope were close enough to one another that the land wagon's meter-tall tires should be able to cross them.

Ray breathed a sigh of relief. The warm, dense air reminded him of Florida. He unzipped his mission uniform, a one-piece body suit like something a fighter pilot might wear, and pissed off the side of the vehicle. More relief.

The terrain had grown wooded in the foothills and soaring conifers surrounded the pool. Ray dropped back through the hatch and collected a pair of twenty-liter water jugs. He might as well replenish his supply while he was here.

The cold water made a satisfying glug-glug sound as Ray filled the jugs. Adeline would have loved this spot. There was shade, fresh water, and the gentle swish of wind in the treetops. He decided to come back after completing the mission. He could live out his days in this picturesque little glen. He looked around for the best place to park the land wagon. There was more room on the other side of the river.

Across the pool, some thirty meters away, huge orange eyes watched him from the shadows. Ray froze.

He didn't need ID cards to recognize this dinosaur. *Tyrannosaurus rex*. It waited, motionless, ready to ambush anything that came close. Like Ray.

Vertigo swept over him. He felt like he was falling into the water. The mission didn't matter. That motherfucker was going to eat him.

The dinosaur's nostrils flexed, as if tasting the air. Scruffy black quills grew from its neck. Crimson tangles of feathers covered its flanks like fur and two flaps of skin hung from its jaw where its lower lip had been torn.

Ray's sphincter clenched tight enough to bend metal. He rose slowly, leaving the water jugs on the shore. He could come back for them later. If he lived. Ray backed slowly toward the land wagon, one excruciating step after another.

Eyes the size of tennis balls rotated in their sockets, tracking him.

Sweat dripped down Ray's face. He was five meters from the ladder.

The Tyrannosaurus burst into the pool like a freight train. A spray of water doused Ray. There was no time to climb the ladder. He dove between the back wheels and crawled toward the front, expecting jaws to clamp on his feet and drag him out. The ground trembled as the dinosaur stomped ashore. Ray froze between the middle wheels, keeping himself centered under the vehicle. He gasped, desperate to get enough air in his lungs.

The Tyrannosaurus sniffed the ground between the rear tires. Its breath smelled of sulfur and rotten meat. Ray rolled over to look back. A long pink tongue snaked out and probed the ground beneath the land wagon. Ray brought his heel down on the tongue as hard as he could. The Tyrannosaurus made a wet hissing sound and withdrew its head.

The beast pushed against the back of the vehicle. Metal screeched as the land wagon slid forward on locked tires. Ray scrambled backwards on his elbows to stay under the middle of it.

A sharp rock dug into his back.

The Tyrannosaurus walked around the land wagon, stopping between the vehicle and the river to sniff the wet dirt where Ray had pissed earlier.

Ray grabbed the rock from beneath his back and crab-crawled to the rear of the vehicle. He peeked out. The monster's tail thrashed in the air above him. Fear pricked up and down his spine.

Leaning on his side, Ray chucked the rock into the pool. It plunked into the water.

The Tyrannosaurus jerked toward the sound.

Ray spotted another rock a meter behind the vehicle. His chest compressed. He would be completely exposed. He scrambled out, grabbed the rock, and tossed it.

Sploosh.

The Tyrannosaurs stepped into the water, its tail smacking the land wagon.

Ray crawled on his knees and picked up two more rocks. If he could just get inside, he could drive up the rocky slope. He tossed one rock and then the other, right over the dinosaur. They splashed beyond it.

The Tyrannosaurus ducked its head underwater, searching for the source of the splashes.

"Get 'em, dumbass." Ray climbed the rungs, dropped through the hatch, engaged the motor, and slammed the accelerator. His heart hammered in his chest as the land wagon surged forward.

The Tyrannosaurus reeled around and burst from the water, following him.

The land wagon bounced onto the rocky incline. Ray clutched the wheel, trying to find the best line up the cascade of boulders. Granite scraped the underbelly. The slope was steeper than it looked, pressing Ray's sweat-soaked back into the captain's chair. He prayed the land wagon wouldn't tip over.

The head of the Tyrannosaurus filled the rear viewscreen.

Ray worked his way right, lurching up the rock fall and across to the other side of the river.

The Tyrannosaurus stopped at the base of the slope and lifted a clawed foot onto one of the boulders. The rock shifted beneath its weight, causing the dinosaur to step back onto the flat ground. Ray watched the rear viewscreen as the Tyrannosaurs tried another boulder, but it couldn't find stable footing on the rocky slope.

When the land wagon's tires struck dirt on the opposite side of the river a hundred meters upstream, relief washed over Ray. The Tyrannosaurus paced at the bottom of the rock fall. It only needed to cross the pool and walk up the slope on the far side to pursue him, but it didn't seem to understand this. Thank God for lizard brains.

Ray drove north until night fell and then turned back to the east, finally stopping when he reached the dunes. As the adrenaline dissipated from his system, he wondered if he would ever feel safe again.

***

The dunes were a blast. The land wagon climbed each one and barreled down the other side like a roller coaster. Ray wished he could share this with someone. "Hold on, Addie!" She would have screamed with glee, both hands in the air above her head.

When he crested the final dune and saw the open expanse, he parked and climbed out.

Charlie had told him an inland sea covered the middle of North America during the Cretaceous, and by God, there it was. Green waves lapped at a broad, mustard-colored beach. A crisp breeze brought the smell of salt and seaweed.

The plan was to bury the time capsule along the coast in the area that would someday become the city of Denver. The capsule contained a detailed history of the apocalypse, naming a trio of world leaders who had conspired to escalate tensions for their own political gain. Damning details about the three men would provide enough evidence of their corruption to prosecute them before they seized power, thus preventing the war. That was the theory, anyway.

Ray went to the back of the land wagon for a snack, craving peanut butter. He stopped to look at the time capsule, secured in a case on the wall like a fire extinguisher. Charlie had written "Break Glass to Save World" on the outside with a marker. Hilarious.

The capsule itself could not be opened without modern tools, to prevent tampering by Native Americans or early European settlers. In addition to details about the end of the world, the capsule contained the address of the White Rock Institute in Los Alamos and instructions about sending someone back in time. After all, if they prevented the war, they wouldn't have any reason to send it back. But if the capsule wasn't sent back in time, nothing would stop the war.

Ray's head hurt thinking about it.

It was all a long shot anyway. The capsule might not survive the next sixty-nine million years. It might never be found. It might not be delivered. Worst of all, Ray would never know if he had succeeded.

All he could do was his part, but not until he had something to eat.

Thirty minutes later, Ray wasn't just hungry, he was also annoyed. A thousand kilograms of high-density foodstuffs and not a single container of peanut butter. He couldn't open the time capsule, but maybe he could scratch a message on the outside. "Pack peanut butter." Would they send him some? Could he alter the future that way? Would the contents of the land wagon change suddenly, based on his message?

Ray settled for the closest thing he could find; a tube of applesauce so dense it was chewy. Gagging, he pressed the accelerator and slid down the final dune onto the sand flats.

"Don't be silly," Ray told himself. If he was going to leave a message asking for more supplies, he ought to come up with something better than peanut butter. Whiskey maybe.

He cruised along the beach at sixty kilometers an hour, which felt like flying after the previous two days. The smooth sand gave him a comfortable ride and the slate sky made the world feel big.

Adeline had been changing planes in Hong Kong when the airport was nuked. Before her trip, they had gotten into a fight, the details of which barely made sense in hindsight. Ray should have simply swallowed his pride and apologized. Their conversations had been tense before she left and terse over the phone. When the first missiles started flying, Ray couldn't reach her. He hadn't been able to say goodbye. He hadn't been able to tell her he was sorry.

Seventeen nations had been attacked. Three billion people killed. That left four billion who would die slowly from radiation and starvation.

Ray would give anything for one more day with Adeline. If she hadn't been overseas, he would have insisted on bringing her back in time with him. They could explore the Cretaceous together. She would have seen it all as one big adventure.

Rebecca might have prohibited Adeline from joining him. She thought that sending more than one person posed a greater risk to the timeline. Ray looked at the photo on the dash. "You wouldn't let her stop you, would you, babe?"

A mass on the beach ahead caught Ray's attention. "Is that seaweed?" It stretched from the dunes to the surf. Ray decelerated as he drew closer and saw that the mass was moving. Definitely not seaweed.

More than a thousand bird dinosaurs clustered on the sand, each the size of a small terrier. They were like miniature versions of the Greater Yellow Glasscracker, but white with a dash of grey on their shoulders and bright blue snouts.

Ray thought for a moment about barreling through them, but he couldn't risk killing any. He slowed down, hoping the flock would scatter, like a field full of geese chased by a dog.

A thousand blue heads turned in his direction.

Ray slowed to twenty-five kilometers an hour. He was fifteen meters from the edge of the flock when they finally started moving. They came straight at him, like a school of piranhas.

The little bastards swarmed the wagon, plinking against the metal body. Ray sped up to forty kilometers an hour. He didn't want to crush them, but he had to get through.

They held onto the edges of the hood and several hopped to the base of the windscreen, where they gripped the wiper arms and pecked at the glass. Ray flicked the switch and the single wiper swished three of them away.

He passed through the flock, but the land wagon was covered, furry with the little fuckers. Ray pressed the heel of his hand against the steering wheel. The horn blared, but the Blue Heads didn't seem to care. He shoved the pedal to the floor and sped up to seventy-five kilometers an hour. Blue Heads flew behind him as the slipstream plucked them off.

A few still clung to the vehicle, their claws gripping seams in the hull. Ray had to shake them all before he could ever hope to exit.

He swerved into the surf. Spray kicked up under the wheels and the remaining dinosaurs disappeared, blasted off by the water. He checked the rear viewscreen and laughed. A wake of bouncing Blue Heads tumbled in the breakers. They looked dazed.

"Serves you little shits right. Sorry, Adeline."

***

The biggest animals Ray had ever seen marched twenty meters offshore.

"They look like *Brontosaurus*," Ray said to his wife's photograph. "But I can't find *Brontosaurus* on the ID cards. The closest match is called *Alamosaurus*." He wondered if talking to a picture was good for his mental health.

The behemoths advanced along the coast with their long necks lowered, slurping up sea grass. Four adults walked in formation with a pair of juveniles between them. Their tails spiraled in the air behind them like tiny propellers. *Pterodactyls* flitted about the backs of the larger ones.

"What a stupid name." Ray held up a mocking finger. "Remember the *Alamosaurus*!"

Adeline always sought out local wildlife wherever they traveled. He had surprised her on their twenty-fifth anniversary with a trip to the Galapagos Islands.

"You would love these guys," Ray said, watching the herd out the side window. "But I'm afraid I'm going to have to call them Big-ass-o-saurs."

The land wagon rolled on.

Ray parked at dusk and launched the Stargazer program. His last reading had put him a hundred and fifty kilometers from Denver and he had driven that far since then.

"Bingo." The software put him at the thirty-fifth parallel, which was south of Denver in modern times, but the Skygazer program took into account how much the North American plate would drift over the next sixty-nine million years. Ray decided to bury the time capsule first thing in the morning.

After an extraordinarily bad dinner of freeze-dried chicken cubes, Ray settled down on the floor and slept. He dreamed that he and Adeline owned a ranch with a herd of Big-ass-o-saurs. They were branded with a sideways "8," the symbol for infinity.

Ray rose the next morning, stiff from his bed on the floor, and climbed to the rooftop hatch, inhaling a deep breath of sea air.

He turned to look at the ocean and faced a wall of teeth.

The Tyrannosaurus stood beside the land wagon, its head looming over the rooftop. The same Tyrannosaurus. Two flaps of skin hung from its torn lower lip.

It lunged, twisting its head sideways.

Ray let go of the ladder and dropped to the floor of the land wagon. Teeth as big as carving knives clamped shut where his head had been. Slimy spittle rained down on him.

Metal screamed and plastic fittings exploded as the Tyrannosaurus chomped off the hatch.

Ray scrambled to the captain's chair. The land wagon rocketed forward. "That fucker followed me."

He sped up to seventy-five kilometers an hour. Wind roared through the open hatch. The Tyrannosaurus stomped behind him. It wasn't gaining, but it showed no sign of abandoning the chase.

The range indicator on the dashboard showed twelve hundred kilometers remaining. The Tyrannosaurus couldn't possibly pursue him that far, could it? Every second took Ray away from his target location.

A churning mass stretched across the beach ahead. Another flock of Blue Heads. "I got an idea," Ray told the photo. He would lead the Tyrannosaurus right to the Blue Heads, and they would pounce on it, just like they had covered the land wagon.

Adeline would have liked his plan. Ray was learning.

He slowed down, allowing the Tyrannosaurus to catch up as the land wagon approached the Blue Heads. This flock looked smaller than the one he encountered yesterday, but there were still hundreds. Plenty.

Ray steered toward the center of the mass. The Blue Heads parted, giving him an opening. Some would probably attack the land wagon, but no matter. Ray knew how to clear them off.

As he entered the flock with the Tyrannosaurus close behind, the Blue Heads scattered. "Crap." They weren't swarming the Tyrannosaurus, they were fleeing from it. His plan wasn't working.

"Come on guys." Ray made a wide circle, corralling a clump of Blue Heads. He drove them toward the big predator.

The Tyrannosaurus, now visible out the side window, entered the flock. It loped along and then lunged to one side, coming up with a mouthful of bird dinosaurs. Carcasses dribbled from the monster's jaws and it snapped in the other direction, taking out several more. Blue Heads fell everywhere.

Ray continued his wide circle until he reached the hard sand at the edge of the surf and pointed back the way he had come. The Tyrannosaurus stood in a mound of bloody bodies. It opened its jaws and roared as the land wagon passed, a deep booming *BRAAAM* that Ray felt as much as he heard.

As he drove away, Ray watched the monster tear into its freshly-killed feast on the rear viewscreen.

***

Sea water seeped into the bottom of the two-meter hole. There was no point in digging deeper. Ray tossed the shovel aside and climbed into the land wagon, which was parked at the base of a dune, right on the thirty-fifth parallel.

The time capsule looked like a giant pill, almost a meter long and made of some shiny alloy that had been engineered to last for millions of years. Except for a hollow cavity in the center that contained the important information, the capsule was solid metal. It weighed more than a bag of cement. Ray held it on one shoulder and climbed through the hatch, his back spasming as he reached the top. He rolled the time capsule across the roof where it plummeted to the sand, then he stood and stretched. The beach lay empty in both directions. All that remained was to bury the capsule. Ray had done his part, though he would die here without ever knowing if the plan worked.

He could live here too.

The Tyrannosaurus was out there, several kilometers to the north, but Ray had escaped from it twice. He could do it again. He would study the dinosaurs and learn everything about them. He would sample the plants eaten by herbivores until he found enough to supplement his food supply. He would figure out how to avoid the most dangerous species. He could survive.

But he would be alone.

"I miss you, Adeline. And I love you. And I'm sorry." He said the words aloud as he looked down the silver cylinder in the sand. He hadn't been able to tell her that.

Maybe it wasn't too late.

Ray climbed back into the land wagon and found a screwdriver. He didn't know if he'd be able to scratch the surface, but he had to try. It worked. He spent the next hour carving his message on the side of the time capsule.

I miss you Adeline. And I love you. I'm sorry.

The words were clunky, as if a child had made them, but they were his. He hoped the scratches would survive the ages. He hoped someone at White Rock would pass along his message before the war began.

Ray dropped the time capsule into the hole and used the shovel to bury it. He patted the sand tight after a long sweaty hour. His job was done.

As he climbed the ladder on the back of the land wagon, a wave of dizziness swept over him. Ray hitched his arm around a rung and took a deep breath. It felt like the world was spinning. Had there really been a nuclear war? Or was he here to prevent a war? He couldn't remember. For a moment, he wasn't even sure where he was.

A salty breeze blew by and he focused on what he knew for sure. He had completed the mission and he understood what to do next. He would retrieve the water jugs and then go west to scout out a suitable place to park the land wagon. He had enough food to last for years. He could do this.

Ray climbed inside and went straight to the captain's chair. The dizzy feeling subsided.

"Mission accomplished," came a familiar voice from the back.

Ray turned around, afraid to look, but too desperate to stop himself.

Adeline stood by the bed, wearing a blue mission uniform that matched Ray's. She gave him a thumbs-up. "Let's go have an adventure."

The End

SAURIA

By Tim Curran

By the time Felix got to him, Ritchie had bled out. The Utahraptor had disemboweled him, torn off his right leg, and nearly decapitated him by chewing out the soft white meat of his throat. Ritchie was mangled and crushed, knobs of white bone thrusting from his perforated red remains. He had one eye left in his blood-spattered face, so clear, so blue, and it stared up at Felix as if he had died wanting to know *why*.

Felix felt his breath catch in his throat, a single hot tear rolling down his grimy cheek. Something white clenched in his chest.

Oh, kid...Jesus, Ritchie, don't go out on me like this.

But he had already gone out.

Felix was crouched down by him, there on the edge of the deserted town, Paynesville, trying to make sense of what had happened and formulate what might come next.

He felt a hand on his shoulder. "He's gone," Doc said.

Felix swallowed. "He was a good kid, you know? He was a really good kid." He swallowed again. "That fucking raptor came out of nowhere. It was so fast."

Doc nodded. "It's what they do. You let down your defenses for one minute and...well, that's all it takes."

The others—Dane, Misty, Ugly George, and Fly—had gathered in a loose circle behind them. They'd liked Ritchie, too. Maybe not as much as Felix, but they felt his loss. No one liked to lose anyone off the team. Every time one of them died, it made them feel their own mortality.

"Do you want to bury him?" Doc asked.

Felix did. God knows, that he did. But if they waited around to do that, then the pack would slip away completely, if it hadn't already, and they'd never clean them out before sunset.

"No, we don't have time for that."

It hurt him to say this because he knew that by the time they hunted down the pack and sorted them out, scavengers would get to Ritchie's body and strip it down to bones. It wasn't like it had been before the Big Impact, now everything was meat on the hoof.

"Let's go," he said.

They piled in behind him as he led them back into the town in the direction the pack had taken. There was a logical course of action here, he knew. The Utahraptors were much like leopards that he had read about many years before. They would charge out, gore their prey with claws and teeth, then run off and hide. Wait. Let their prey bleed and weaken, then they'd return, finish them off, and feed. It was the age-old strategy of the predator and it reached far back to the Mesozoic and probably beyond.

Now, with that in mind, if he and the others were to set up a blind in the nearest thicket and wait it out, the pack would return. But Felix didn't like the idea, sound as it was. The idea of waiting, sitting there, doing nothing…no, he just wasn't up to it. He had to find the pack. He had to kill them. It wasn't just his job now, it was an obsession.

"We should proceed very carefully," Doc said, the .300 Savage cradled in his arms. "They've tasted blood. They'll do whatever it takes to taste it again."

"That's what I'm hoping, Doc," Felix said. "Then we're going to kill them all."

"Keep your head," Doc warned him. "Don't let Ritchie's death color your judgement."

Good old Doc. The sage. Always full of good advice.

"I won't."

He put a hand on Felix's arm. "Just remember: they're smart."

Felix nodded. He knew. He knew, all right.

There were things that Doc wanted to say to him, but he was holding back. Doc had told them all not to scout ahead of the team, that it was dangerous, but Ritchie did it anyway and mainly because he was trying to impress Felix whom he looked up to. Now he was dead. Now Felix was hurting. Now they were all disturbed. They had grown to believe in luck. That when it was good, it was good; but when it turned bad, it would keep getting worse.

Everyone was scared now.

If not that, then concerned, threaded with anxiety.

Felix watched Doc looking them over. They respected his brain and his age, the fact that he had been a paleobiologist before the Big Impact, but they knew he wasn't in charge of this outfit. Maybe if he had been, there would have been a lot less dying. But Felix claimed that right. He was a hothead, a quick gun, and an opportunist, but nobody had ever acquainted such things with common sense or basal intelligence.

Right then, as he led them deeper into the green tangle of the town, he knew he was making a mistake. Just as Doc thought, he was turning this into a vendetta. That's not how you did it. When you hunted dinosaurs for a living, you didn't stalk them, you didn't run after them—you let them come to you. You baited them into carefully prepared killing fields, then wasted them.

To meet them on their own ground, to think even for a moment that your instincts were anywhere near as sharpened and lethal as theirs, was a huge mistake.

***

Not twenty-four hours before, Felix leaned against the hood of a Jeep, listening to Mayor Penwick—a round, bulbous, red-faced little man—going on and on about the new world, the rebuilding of society, how it would start in places like this with baby steps rather than giant leaps of any sort. Open hearts and ready hands and all that.

"And the first step is down there," he said. "Right down there."

They were standing on a gorse-covered hilltop looking into a gentle sloping valley below. Using binoculars, Felix studied it all in some detail. Dead center of the valley was a town called Paynesville. It had once held some 5,000 people. Now—at least as far as Penwick knew—it was empty. Felix walked down the red clay road, taking in the town from every possible vantage point his position would allow, as his boots kicked up clouds of red dust.

It looked like a nice town, he figured. There was a long, L-shaped main drag with plenty of stores and shops, squared-off blocks of ranch houses and older two-stories, some garish Victorians sprinkled liberally about, church steeples thrusting up amongst the trees. He saw a couple schools, a warehouse district sidling up to train tracks. A few parks. Ballfields. Same old, same old. A nice town, maybe a little green with all the Mesozoic foliage pressing in, but still a nice town.

What bothered him most was the heavy forest pressing in from all sides. Some hardwood, but mostly conifer and invasive Cretaceous scrub.

"The Big Impact was hard on us," Penwick admitted.

"It was hard on everyone," Felix said.

The Big Impact, as it was generally known, was the result of something science had feared for years: an asteroid impact. The asteroid in question was eight miles across when it entered the Earth's atmosphere. It struck the Changbai Mountains of Manchuria, creating a shock wave that was felt hundreds of miles away. The resulting seismic activity, firestorms, and erratic, devastating weather patterns killed millions. Huge amounts of debris were thrown up into the atmosphere. The sun barely peeked out for a month. Crops failed. Infrastructure collapsed. Millions more starved or were the victims of raging pandemics. All in all, two thirds of the world's population was eradicated. In the coming months, millions more died. A conservative estimate claimed that one quarter of the pre-impact population had survived. And as terrible as the impact was, it created a magnetic chain-reaction that (it was theorized) opened some sort of time rift to the late Cretaceous Period. Suddenly, the world was not only being overtaken by prehistoric flora but overrun with Cretaceous animals. The riddle of the disappearance of the dinosaurs from the fossil record was solved—they hadn't gone extinct at all, the majority of them had been funneled far into the future.

The irony of it all was that the very thing that was thought to have killed the dinosaurs, had brought them back again.

"We've sent people in there with guns, but they never come back. I'm hoping it'll be different with your group."

Felix nodded. *Shitkickers,* was what he meant. *Trigger-happy rednecks with guns that went after animals with names they couldn't pronounce.*

"We'll get 'em for you."

"I want to get my people in there," Penwick said. "Get them in there so we can reclaim our town and clean it up. Put things to right."

"But you don't care much for the wildlife," Felix said, watching a group of graceful-looking saltasaurids grazing happily amongst the lush vegetation in what had once been a football field adjacent to one of the schools.

"No, it's infested by those terrible animals."

"The dinosaurs."

"Yes," Penwick said, a hateful, devilish look coming over his features. "And that's where you and your people come in."

***

Felix led his crew away from the soft green jungle that was creeping in closer day by day, and deeper into the town itself.

The day had gone from bright and sunny to overcast and gray, a dull, murky haze obscuring what waited ahead. The neatly squared off streets and trim houses were going to rot as the Cretaceous infestation assimilated the world of men. Foliage that was lush and dank had taken over yards, ballfields, and playgrounds, all of it a vibrant emerald green. Huge cycads with scaly emerald trunks and crowns of drooping fronds had displaced oaks and maples. Primitive conifers towered over immense club mosses and flowering shrubs that appeared invasive and parasitic, vines of them engulfing houses. Hairy green creepers even grew across the streets.

"Looks like a rainforest," Fly said.

"Another couple years and there won't be any town," Doc told them.

"Probably won't even take that long, Doc," Dane said.

They passed over a bridge and a swarm of large orange wasp-like insects flew overhead, a few small insectivorous pterodactyls giving chase. Everything in the green, primordial world of Paynesville was vibrantly alive, buzzing and rustling, chirping and piping. The streets were potholed and cracked open, pools of dirty water filling dips.

A flock of ornithopods broke cover suddenly, nearly giving everyone a heart attack. They were small with iridescent blue plumage and bright red staffs of tail feathers. They charged across the road, chirping loudly. They looked like pimped-up chickens. One of them paused, cawing angrily at the intruders, challenging them. Fly kicked a stone at it and it shrilled, racing off.

The river was steaming and brown as tea. Giant horsetails and immense ferns shrouded its banks. There was a great break in them, about fifteen feet wide, and the drag marks were evident. It looked as if someone had beached a tank there.

"Croc down there," Doc said. "Big one. Maybe a *Deinosuchus*. Keep away from the banks."

Felix paused about half a block from the bridge. How the heck were they supposed to track anything in this green hell? Huge maples had once hugged the streets. They were still there, but leafless now and withered, looped with hanging parasitic creepers.

"Something?" Doc asked.

Felix shook his head.

He wasn't saying much and that was because he had the worst feeling down in the pit of his belly. They had cleaned out towns before. A motivated man with some good people, the proper weapons, and a plan could always best the dinosaurs. Most of them were dumb as any other animals, though a few were far-too crafty for their own good. But this time he was worried about what they were facing and that his little group was beginning to crumble from within.

He lit a cigarette, studying a flock of large birds in the distance. When he turned around, Dane was studying him with what seemed lethal intent, a .416 bolt-action Rigby at the ready.

"Something you want to say?" Felix asked him.

"Just waiting for your orders, boss."

Felix reluctantly turned away from him. Doc looked nervous. He didn't like any of it either. He knew there was trouble and he knew there *would* be from the moment Dane came in with Misty. *I'm not sexist or anything,* he'd said, *but I'm telling you a woman in this outfit is not a good idea. And especially one like her. She might be with Dane now, but you look in her eyes you can see she has plans.* Good old Doc. He always knew. He could always smell trouble coming around the bend. He was older than the rest of them, pushing sixty, educated and experienced. And wise. Felix figured he should have heeded his warning and kept Misty out. He should have done at least that. But he hadn't. No, now he'd slept with her. Dane wanted to kill him and the others…well, he had a feeling that they had lost more than a little respect for him.

"Not good," he said under his breath.

"What's that?" Doc asked.

Felix licked his lips, swallowed, tried to pretend he couldn't feel goddamn Dane standing behind him with a loaded weapon. "This place…something wrong about it. Hate to sound like a cliché here, Doc," he said, pulling off his cigarette, "but it's awful quiet."

"Yes, it is."

"Of course," Ugly George told them. "Ain't no people here."

Felix smiled. Oh, George. To be that gloriously, wonderfully dumb. There must have been a certain comfort in it. But *people* wasn't what Felix was worrying about.

He moved down the street, over fallen trees and around rusted vehicles. He hadn't gone far when he smelled a perfectly vile odor of spilled blood. It was an odor he knew well by that point. The others caught a whiff of it, too.

"God, that smell," Misty said.

Felix came to what had once been a vacant lot, he guessed, but was now just scrubland. In it, was the badly worried carcass of a medium-sized Utahraptor. Its flanks were stripped down to the bone, its spinal vertebrae laid bare. Most of its neck and hindquarters were missing. Something had fed upon it and fed well.

If everyone was nervous before, they were scared now. Unless there were a few stray large theropods hiding in the woods that they did not know about, then the Utahraptor pack should have been the dominant predators here.

But apparently they weren't.

Felix studied the slouching houses, the drooping greenery, the clotted masses of undergrowth. He felt very apprehensive.

It's out there, he thought. *And it's watching us.*

"What the hell could take down one of these things?" Fly asked.

The very idea was ludicrous and they all knew it—the Utahraptors were apex predators, lethal killing machines. They were not prey.

"Doc?" Felix said.

Doc shrugged. "Judging by the wounds, it doesn't look as if it was attacked by anything larger than itself. It may have been old or sick, diseased...who knows? The pack might have killed this one themselves. We know so little about their social structure and behavioral mechanisms."

The others relaxed a bit when Doc told them this, but not Felix. He became even more uneasy. When the others were out of earshot, he said, "That's some nice bullshitting, Doc, but what do you think *really* happened?"

"I don't know. I just don't know. I've never known them to turn on one another...but who can really say?"

"Quit it, Doc. Tell me what you're thinking."

"I think we've got a predator out there, a real monstrous beast that is so brazen it will even attack a 'raptor pack. It must be savage, fearless, and very fast, I should think."

"Which puts us in a bad position."

"Yes, it does. I think we should withdraw to some more open country."

Doc was right, of course. Pack it in, get out, come back first thing in the morning, set up some hides out in the fields, bait the animals and draw them in. That was the thing to do. Felix knew very well that that was the proper course of action...yet, he kept seeing Ritchie's mangled body in his mind.

"Let's stand down for a bit," he told the others. "See what shows up for the carcass."

They all have to go. That's what Penwick said, so it might as well start here and now.

The day was hot and moist, humidity hanging in the air like a warm, wet rag. The haze was thickening.

Felix waited with Doc, watching the dead Utahraptor twenty yards away, and the crew.

They smoked and whispered, giggling now and again, swearing and insulting each other. Things were chilly between Dane and Misty. She kept trying to kiss his ass, but he would have none of it. Ugly George watched her with bovine eyes, lovestruck. He was just the sort of big, goofy idiot with a heart of gold that someone like Misty could exploit expertly.

It's all turning into a soap opera, Felix thought.

An hour later, about the time everyone was getting very ancy, there was a shrill screeching and piping as a dozen pterosaurs descended from the sky on purple reticulated wings. They were medium-sized flying reptiles with ten-and twelve-foot wingspans. Greedy, selfish beasts that tried to covet the dead 'raptor like seagulls with French fries—they squawked and pecked at one another, dipping their toothed crimson beaks into the meat, tearing out long, juicy strips which they tried to crawl off with, wing-walking like bats, each one trying to steal from another.

"Goddamn shitbirds," Fly said. "You want me to pop a few?"

Felix shook his head. "No, this is a bust. No sense wasting ammo on those fucking things."

It would only make matters worse and he knew it. The pterosaurs would attack anything alive with suicidal abandon, scavenge carcasses, and even eat one another if the opportunity presented itself. As Fly often said, if there were still fast food joints around, the shitbirds would have been in their glory feeding out of dumpsters.

"Hey, Doc," he said, watching the birds tear at a bloody shank, fighting and shrilling, two of them playing tug of war with a prime cut, "you sure we didn't evolve from those things? I'm seeing a lot of human behavior in them."

Doc laughed. "I'm pretty sure."

***

They found three more dead Utahraptors and everyone was spooked. The first had been partially eaten and you could understand that. It had been killed for food. It was what predators did. But these other three...they did not appear to be eaten at all, just savaged, mauled, and mutilated. As if they had been killed by something that just liked to kill, a creature that murdered for sport rather than sustenance.

"What do you make of it, Doc?" Felix asked when they took up the trail again.

"My assessment has not changed," Doc told him. "We're dealing with a predator that's very fast, very smart, and very dangerous. I can't imagine what it might be. Can you?"

No, Felix couldn't.

Part of him didn't want to. In fact, it was *afraid* to.

Felix and Doc, in their own way, were having a conversation about something without actually having one. In the past, now and again, they had come across things like this, things they simply could not explain. Evidence that hinted at some sort of super predator, an X-Predator: nameless, deadly, and quite possibly intelligent. It was Doc's opinion that at the tail end of the Cretaceous, a sort of ultra-predator had evolved, something which left absolutely no trace in the fossil record. This creature had been funneled into the future along with the rest during the aftermath of the Big Impact and it was here now, among them.

"Shadows are getting long," Misty pointed out.

"Yeah, we better pack it in," Fly said.

Felix nodded. They were concerned and they had every right to be.

"Okay. Let's get back to the trucks."

He was waiting for some smartass comment from Dane, but he got nothing. They backtracked through the town and over the bridge. The entire way, Felix had the worst feeling that they were being watched. But as to whether that was just his nerves jumping like live wires or a very real intuition of danger, he did not know.

Finally, the trucks were in sight.

"Thank God," Fly said.

"Wait," Doc told them, holding up a hand. "Just wait."

But the others did not wait. They strolled leisurely to the trucks. Whatever Doc had picked up on and what Felix was beginning to suspect, was lost on them.

"Hold up," he called out to them.

The trucks were parked off the main road, near the tree line, and he suddenly got a very bad feeling. This wasn't what he had been feeling before, this was the real thing. It went right up his spine and curled up in his belly in a shivering cold mass.

Listen, he told himself. *Just listen.*

The silence.

That was the thing you had to be aware of when it came, Felix knew. Because when the forest went quiet, that's when trouble was coming. It was an acuity you had to develop and a sense you had to sharpen—noise was good, lack of it was as deadly as a razor against your throat.

In his experience, which stretched back ten years to the Big Impact, Cretaceous dinosaurs were not quiet by nature. They were not only loud, they were fucking LOUD. Constantly chirping and chittering, whistling and screeching and squawking. It was like living in a world overrun by giant birds which, essentially, it was. Point being, they were rarely quiet. The only thing that seemed to shut them up was the presence of predators, particularly pack hunters like raptors or a large theropod.

And it was goddamned silent out there now.

It wasn't natural and he knew it. It was nearly sundown and dinosaurs, like birds, became especially noisy at the end of the day. They were never quiet like this.

"Something smells bad," Misty said.

And it did, Felix knew. A smell he knew very well—the gamey blood and meat smell of a large predator, a creature that brought death and fed upon it.

"Pull back!" he cried out to them.

The words left his mouth about the same time that a massive theropod dinosaur charged from the trees. Despite its size—it had to be thirty feet long and an easy 3,000 pounds—it moved with amazing grace and agility. Oh, you could hear the thumping of its feet and feel it right into your bones, but the earth did not shake the way the science fiction writers had always thought. This beast, possibly a T. Rex, was incredibly nimble and sprightly as it closed in to slaughter them.

It was a terrible machine of dread, hissing and snarling, the dying light gleaming off its leathery copper-scaled flesh. Its massive hindlegs propelled it forward and it didn't seem to run so much as hop with immense strides, closing the gap between the tree line and the trucks in what seemed seconds, rushing forward like a rocket, massive skull jutting forward, tail held straight behind it like some kind of counterbalance.

Felix brought up his Westley Richards .577 Nitro, trying to get a clean shot, but he was afraid of hitting someone.

Misty broke and ran, as did Dane. Ugly George ran into Fly, pivoted, and smashed right into one of the trucks, pancaking himself. And by the time he found his feet, the beast was on him. It snatched him in its jaws which were lined with teeth like steak knives. He screamed as the jaws clamped down, his bones snapping and splintering, an enormous cloud of blood forced from his mouth like a gory cartoon balloon.

By then, Doc had gotten off several shots from his .300 Savage. At least one of them had hit the beast, more of a glancing shot than anything, tearing a bloody trench in its hide. It led out a shrieking/squawking sort of noise that was guttural and deafening. The bullet didn't hurt it—it pissed it off.

"WATCH IT!" Felix screamed. "WATCH IT!"

The beast was angry. A split-second after it cried out, it brought up one of its massive feet and kicked out, catching one of the trucks in the quarter panel and flipping it right over...on top of Fly, who screeched like he was being boiled alive, a twisted sculpture of red pulp.

Felix sighted in on it.

The .577 was a double rifle. It held two massive rounds that had been originally designed to drop rhino, elephants, and other dangerous African wildlife. That meant he had two chances. If he wasted either shot, the beast would kill them all.

It leaped up on top of the overturned truck, its tonnage nearly flattening it, squeezing Fly's remains out from underneath it like toothpaste from a tube. It bellowed and hissed, swallowing Ugly George's well-pulped remains in a single gulp.

The others were shooting by then, but only angering the creature with their small arms.

It was going to charge down on all of them now.

It would macerate them in a fit of rage. It was the tyrant king and brooked no interference or defiance from its prey; all must bow down before it and accept the baptism of its unearthly hunger and red-stained teeth.

As it made to leap, Felix fired.

He took it right in the chest, blowing a huge bloody and blackened hole in its pebbled flesh. It rose up to full height, its gigantic tail sweeping back and forth, its entire body trembling. It let out one last gargantuan roar and fell right over, crashing into the earth and shaking the ground. It undulated like a massive snake, trembled and went still. With one last convulsive shudder, its tail whipped back and smashed into the other truck, flipping it over, smashing it into the other flattened one. Then it vomited out the slashed, broken, and mangled remains of Ugly George—along with other half-digested things—in a foam of blood.

That was it.

The tyrant king was dead.

But so were Fly and Ugly George.

Everyone stood there for a time as the sun went down and the shadows covered the horror before them. Misty began to make a high wailing noise like the death song of a warrior.

***

There were sounds in the darkness and every one of them was like a knife cutting into Felix. He had lost two of his team, which was bad enough, but now they were hunkered down behind a fallen tree, surrounded by...*something.*

They had tried hiking their way out of the little valley that the town sat in, but they were being hunted by something that was not one thing but many things.

They were trapped.

The road out was flanked on both sides by heavy growth. If something was waiting for them, it would be on them before they could hope to draw their weapons.

"Any ideas, Doc?"

"I recommend staying put," he said. "Either that or we try getting into the town and hiding out in a house or a building. But that will involve a certain risk."

"We'll stay here."

"All night?" Misty said.

"Yes, all night, dammit," Felix told her.

She muttered something under her breath.

"Shut the hell up," Dane told her. "You heard the big boss man. We have to do what the boss man says. We're expendable."

Felix sighed. "Now's not the time, man."

"Sorry," Dane said. "I get pissy when someone fucks my girlfriend."

"I'M NOT YOUR GODDAMN GIRLFRIEND!" Misty shouted, her voice echoing out in the darkness. "How many times do I have to tell you that? I told you we were done a week before...a week before I had anything to do with Felix."

"Okay, whore."

"Fuck you!"

"Please," Doc said. "We need to keep the volume down."

Previously, on The Young and the Restless, Felix thought with distain.

Misty was devious. She had come in with her tail in the air like a cat in heat. She had gotten Dane to fall in love with her, flirted with Felix blatantly, slept with him—something he still regretted—and now'...God only knew what her agenda might be. Dane and Misty were still going at it, insulting and threatening each other in whispers. Forty-five minutes later they were kissing and giggling.

Christ.

People and their fucking glands, Felix thought.

"Doc," he said. "I don't care for waiting in the darkness like this. We need an edge and I'm going to get us one."

"What do you mean?"

"The trucks. There's a set of NV goggles in there. We need them and I'm going to get them."

Doc said, "Okay. Be careful."

He obviously didn't like the idea, but he realized the practicality of having some night vision. Without another word, Felix borrowed the .300 Savage from him and slipped out into the darkness. The stars were bright and that was something. The dark outlines of the smashed trucks and the dead theropod were easy to pick out. He just hoped nothing was lying in wait for him.

He moved in closer, his heart pounding hard in his chest.

He heard a slurping over near the trucks. It made his breath catch in his throat. He stepped quietly over there. Something was moving near the truck that had squashed Fly. He could smell the death stink of the theropod—like cold blood and hot decay. He heard a rhythmic sort of tearing sound and could see something pecking away at what must have been Fly's remains like a rooster searching for grubs.

As he closed in on it, it scampered away.

The truck. He was close now, but he sure as hell was not alone. He heard a trilling squeak behind him. He turned slowly. Something was there, stalking him, moving in for the kill. He sensed movement and brought up the Savage, firing. In the muzzle flash, he saw a raptor leaping at him, claws extended, jaws opened to reveal bloodstained teeth. Then the bullet punched into it. It screeched, hit the ground, and died quivering.

He heard the rest of its pack run off.

On his belly, he crawled into the overturned truck and found the NVGs.

Quick. Go!

Dappled by shadows, he moved back towards the others. Right away, he felt a terrible sense of urgency. Something was happening or about to happen. He could feel it inside him as if some preternatural sensory network had been activated. He'd felt it before during times of danger and he knew better than to ignore his instincts.

He paused, fumbling with the NVGs. He nearly had them on when he heard a scream rip through the night. It was a horrible sound—a piercing, perfectly insane screech of madness and agony, as if Misty were being burned alive at the stake.

"MISTY!" Dane shouted. *"MISTY! MISTY! WHERE THE HELL ARE YOU?"*

And that's about all he got out. Doc cried out and there was a noise like an axe cleaving a melon, the sounds of something sprayed into the grass. Then Felix had the NVGs on and in the green field, he saw a blurring motion as something dragged Dane away into the night with incredible speed. Doc fired a few times but it was hopeless.

Both Misty and Dane had been taken literally in the blink of an eye.

Felix ran over to Doc.

"They're gone," Doc said, his voice cracking. "So fast...oh my God, so unbelievably fast."

Felix scanned the fields around them. There was nothing, not a hint of movement. Their speculative X-Predator had attacked and withdrawn before there was any hope to react.

Doc was mopping blood off his face, mumbling in a broken voice how whatever it had been had gotten Misty and with such speed and ferocity that she had not muttered a sound beyond a single choking gasp. Seconds later, she screamed out in the field as she was pulled away into the night. Dane had run out there after her and the predators had gotten him, too.

Felix kept turning in circles, trying to maintain a 365° field of acuity so they could not sneak in to finish the job on he and Doc. He could see their trails in the grass, along with a lot of sparkling wetness.

"We have to wait for sunrise," he said.

"I'm praying we make it that long," Doc managed.

The night drew out, a phantasmagoria of skulking shapes and slithering shadows, things that were real, unreal, and sometimes a little of both.

Finally, after an eternity of darkness, dawn broke.

***

At first light, they got going. A quarter mile into the dripping, dense green hell of the forest, they ducked beneath vines and slashed at waterfalls of glistening green creepers hanging from the low-lying branches of immense, primitive conifers. There was a profusion of spreading ferns and lush angiosperms, occasional scaly-trunked Williamsonia and great algae-slicked pools of sucking black mud. It was like stepping out of Indiana into the primeval wastes of Borneo.

Felix led mainly by instinct, going completely by feel. But he was right on target—they found Misty first as if she had been left for them.

"Christ," Doc said.

She had been partially devoured, her face stripped to the skull beneath, the flesh chewed from her throat and breasts, her body cavity opened and emptied. Her protruding bones were gouged with claw marks and punctured by teeth. She had been partially buried, perhaps to ferment and soften. There were ants and beetles covering her, six-inch worms feeding on her tongue.

"Her legs and arms are gone," Felix pointed out.

"I have the worst feeling it was not out of hunger but out of amusement."

"Meaning?"

Doc looked at him, waving flies away from his face. "Meaning that our X-Predator is, as we have guessed, not only calculating but sadistic."

They pushed on and found what appeared to be a game trail. Felix was struck by the perfectly absurd idea that they were being led into a trap, baited in. Five minutes later, they found one of Misty's arms. Then one of her legs.

It's drawing us in. It has to be drawing us in.

Then something moved just ahead. It was one of the beasts. Felix fired and missed. *Dammit!* He charged forward only to see the cruel eyes of his adversary glaring at him from the thick vegetation. He fired and missed again.

As he turned back, he saw Doc was not alone.

One of them was waiting there amongst the ferns.

Jesus.

It stood about six feet tall, maybe fifteen feet in length, serpentine and streamlined, not feathered (as he had thought) but set with tiny spine-like proto-feathers. Its flesh went from a beaded green at its back to an indigo blue at its snout and a pale gray at its underbelly. Its head was cocked at the end of a long angled neck, wicked blood-red eyes studying him from beneath bony ridges. Its chest expanded as it breathed, nares on its snout opening and closing.

It was an absolutely marvelous animal. There was a row of triangular dorsal spikes that ran down its neck and back and terminated at the tip of the sweeping tail. Its forepaws were set with scythe-like claws as were its splayed triple-toed feet. Nature had designed it to one end—to kill, with speed, power, and precision.

Felix slowly reloaded his rifle, struggling to grip it in his sweaty hands.

The beast flinched.

It made a low growling sound in its throat.

Its body rippled with muscularity.

The jagged teeth jutting from its jaws gave the impression that it was sardonically grinning.

"Easy," Doc said. "Don't startle it."

Then it leapt, knocking him to the soft, moist ground in a flurry of claws. He had no idea where his rifle was, because the hand that held it—and the arm itself—had been taken off at the shoulder joint. He was gagging on the blood that bubbled up his throat, filled his mouth, and spilled down his chin, glazed eyes watching the red-stained snout of the beast yank out his intestines.

Felix fired and missed and then something hit him from behind, knocking the wind from him and the rifle from his hands and sending him into dreamland.

***

When he came to, he was in the lair of the beasts.

It was a long, low cave, the scraps of their meals scattered in all directions—bones and rusting weapons, old boots and torn shirts. Yes, the detritus of those that had come to hunt them.

One of them was poised above him, watching him. Though his modern, reasoning brain knew what it was, a much older fear-laced network was at work here, sending him ancient images of primal flesh-eating monsters.

The creature did not move.

It barely seemed to breathe.

In the light coming from the entrance, he saw it quite well. Its eyes were yellow with the slit pupils of a lizard. It stood maybe five feet in height, its twelve-foot streamlined body covered in a plumage of red-brown proto-feathers that nested together rather like the spines of a porcupine. Its snout was narrow, a brilliant blue, as were its paws, splayed feet, and underbelly. Leaning forward on muscular hindlegs, its forepaws were set in a defensive posture, the triple claws of each gleaming like meat hooks.

As it stared at him, it angled its head which was set with a backward sweeping spiky crown of red feathers which resembled a punk rocker's Mohawk. Felix's brain registered about a microsecond of amusement at this before flooding him with the ice water of pure terror.

His mind had time to think one thought: *I'm going to die. This thing is going to kill me.*

The thing in question had never been completely described by science. It was known only by fragmentary fossil evidence found in the Montana badlands—a weathered tooth, a single spinal vertebra. But now here, in this place, out of time, it revealed itself. An adult dromaeosaur of the late Cretaceous, a predatory theropod whose family included the Deinonychus and Utahraptor, but who had evolved well beyond them.

The muscles of the beast twitched.

It made a low grunting in its throat.

Felix reached slowly down for the .357 Magnum at his hip. The holster was there, but the gun had been removed. As had his knife.

Intelligent, then. Cunning, crafty, and clever.

Felix scrambled away, trying to make for the entrance.

He saw a rippling, fluid shape. Triple-clawed paws slashed him across the face. Letting out a gurgling, unpleasant scream, he sank to his knees, dropping the flashlight. His face was gored with three deep trenches from the claws. His left eye was gone, his septum bisected, his lower lip hanging by a thread. Blood gushed, hotly flooding his face as shock and trauma overwhelmed him.

The beast rushed in, delivering what looked like a lightning-fast kick, but its only purpose was to bring its deadly, retractable hunting claw into action. Each foot had one. It leapt onto Felix, forcing him to the ground, the hunting claws sunk deep inside him. As he struggled weakly, bleeding out, the beast literally ripped him open with its foreclaws, its toothed beak-like jaws pecking at him unmercifully, yanking out strands of tender red meat. The scent of blood triggering biochemical reactions in its brain, it attacked that much more ferociously, tearing and rending and hacking him down to the bone.

The amazing—and horrible—part of it all, was that Felix lived through much of it. At least, long enough to see another seven sets of gleaming yellow eyes as the rest of the pack came in to feed.

That and the clutch of eggs they protected.

Once they reproduced in sufficient numbers, men would be prey and the human race would face its own mass extinction. It seemed almost fitting.

The End

LOST ISLAND

By David Wood

"Is it me, or does the way ahead look a little strange?" Kurtis Kane looked out at the fog blanketing the cobalt waters of the Gulf of Mexico. It was late morning, the sun high and the temperature warm, yet the fog remained.

"Lighten up. You're a science teacher, not a weatherman." His brother, Kevin, clapped him on the shoulder. "It'll be fine."

"It's just weird, that's all." Kane turned his back on the curtain of gray into which they were headed. "Fog should have burned off by now."

"The place we're headed is unusual. The weather is the least of it." If his father, Samuel Kane, found the phenomenon unnerving, he didn't let it show.

"You're going to love this, bro. Take your mind off of those, what are they, kindergarteners you teach?"

"Middle school."

Kevin shrugged, turned, and opened the cooler. "Who wants a cold one?" Without waiting for an answer, he handed a bottle to his father and tossed another to Kane.

"This is nice," Samuel said. "A father-son trip with both of my boys. How long has it been?"

Kane considered the question. "Not since college. So… eight years?"

"Sounds about right. Spring break of your junior year. We were climbing El Capitan. That was when you finally told me what your actual major was."

"Give him a break, Dad," Kevin said. "If he wants to take a vow of poverty, that's his business."

Kane didn't rise. It was territory they'd covered countless times before. Neither of his chosen careers had been lucrative, but they'd been what he considered important work—opportunities to make a difference in a way that being yet another Executive Vice President of Bullshit at Kane Enterprises would never allow.

Samuel and Kevin exchanged a long, knowing look. If Kevin had been thirty years older, the two might have been twins—blonde, blue eyed, sturdily built. Kane was the black sheep, or "brown sheep" as his brother called him, thanks to his dark hair. He stood a few inches taller than the other two, weighed in about twenty pounds lighter. He did however share their blue eyes and what a few of his exes had described as a strong chin, whatever that was.

A chill passed over him, and he realized that they had moved into the fog bank. The cool dampness clung to his skin, and cast his father and brother like filmy gauze.

"Almost there!" Samuel raised his beer and clinked bottles with his sons. "To a successful hunt."

"Cheers." Kevin grinned.

"Cheers," Kane echoed dully. He hadn't hunted in years, but his dad had practically begged him to come along on this expedition, promising it would be the trip of a lifetime.

"Okay, Dad. Don't you think it's about time you spilled the secret details. You haven't told me anything other than we're going on a hunt."

"What would you like to know?" Samuel's grin crinkled the corners of his mouth.

"For starters, where are we going? What place is so secret that I had to sign a non-disclosure agreement before I could hunt there?"

"The island of Bermeja."

That brought Kane up short. "Bermeja? Wait. That island doesn't exist. It showed up erroneously on some old charts. Mexico pretended it was real in order to stake claim to waters where oil was in good supply."

"Yeah?" Samuel inclined his head, his brow furrowed. "You'll have to explain that to the men who live there."

"Is this a joke?"

"Not at all. The legend of the 'lost' island is not factual, nor is the conspiracy theory that the CIA blew it up in order to thwart Mexico's claim on the surrounding waters. I assure you, it's quite real."

"But how?"

"Money and power can do many things, even make an island disappear."

"Money," Kevin parroted, nodding along.

"The perpetual fog and the fact that the island is very small also helps," Samuel added.

Kane wasn't satisfied. "But there have been independent surveys that confirmed it didn't exist."

Samuel flashed Kane a pitying smile, then turned to Kevin. "Independent, he says." He turned his gaze back to Kane. "Son, you pay the right people, do a few favors, call in some markers, and there's not much that can't be accomplished. Mexico has a vested interest in keeping this island a secret. You'll soon find out why."

***

"Dinosaurs." Kane gazed at the horned skull that hung above the fireplace in the common room of the Bermeja Lodge. He wasn't certain of the species, Stegosaurus, maybe, but it was definitely a dinosaur, and not a fossil. This was bleached bone. Had it been a steer it wouldn't have been out of place in a ranch house in the American Southwest. "You're telling me we're going to hunt actual, walking, eating, breathing, living fucking dinosaurs?"

"I'm not all that interested in seeing them fucking," Kevin said. "But hey, if that's your fetish..."

Laughter rang out from the group that sat in a semicircle on comfortable chairs, enjoying drinks.

"Is this an elaborate prank?" Kane looked around for hidden cameras or a B-list celebrity waiting to pop out and surprise them.

"If so, we've all wasted a great deal of money for nothing." Albert Montez, a bear of a man with light brown skin and steel-gray hair cropped in a G.I. cut, was a Texas land baron or something like that. Beside him, his daughter Maya sat, sipping a glass of red wine, her expression unreadable.

Kane had gone out of his way not to stare at the young woman. It hadn't been easy. Even if she hadn't been the only female within hundreds of miles, her big brown eyes and trim, athletic figure would have drawn his attention in any setting. He had trouble reconciling a beautiful young woman with a hunting expedition. He supposed that was gender stereotyping. Still, the thought made him a little sad.

Seated on the other side of Maya was Eric Barnard, a skinny, early twenties type with trust fund written all over him. His popped collar and loud proclamations about the superiority of craft beer over brand name brews had already alienated him from the rest of the group, but he appeared oblivious to their disdain.

Their team was rounded out by Harrison Tomlin, a tall, ebony skinned man, gray around the temples, a wicked scar bisecting his left cheek. He was to be their hunting guide. He drank little and said even less.

"You'll have to excuse my son," Samuel said. "He's taken up science of late. I guess he doesn't believe in anything without testable evidence."

Kane didn't miss his father's emphasis on the words "of late."

For the first time, Maya looked at him with interest. "You're a scientist? What field?"

"Seventh grade biology. And eighth grade chemistry and physics."

She laughed. "Don't seventh graders already spend too much time thinking about biology?"

"Only human reproduction. I try to emphasize the topics."

"Really? Like what?"

Kane grinned wickedly. "Venereal diseases."

Maya made a face. "I hope you're not an expert on that subject."

"Academic knowledge only. I promise." He took a drink. "What about you? What do you do with yourself when you're not blowing holes in extinct animals?" He hadn't meant to sound so coarse, but Maya didn't appear to have heard him. Her attention was focused on the man who had just entered.

"Good afternoon. I am pleased to see you are all settling in." The speaker was a tall, handsome man with perfectly coiffed black hair, a neatly trimmed mustache, and straight, white teeth. He was the very image of the wealthy Spaniard who filled the role of villain in old episodes of Zorro. "I am Santiago Aquino, special attaché from the government of Mexico, tasked with overseeing this very special island."

"When do we get started?" Barnard piped up.

Aquino flashed an indulgent smile, unruffled. "Soon. First, there is business to which we must attend. You all signed non-disclosure agreements prior to your arrival. I must caution you that the government takes these very seriously. More importantly, among the few who know about this place, there are some who believe the agreements are not sufficient." He paused to let that sink in.

"What are you telling us?" Maya asked.

Aquino frowned, considering the question. Kane figured it was an act. Aquino probably delivered this same speech to every group of hunters.

"If you should violate our agreement, it is probable that steps will be taken, not by the government, to silence you permanently. Sadly, our nation has no shortage of capable men and women who would perform that task in exchange for modest compensation." The members of the hunting party exchanged frowns and Aquino held up a hand. "I am not threatening you. I am merely warning you that if you should violate your NDA, we cannot guarantee your safety. So, it would be best if you simply lived up to your word and kept to the terms of our agreement, yes?" He flashed his too-white smile.

"I guess we have no choice," Albert said. "Not that we weren't going to abide by our agreement."

"We're all professionals here." Samuel glanced at Kane as he spoke. "We understand the importance of confidentiality. We're just here for the hunt."

"I expected no less from gentlemen…" Aquino paused, "and ladies of your standing." He winked at Maya.

Kane decided this was as good a time as any to ask the foremost of his many questions. "If I may ask, how is this possible? Cloning?"

Aquino shook his head. "It is actually much simpler than that. The Chicxulub impact wiped out almost all of the dinosaurs, but a few survived."

"How?" Kane pressed. The asteroid that had struck the Yucatán Peninsula nearly sixty-six million years ago, forming the Chicxulub Crater, had such a devastating impact that it caused the mass extinction of dinosaurs all around the world. "The island is so close to ground zero."

"That, we do not know. I can only tell you that the fossil record shows the continued survival of a few species of dinosaurs."

"What kinds do you have?" Kevin asked.

"I will show you." He nodded at a television hanging on the far wall. As they all turned to look at it, he picked up a remote and clicked. The screen came to life, the video feed flashed to a pair of squat, armored dinosaurs who stood at the edge of a stream, munching on thick grasses. "Ankylosaurs. I do not recommend shooting at them. You will only provoke them."

"Is this a live feed?" Maya asked.

"Recorded footage." Another click. "A small herd of bipedal dinosaurs moving across a clearing. Colorful feathers dotted their tough hides.

Kane recognized them immediately. "Hadrosaurs?"

"Correct."

"I still can't believe it," Maya said softly. "They really did have feathers."

"They have much in common with birds, as some famed archaeologists have theorized," Aquino said.

Next came triceratops, followed by a few species with which Kane was not familiar. Most bore a strong resemblance to more familiar dinos, but with minor differences that merited new names. Just as Aquino turned away from the screen, Kane saw something flash across the corner of the screen. He couldn't be certain, but it looked to be the size and shape of a compsognathus, the scavenger dinosaur that grew to approximately the size of a turkey. The thin veneer of colorful feathers only added to the mental association.

"Those are the creatures you are most likely to encounter. A few species, those that are in need of protection due to their limited numbers, are kept on the north end of the island. That section is off-limits for the animals' protection."

Aquino tapped a button and a map of Bermeja appeared on the screen. The island resembled an elongated skull, the north end large and round, twin lakes forming the eye sockets. The lodge where they now sat was located just south of the lakes. Aquino zoomed in on the south end of the island.

"The animals are not restricted in their movements, save for the moats that keep them away from the lodge. They tend to keep to themselves. If you wish to hunt different species, you will most likely have to cover the entirety of the Southern Reach, which is what we call this section of Bermeja."

"How much extra will we have to pay in order to bring a trophy home?" Barnard asked.

Aquino turned a tight-lipped smile on the young man. "I am afraid that is impossible, for security reasons. Your kills will, of course, be prepared and served at the end-of-hunt banquet."

"What does dinosaur taste like?" Maya asked.

"It depends on the animal, but most of them taste like chicken."

Everyone laughed. Everyone except Barnard, who still wanted to take home a prize.

"Surely there's a way we can take something home. A skull, maybe?" Barnard pressed.

"No," Aquino said simply.

Kane frowned at the map. Something was bothering him. "I don't see any predators among your dinosaur population."

"You are correct. Despite our best efforts, the last carnivores died off. That is why hunting expeditions like these help keep things in balance. We could cull the herd ourselves, of course, but the hunting program funds schools and clinics in the poorest villages in Mexico."

"I assume there are limits on what and how many we can bring down?" Samuel asked.

"Mister Tomlin will guide you. While you are on the hunt, his word is law." Aquino looked at each hunter in turn, his gaze lingering on Barnard, whose face turned scarlet.

"Finally, I must warn you that, although you are here to hunt dinosaurs, those are not the only animals you are likely to encounter. The island is home to poisonous reptiles and other native species. Never think you are safe merely because there are no dinosaurs about." A contemplative silence fell over the group. Aquino bade them goodbye and left the room.

Kane's gaze lingered on the screen, where a single dinosaur stood, looking out at the horizon. As Kane watched, the creature turned toward the camera and Kane thought he saw intelligence there, awareness. His breath caught in his throat. What had he gotten himself into?

***

"End of the road," Tomlin proclaimed, parking the Jeep at the end of a paved road. "We hoof it from here."

The group piled out, Barnard leading the way. He moved a few paces into the forest and swung his rifle to and fro, as if he expected to make a kill right then and there.

"You won't find anything this close to the road," Tomlin said, shouldering an overstuffed pack. "It'll be at least an hour, depending on where the herds are."

"An hour?" Barnard whirled around to face the guide. "What the hell?" he snapped as Kane grabbed the barrel of his rifle and forced it straight up.

"Get your finger off the trigger," Kane said through gritted teeth.

"I know what I'm doing."

"You'll stay up front with me," Tomlin told the young man. "Where I can keep an eye on you."

Barnard wilted under the hunting guide's glare. "Whatever. Let's get going."

An hour later, they found themselves kneeling in the midst of a thick stand of palmetto, peering out at a trio of dinosaurs in the distance. The massive bony frills on their heads resembled that of triceratops, but they lacked the long horns.

"They're a variety of ceratopsian," Tomlin said. "Like the trike, but they have stubby horns." He flashed a wolfish grin. "They're nasty sons of bitches. Difficult to kill. Impossible at this range."

He handed Kane a pair of binoculars. Kane zoomed in and focused. The binoculars lent the image a surreal quality, yet he still felt overwhelmed. The powerful creatures moved with a surprising grace for their size. Their flanks heaved with each breath, muscles rippling beneath thick hide and a dusting of silvery gray feathers. Magnificent!

"You've hunted these before?" Samuel whispered.

Tomlin nodded. "You've got to get up close and get a perfect shot, just behind the left foreleg, up high where the heart is. If you miss, you'd better put a lot of lead in the air, because it will come for you."

"I'm guessing we're too far away," Kane said.

"You guessed right."

A shot rang out, deafening in the stillness of the afternoon. Kane had an up-close view of the bullet glancing off the armor plating of the largest dino. Blood and feathers flew. It let out a bellow, turned, and charged.

"What the fuck?" Tomlin ripped the rifle away from Barnard, who was already taking aim for another shot. "There's a ledge about fifty meters that way!" He pointed to the west. "Everybody run for it."

The hunters ran as fast as they dared in the dense tropical forest. Kane fell back to the rear, thinking to protect the others. He doubted there was anything he could do that Tomlin couldn't do better, but taking responsibility for others had been drilled into him over the past several years. By contrast, Kevin had adopted the "every man for himself" approach, sprinted well ahead of the party, and was now scaling the rock wall.

Behind them, Kane heard the thunder of heavy feet pounding the soft turf, the angry bellow of the charging beast.

And then it ended.

"She broke off the charge," Tomlin said, looking. He barely sounded winded despite the sprint through the woods.

"How do you know it's female?" Kane asked, the science teacher in him coming to the fore.

"Just speculating because of her protective behavior. I'm not gonna lift her skirt and find out." He turned and called out to Kevin, who had just reached the top of the ledge.

"You can come down from your perch now."

Kevin paused to catch his breath before climbing down. When he returned to the group, his sheepish expression spoke volumes.

"Sorry, I didn't realize how slow the rest of you are." He winked at Maya, who turned and walked away. "Bitch," he muttered softly enough that only Kane heard. It was a good thing, too, because her father, Albert, looked like he could take Kevin apart with ease.

"Can I have my gun back, now?" Barnard stood, hands on hips. He wore a pith helmet, crisp khakis, and an olive green shirt. He had, of course, popped the collar. He looked absurd.

"Repeat after me. This is my weapon," Tomlin held up Barnard's rifle, "and this is my gun." He pointed the rifle at the young man's crotch.

Albert chimed in. "This is for killing," he flourished his own weapon, "and this is for fun."

Tomlin winked and turned to Barnard. "To answer your question, no, you may not have your weapon back until I'm satisfied you can follow instructions."

Barnard clenched his fists, cocked his elbows, and then relaxed. In the first display of intelligence Kane had seen from the young man, he exhaled slowly, his posture relaxing. "Sorry."

Tomlin nodded. "Don't let it happen again."

***

Kane awoke with a start. He rolled over and pressed a hand to his churning stomach. They'd enjoyed a productive hunt and had feasted on choice cuts of the hadrosaur he'd taken. They'd washed it down with a few too many Noche Buena, a rich, dark lager. Now he was paying the price.

"What was that sound?" Maya whispered. She lay a few feet from him, her face illumined by an orange glow.

It only took a moment for him to identify the source of the light. In the distance, the sky glowed, smoke roiling. Now he remembered what had awakened him. It wasn't his stomach, but a loud boom.

Maya seized his hand. "What happened?"

"An explosion...I think it's the lodge."

Voices cut through the darkness; Samuel and Albert grumbling muzzy variations on the theme of, "What the fuck is going on?"

Kane looked around for Tomlin. "Tomlin, anything on the radio?"

No reply.

A flashlight clicked on, its intense beam slicing through the darkness. Samuel strode forward and let out a curse when the light fell on Tomlin. "The man appeared to be asleep, but the gaping wound in his throat and the blood soaking his sleeping bag told a different story.

Maya let out a gasp and covered her mouth. Samuel took a step toward the body but Kane grabbed him by the arm.

"Let me. I know what I'm doing." Taking the flashlight from his father's hand, he circled the body, inspecting the ground. He quickly found what he was looking for.

"Footprints. Someone walked right up to him, did the deed, and then headed into the forest in the direction of the lodge." He moved the circle of light along the path the presumed killer had taken.

"What are you, an Indian scout?" Maya asked.

Kane shook his head. "I worked in law enforcement for a while. This isn't my first crime scene."

"Who would have done this?" Maya asked.

Albert piped up. "Barnard or Kevin. They're both missing."

Samuel and Maya reacted with surprise, but Kane was distracted by movement in the underbrush. A dark shape scurried out into the light, resolving into the form of a small, feathered dinosaur the size of a chicken. Two more followed in its wake. They scurried over to where Tomlin's body lay. The largest of the three gave the man a sniff. A long tongue flicked out, tasting the blood. Its head flicked to the side, birdlike, and it let out a chirp. The two smaller dinos answered, then the three began tearing at Tomlin's ruined throat.

Behind him, Kane heard his father lose most of last night's meal. Maya grabbed her rifle, intent on shooting the scavengers.

"There's no point," Kane said. "There are bound to be more of them, and we can't take his body with us when we go. Besides, a shot might alert whatever else is out there."

"Like what?" Albert asked.

"These are scavengers that feed on carcasses. Ask yourself, if the animal population is strictly controlled, select creatures regularly harvested, what is there to support a population of compies, if that's what these are?"

Maya nodded. "There must be a population of predators on this island."

"The north end? The part that's off-limits," Albert said.

"I guess when the lodge blew, it opened the gates that held them in," Maya said.

Samuel scratched his beard. "Seems like they'd have redundant systems, failsafes. Shouldn't take a chance, I suppose." He let out a long sigh, deflating. "I'm sorry, son. I truly thought this would be an adventure."

"It is," Kane said. "Let's find Kevin and then make our way to the docks." He picked up his rifle and ammunition and followed the footprints into the forest. The others followed his lead, grabbing their weapons and falling in behind him.

About twenty meters away, a second pair of footprints joined those they followed. Out of the corner of his eye, he saw Maya flash a concerned look at him. There was no need to reply. They all knew what it meant—Kevin and Barnard were working together. And considering the comparative sizes of the prints, he was almost certain it had been Kevin who murdered Tomlin.

"What the hell are they up to?" he whispered.

"I'm sorry," Maya said. "It's not easy finding out a family member is an asshole." She glanced back at her father. "I've hated that bastard for as long as I can remember."

"Why are you here?" Kane snapped.

Maya was silent for a long while. "I work for a non-profit. Dad pays me a generous stipend on the condition that I come home for major holidays and I spend one week pretending we're a happy family. I'd tell him to fuck off, but…"

She didn't get the chance to finish. At Kane's four o'clock, something crashed through the undergrowth. He whirled about in time to see a large theropod charge them. It was a good five meters from the point of its snout to the tip of its tail. It stood on two powerful hind legs. A triple line of bony protrusions ran from the base of its skull down along its spine and tail. They jutted up from a blanket of thin, mottled green feathers. Thick patches of black feathers ringed its eyes like a mask. A bladelike horn thrust up from its snout, and two smaller horns jutted out above its eyes. Teeth like daggers gleamed in the dim light.

Even as he raised his rifle, he remembered its name. Ceratosaurus.

Samuel stood directly behind Kane, blocking his line of fire. Before Kane could draw a bead on the dinosaur, it attacked. Moving with surprising speed, it struck at Albert, its powerful jaws slicing off the man's right arm.

Albert screamed as blood spurted from his ruined arm. His rifle clattered to the ground, hand still gripping it. He reeled backwards, gouts of blood spraying in a circle like a lawn sprinkler.

Kane squeezed off a round, but the ceratosaur lowered its head, bobbing birdlike, and bit deeply into Albert's gut, tearing out a mouthful of vital organs. Intestines dangled from the corners of its mouth like spaghetti noodles. Samuel, spewing invective, opened up with a wild burst of gunfire. Most of the bullets went wide, but a few found their marks.

The ceratosaur, its jaws still clamped around a mouthful of Texan, let out a shriek and fled into the undergrowth. Samuel, roaring incoherently, chased it with a stream of bullets.

"Dad! You're wasting ammo!"

The sound of Kane's voice got Samuel's attention. "Right." Breathing heavily, he turned to Maya, who stood motionless, eyes locked on what remained of her father. "I'm so sorry about your dad."

"It's okay. He was an ass, but he was my dad." She knelt beside the body, reached into a pocket, and drew out an old Zippo lighter. "He was awful in a lot of ways but he was my dad."

Kane didn't know what to say, so he turned and led them through the forest. In the distance they heard shouts and bursts of gunfire.

"Kevin and Barnard?" Maya asked.

Kane shook his head. "Too many voices. Got to be security." He returned to tracking. An occasional footprint was enough to tell Kane that both Barnard and Kevin had come this way. For what reason, he still didn't know.

"Kane," Maya said, "I think we're being followed."

Kane looked back just in time to catch a glimpse of a dark shape moving toward them. He glimpsed its feather-flecked hide, caught a glint of firelight reflected in its eyes.

"I got this. You two watch our flanks!"

The last three words were drowned in a torrent of gunfire as another ceratosaur charged them and the three hunters opened fire. Bullets tore into its tough hide, pinged its thick skull. Kane took careful aim at the spot where he thought its heart would be, and fired.

The dinosaur let out a shriek. Blood and feathers flew. It slowed its pace, but kept coming, the hunters retreating before its charge.

"It's not dying!" Maya shouted.

And then it fell in a heap.

Relief tinged with regret at killing such a magnificent creature flooded through Kane.

Samuel turned to him and grinned. "Well, that was… Aaaah!" He let out a bloodcurdling cry as, with viperlike quickness, a head popped out of the forest cover and bit him just below the rib cage. He fell to the ground, still screaming.

Kane fired at the creature that, even now, tensed to spring. A hail of bullets, and then his weapon ran dry. It was enough. The dinosaur, a juvenile ceratosaur, lay twitching in a pool of blood that was already soaking into the soft earth.

"Keep watch," he told Maya, then turned and knelt beside his father.

It was a grisly sight. Blood poured from the deep, ragged wound. He knew immediately it would prove fatal. Still, he began stripping off his shirt.

"Hang on, Dad. I'm going to bandage you up."

"Stop," Samuel rasped.

"I'm going to take care of you." He was proud that his tone betrayed neither the certainty of his father's imminent demise, nor the regret he felt at never having bridged the gap between them.

"Listen," Samuel said with surprising force. "No time. I'm already dead. My body just hasn't figured it out."

A sudden wave of grief pinched the back of Kane's throat and his eyes misted. "All right."

"I left the company to you. Kevin… no imagination… doesn't think deeply… a yes man. A schemer." He shuddered as a wave of pain surged through him. "The portals," he gasped. "Don't let him…" His eyes closed.

"Dad? What portals?"

Samuel was gone.

Kane couldn't begin to wrap his head around what his father had told him. The company was… his? And something about portals? He felt Maya grip his shoulder.

"Come on," she said gently. "We've got to go."

***

"We're not going that way." Kane peered down a gentle slope toward the docks. A half-dozen dinos, velociraptors, barred their way. They milled about, occasionally snapping at one another, but never straying far from the shore.

"It's like they're standing guard," Maya said. "What do we do?"

Kane shrugged. "Work our way north and then follow the shoreline down."

Maya smirked. "I hope dinosaurs can't swim."

Going north required passing the lodge, which necessitated crossing the moats that bisected the island. When they reached the bridge that spanned the first moat, Kane was pleased to see it had not been damaged by the explosion. He looked around to make sure no dinosaurs were about, then reached out to take Maya by the hand.

"What are you doing? I can walk just fine by myself."

"Oh, sorry."

"Here, make yourself useful." She shoved her rifle into his hands. "I've seen you shoot. You're better than me." She grimaced at the admission. "Only a few bullets left in the magazine, so make them count."

It didn't take long for Kane to exhaust the remaining rounds. No sooner had Maya stepped out onto the bridge than a dark shadow swooped down upon her. Kane fired instinctively, ripping through the creature and sending it tumbling down into the moat.

"What the fuck?" Maya pressed her hands to the top of her head as if checking to make sure everything was still there.

"Pterodactyl," Kane said. Down at the bottom of the deep concrete moat, the body of the flying reptile was easy to spot. "But that makes no sense. How could they keep flying creatures on the island?"

"They didn't keep them on the island," a voice said. "That thing came through the portal."

Barnard stepped out onto the bridge, blocking their path. Gone was the petulant trust fund kid. Now he moved with a calm, self-assuredness. His grin was that of a predator.

"What the hell?" Kane said. He and Maya backed away from the bridge. "Where's my brother?"

"Looking for the portal. I think he plans on going through."

"What portal?" Maya asked.

"Haven't you figured it out?" Barnard sneered. "The dinosaurs are not survivors from the Late Jurassic or whenever the hell they were supposed to have lived here. They come here through a portal that connects our world to the past."

The words were insane, but somehow Kane believed him.

"Your father knew," Barnard said. "Where are he and Albert? Dead? That would save me some trouble."

"Why are you doing this?" Maya asked.

"Kevin's obsessed. He's tried to access Kane Enterprise's files on portals, but he's been rebuffed at every turn. Apparently your dear old dad didn't trust him."

Kane didn't miss the fact that, like Samuel, Barnard had said "portals" plural. "And what's your reason?"

"Me? My motivation is simple. Revenge." He didn't wait for them to ask him to elaborate. "The woman I loved came here on a hunting trip with her old man. She came back in a closed casket. But I opened it." He shivered. "So, to paraphrase David Keith, I'm 'burning it all down, baby.'" He bared his teeth, eyes wide and gleaming maniacally.

"That's got nothing to do with us," Maya said. "We just want to get out of here."

Barnard made a clucking sound and waggled his finger. "Sorry, but you know too much. I do want to have a life when I get back. So, I'm afraid I'll have to dispose of all witnesses."

Kane knew this was the moment. When Barnard reached for his waistband, Kane hurled the empty rifle in the man's direction and charged. Barnard dodged the flying rifle and managed to get his pistol clear of its holster, but couldn't take aim before Kane seized his wrist.

Kane was the bigger man, but Barnard was surprisingly strong and agile. He twisted and nearly managed to tip Kane off-balance, but Kane held on and drove the lighter man backward like a football player hitting a blocking sled. Barnard head butted Kane across the bridge of the nose. Pain blossomed across his face and wetness poured from his nostrils, but Kane kept pushing Barnard inexorably back across the bridge and toward the burning building.

Barnard realized what was happening when the heat became unbearable. He shifted his weight and tried again to throw the bigger man off-balance, but Kane had plenty of practice at this sort of thing, not to mention extensive training in judo and jiu-jitsu. When Barnard twisted, Kane used the motion against his opponent. He slammed Barnard's gun hand against a burning section of wall. Barnard let out a cry of pain and rage, dropped his pistol, and somehow managed to break free.

Kane turned to meet his attack, but Barnard was fast. He snapped off a roundhouse kick that caught Kane in the knee and followed with a sharp jab to Kane's broken nose.

Kane blinked away the pain in time to see Barnard shift his feet and drive a sidekick at Kane's midsection. He had expected the attack. Barnard wasn't strong enough to force Kane bodily into the fire, but a well-placed kick could do the job. He pivoted, and the kick struck him a glancing blow. He caught Barnard's leg, held on, and drove forward, this time pushing the younger man away from the fire.

Barnard struggled to remain on his feet, or foot, as things now stood. He didn't realize what Kane was doing until it was too late.

"What! No! Noooo!" His arms flailed, hands snapping closed as if grasping an invisible rope, and he plunged into the moat.

"Nice job," Maya said. "I would have helped you out, but I figured you had it under control."

"Thanks. Now let's get the hell out of here."

***

Between the spreading fire and the dinosaurs that roamed the island, making their way to the shore proved to be almost impossible. They soon found themselves hiding in a maintenance shed as a familiar sight strode past them.

"Was that a T-Rex?" Maya whispered.

Kane nodded. "Remember, they track movement, so wait until it's well out of sight before we go."

"Trust me; I couldn't move right now if I wanted to."

Kane waited until he was certain the apex predator was gone, and then he peeked around the corner of the shed. In the darkness, his eyes caught sight of a flickering blue light. It came from a cave set in a low hillock. A massive security gate stood open beside it.

"That's the portal. It's got to be," he whispered. "As if to confirm his suspicion, a velociraptor sprinted out of the cave and off into the darkness.

"Who cares? Let's go."

"We should close it. Permanently."

Maya fixed him with a flat stare. "I don't know whether to begin with 'why' or 'how.' Dealer's choice."

Kane frowned. He couldn't explain it, but deep down he knew he ought to close off access to the portal. "Whatever Kevin wants with it, it can't be good. He's not the ethical type. Besides, the fewer dinosaurs out here stalking us, the better."

"Okay, let's move along to the 'how' of the situation."

"We've got all the makings for a nice bomb right here in the shed." His sweeping gesture took in several bags of fertilizer and a variety of other items.

"You know how to do that? From your law enforcement days?"

"That and a basic knowledge of chemistry. Let's go."

***

Thirty minutes later they stood at the mouth of the cave, ready to set off the bomb. Kane had not had time to inspect the portal, except to ascertain that it appeared to be a naturally-occurring phenomenon. The blue glow emanated from the bedrock. Some sort of crystal or previously-unknown mineral, perhaps? He wouldn't figure it out standing here. He needed to blow this thing before something hungry stepped through and made him a midnight snack.

"You think it will work?" Maya asked.

"No idea if it will destroy the portal, but it will definitely collapse the passageway. Now, get as far away as you can." He took hold of the wires that would detonate the bomb, and knelt, ready to touch them to the battery he'd scavenged from a four-wheeler.

"Don't do that, brother." Kevin's voice rang out in the semi-darkness. "If your hand moves toward that battery, I kill the girl."

Kane froze. Did he dare try and set off the bomb, trusting that the blast would distract Kevin long enough for Maya to get away? Was he certain the bomb would even go off? He knew the theory but of course he'd never made one.

"Kevin, why the fuck are you doing this?"

Light from the dying fire at the lodge danced on Kevin's sweaty brow. He looked like the devil. "Making my own way, little brother. Dad's not going to leave me the company, so I'm going to find and take control of the portals myself."

"Why? What is the deal with these portals? What do you even want with them?"

Kevin shook his head. "I'd explain it to your dumb ass but I don't see the point. You're both going to be dead in a moment. Now, slowly put the wires down, or I shoot her in the gut. She'll die slowly and painfully. I'll let you live long enough to hear her scream."

Kane laid the wires on the damp ground, scanning the area with his peripheral vision, searching for a weapon. Nothing.

"Good. Now go stand beside your girlfriend."

Kane did as instructed, glaring at Kevin all the while. "Why don't you put that gun down and fight me like a man? Don't be a little bitch."

Kevin flinched. His buttons were easy to push. He lowered his pistol for a fraction of a second. Kane took a few steps toward him, but Kevin raised his weapon again. "Nice try."

Kane tensed. He could see only one option. He'd charge Kevin, probably get shot, but it would give Maya a chance to get away.

"Not yet." Maya's soft whisper scarcely reached his ears. He froze. "If you're going to open the portal," she said to Kevin, "you'll need this."

Kevin frowned. "What's that?"

"It's sort of a key. I stole it from Aquino's office. I'll give it to you, but you have to let us go."

"Let me see what it is and I'll consider it." Kevin sounded doubtful.

Everything seemed to happen at once. A light blossomed over Kane's shoulder, then arced through the air to land at Kevin's feet. Kane had a moment to recognize Albert's Zippo lighter before something charged. Something huge. The T-Rex!

Drawn by the light and motion, it attacked Kevin, snatching him up in its jaws as the screaming man emptied his pistol into the dinosaur. The T-Rex let out a high pitched shriek and dashed back into the cave, carrying Kevin along like a dog with a bone.

"Let's go!" Maya shouted.

"Not yet." Kane returned to his makeshift detonator, grabbed the wires, and touched them to the battery terminals.

The world erupted in fire and smoke.

***

He opened his eyes to see the gray morning sky hanging above him. A gentle rocking and low hum told him he was lying on the deck of a boat. He made to rise, but a stabbing pain in his head sent him back to the deck, groaning.

"You're awake." Maya's face appeared above him, grinning.

"I take it the bomb worked." His voice sounded odd, then he remembered his nose, broken in the fight with Barnard.

"You collapsed the cave, but a chunk of flying debris caught you on the head. You're lucky to be alive."

"Lucky. That's me." He squeezed his eyes shut and took a few deep breaths. "How'd you get me to the boat?"

"A couple of security guys found us. We're getting the hell out of here."

Kane made another attempt at sitting up, and this time managed it. He felt Maya snake her arm around his waist, and he returned the gesture.

"What do we do now?" she asked.

153

He considered the question. He was now owner of Kane Enterprises. At least, he would be when all the legalities were settled. But it wasn't business that was on his mind at the moment.

"I could use your help with a project," he said.

Maya quirked an eyebrow. "What project?"

"Both Dad and Kevin mentioned multiple portals. I'm going to find them."

The End

JEREMIAH'S PUZZLE

By Alan Baxter

Caroline Ardern watched the trio of tweed-clad adventurers and wondered again what the hell she was doing in a musty old mansion on the edge of the Yorkshire Moors. It had seemed like such a good idea at the time, in the bustling offices of the Advertiser back in London. Now she couldn't help thinking she'd stumbled into a satirical gotcha show. Some kind of candid camera throwback to the eighties where a grinning idiot of a host would leap out any moment and play back all her incredulity on a big screen.

"It's got to be something more than a mere trinket," Jeremiah Fotherington-Smythe insisted. He had a florid face, vein-mapped nose, and a belly that strained the buttons of his waistcoat. At a little over sixty, he embodied every kind of upper-class excess. "I didn't trek through eighty bally miles of Amazonian jungle for a damned ornament!"

"Maybe you did," Callum Barker said. The man was everything Jeremiah wasn't. Barker was whip-thin, angular, dark-eyed and haired. He could easily have dressed in robes and passed as an evil wizard in a live role-playing game. "Why does it have to be special?"

Jeremiah's face scrunched in frustration, his lack of chin highlighted by the action. "Hundreds have tried to find that fabled temple. I might look like a fat and useless blueblood, but I've made a life of this kind of thing. I'm no amateur! I've been to places and done things regular people couldn't imagine. Four men died on this damned expedition, for God's sake!" He tossed the offending item to his cousin.

Callum Barker caught the black and gold metallic rectangle and looked it over. It was about the size of a child's lunchbox. "Just because you tracked down an ancient map, and that map led you to a previously undiscovered temple of dark lore, dedicated to who-knows-what ancient god, and just because in that temple you found this item in a place of reverence, doesn't mean it's anything more than pretty, Jer."

Jeremiah huffed like an impatient walrus. "Nonsense!"

"These people revere the sun rising, for Pete's sake," Jacob Miles-Wentworth said, leaning casually on the massive mantelpiece, sipping brandy. He smirked, emphasizing his ratty features and nervous small body. "They think an aeroplane flying above is a giant silver bird. Why wouldn't they worship that just because it's pretty?"

"I refuse to accept it," Jeremiah said, but his face betrayed the lie as he went to help himself to a large Courvoisier.

Caroline shook her head and checked over her notes again. She had all she needed for an article on the man's great expedition, including a large number of photographs from his stock, and permission to use them. She could put together a fascinating feature. Maybe it was time to call it quits. Perhaps the item recovered would remain a mystery. In fact, maybe that could be the angle. *Mysterious Ancient Artifact Defies Explanation.* That could work. She drew breath, about to excuse herself and thank Fotherington-Smythe for his time, when the study door opened and a pale young man with long black hair and an indecipherable t-shirt loped in.

"What's happening?" he asked, his voice like a mudslide.

Caroline had never seen such disdain for the entire world so succinctly worn on a single face before. And the boy couldn't be much more than eighteen or nineteen.

Jeremiah turned, smiled. "Ah! Gents, this is my nephew, Simon Grant, come to stay for a couple of weeks over his uni summer break."

Caroline shook her head. Gents. Like she wasn't even there. What did it matter? She didn't need anything else from them.

"This place is duller than Leeds," Simon said, heading for the drinks bar in the corner. He moved the way Caroline imagined kelp might if it could walk.

As Simon poured himself half a tumbler of brandy, he caught sight of the box Callum Barker still held. "What's that?"

Barker tossed it over. "A useless bit of tat your uncle brought back from the Amazon."

Simon caught it, turned it over as he took a couple of deep gulps of the dark liquor. "It's a puzzle box," he said casually.

Caroline's eyebrows shot up. Had things suddenly got interesting?

"What's that?" Jeremiah asked.

Simon held up the box, light catching on intricate filigrees of brass or copper. The wood of its construction was dark, almost black. Ebony, Jeremiah had postulated earlier. Simon sniffed, nodded. "Like the ones in Darkborn Saint."

"What's that?" Jeremiah repeated.

"Video game. PS4? Never mind. It's not exactly the same, of course, but the principal is there. These small metal nubs shift along the brass tracks if you press them in and slide them." Simon demonstrated, sliding a tiny piece of the seemingly immobile design.

"Good god," Jeremiah said. "It never occurred to me it might move. I thought it was just locked somehow."

Simon shrugged. "It is, I expect. And you open it by solving the puzzle." He went to hand it over, but Jeremiah pushed it back at him.

"Keep going, lad. See if you can get in there."

Simon realized the attention in the room had become intense. Everyone, even Caroline, had moved closer to watch. "Okay," he said, somewhat nervously. He gulped the rest of the brandy and put the glass down, then perched on one arm of a deep red leather wing-backed chair. He cocked one foot up onto the opposite knee and turned his full attention to the box. For a moment he traced its swirls and designs with a fingertip, investigating the pattern. As expectant silence grew heavier than grief in the room, he turned the box over, turned it back, then smiled.

"See here?" He pointed to a small circular indentation in the center of one flat side. "This is where all these small brass knobs need to go. You get them all in here and it makes a kind of rosette. I bet that unlocks the box."

"Can you do it?" Jeremiah asked.

"Come on, lad," Callum Barker said. "Show us!"

Caroline surreptitiously took her phone from her pocket and began videoing the young man's long, slim fingers as he pressed each brassy dome and slid it carefully left and right through the maze of filigree. He grunted in frustration as he met dead ends, but reset, started again. Then the first small metallic bulb slid into the center circle and clicked. Simon grinned, began moving his fingers more confidently. As each knob reached the center, it made a soft but decisive clunk. Jacob Miles-Wentworth, Caroline noted, had remained leaning on the mantelpiece. He held his brandy glass in one palm, gently swirling the drink around and around. The smirk hadn't left his face. Caroline realized it was probably permanent. Not an actual smirk, it was just his face.

She looked back as Simon made a noise of satisfaction and the box clicked again. "One to go," he said, focused.

He turned the box over, gently depressing and shifting the last brass dome. It moved smoothly, but regularly stopped against thin lines of filigree. Simon frowned, backed up, tried a different route. Three times, then four, he came to dead ends.

"Take your time," Jeremiah said. "You'll get it."

"Oh wait!" Simon sat up straighter, shifted his grip on the box, and moved the entire web of filigree a little to the right. It slid easily, then quick lines of blue light flickered all around Simon's fingers. "Jesus!"

The box made a thump as it hit the floor and Simon sat sucking the fingertips of his left hand. "Bloody thing shocked me!"

Jeremiah retrieved it. "Static, maybe?"

Simon gave him a cynical look.

"Well, whatever." Jeremiah handed the box back. "Go on. Please?"

With a wry twist of his mouth, Simon took the thing and shifted the last tiny button into place. As it clicked in, the now complete rosette lit up with sparkling blue like arcing electricity. With a cry, Simon tossed the box away. It hit the thick rug at Jacob Miles-Wentworth's feet, still sparking and crackling. Jacob finally moved from his post, sidling away from the box as it began to buzz softly, then whine. Caroline backed up into one corner of the large room, ensuring she got it all on video.

The box seemed to leap, flickering with blue and white sparks, then it fell open like a book and hit the rug again. Incandescence burst up from it, hot and blinding. The men threw up their arms to shield their eyes, staggered back from the sudden assault. A sound like tearing canvas amplified through stadium speakers made them wince and cry out in pain, then wind whipped through the room. With it came a sulphurous stench and the sounds of wildlife, screeches and howls, clicks and flaps. As the brightness faded, those gathered saw a rent in space like a vertical eye, a sharp-ended oval in the middle of Jeremiah Fotherington-Smythe's study, floor to ceiling, and through that portal was another world. Dark, stormy clouds scudded high. In the distance, a volcano belched black smoke as bright red lava ran down its sides like candle wax. Nearer stood huge ferns and towering trees, with thick waxy leaves. Deep grasses, dark and wide-leaved, covered a floor of ochre sand and rock. The five people in the study gasped as a huge bird, wide wings of stretched leather behind a long, bony head, swept by.

"That's a fucking pterodactyl," Simon said.

"Bit more than a bloody ornament, what?" Jeremiah said, moving closer to the portal. It seemed to stand out of the open box lying on the rug, as though the box projected it, only it was no fancy image. The thing was undeniably real. Its edges flickered and burned, a kind of white strobing tear in reality. As Jeremiah got closer and reached out one hand, as if to try to touch the other side, sudden movement made him leap back.

A creature about the size of a medium dog bolted through the flickering gap and into the study. It stood on powerful back legs, tiny arms waved. It had a long head with a sail of bone at the top and a kind of bony beak that snapped in fear and alarm as it bounced off a leather chair and crashed into the drinks bar. Bottles and glasses rattled and shook. Its body was covered in iridescent feathers of blue and green.

"Bloody hell," Jeremiah said, moving in a crouch to corner it.

"Look out," Simon said, as another came running through.

Then another, then a fourth. They careened around the study in mad panic, bouncing off furniture and people alike, running randomly, snapping and keening a high wail. The door Simon had entered by still stood open and one streaked through it. The others, seeing it go, made a beeline for the same escape. Then another came through from the world beyond the portal, then two more.

"Hey," Caroline started, but Jeremiah shouted over her.

"Shut the bally door! Don't let these things run rampant through the house!"

A squawking rang out and half a dozen of the shimmering small dinosaurs burst through all at once, eyes wide, bony beaks clacking. The room seemed suddenly filled with them and they tore through, all heading out the door into the hallway beyond.

Jacob Miles-Wentworth moved to stand in front of the portal, looking into the lost world beyond. "This is the kind of thing that'll change the world," he said, dancing aside as another shimmering creature rushed through.

Caroline had pressed herself deeper into the corner, still videoing. But gut-roiling fear made her weak. Finally she found her voice again as Jeremiah, Callum and Simon all reached the study door. "What the hell are they all running *from?*" she yelled.

The three by the door stopped and turned, and Caroline's answer ducked through the glimmering portal. Filling the opening, literally stretching the sides of it, a giant scaled head with dark striped feathers cascading down its back, drove into the room and opened a mouth the size of the fireplace behind it. Sharp white teeth, each as long as a grown man's forearm, bristled in that maw as the creature roared a bellowing screech. Jacob Miles-Wentworth stood frozen not six feet from it, his trousers darkening instantly as his bladder opened. It was the last thing he did. The creature ducked, like a giant chicken pecking at grain, and snapped Jacob Miles-Wentworth away in a single bite. All that remained were two legs, severed just above the knee, gouting blood. The two separated limbs fell over as the giant beast swallowed and raised its huge head to screech again, crashing into the ceiling, knocking plaster flying. It took a step forward, pushing through the portal like some sickening parody of birth. A huge, clawed foot slammed into the floor, splintering the wooden boards like balsa. Then another and the creature was through. The Tyrannosaurus Rex, Caroline told herself, shivering in terror. Call it what it was. A fucking T-Rex had just stepped into Jeremiah Fotherington-Smythe's study.

She looked towards the door and saw the others had gone. Cowardly bastards had bolted, leaving her the only one in the room. Jammed into the corner, frozen in fear, she remembered a scene in *Jurassic Park*, where the cast had been told to stay still, the T-Rex only sees movement. Was that true? She had no choice, she couldn't have moved if she wanted to. The beast suddenly strode forward, shaking the house with its weight. However big this room was, the creature hunched and seemed to fill it, tearing out the ceiling with its back. It ducked its head towards the large doorway but was far too big to fit through. Regardless it pushed on and tore half the wall out with it as it barreled into the hallway and crashed through the house beyond.

Freed from her paralysis, Caroline ran to the impossible portal, praying nothing else would come through. She dropped to the floor and grabbed the box, ignored the stinging sparks of electricity that bolted up her arms, and slammed it shut. The portal winked out, the study dropping into sudden stillness and quiet but for the rain of dust and plaster where the T-Rex had punched through the wall and wrecked the ceiling. She managed to take one breath of relief, then the beast's high-pitched roar echoed through the house again.

Sudden concussive blasts sounded, from not too far away. Gunshots, a pistol maybe. Then a louder blast, surely a shotgun. Then another. Then several in quick succession. Well, she'd wanted a story. Every sensible part of Caroline Ardern screamed at her to leap through the study window, run down the long, graveled driveway of Fotherington Manor, and get in her car, put her foot down, and not stop until she was safely back in London. But the journalist in her couldn't turn away from this story. Could it? She swallowed, turned left and right, indecisive. More shots rang out, then shouting. Then the high-pitched scream of a man in mortal agony.

"Fuck this!" Caroline hissed. She crouched by the box, now inert on the rug, and used her phone to quickly take numerous pictures. She snapped shots of the gruesome remains of Jacob Miles-Wentworth, then the destroyed wall where the Rex had smashed through. "That will have to be enough," she said, to convince herself, then ran for the window. She saw her car parked only a hundred yards or so away. More shots rang out as she opened the window and clambered onto the wide sill.

The echoing, screeching roar of the T-Rex rang out, close enough to deafen her. Caroline fell back into the room as the beast thundered past, not ten feet from the open window. She lay on her back, looking up into its enormous shadow, and then it was gone.

"Jesus," she whispered. "It's out there."

Noise behind drew her attention, scuffling and sobbing. She turned to see the source of all this mayhem, Jeremiah Fotherington-Smythe, stagger into the room. His face was white, eyes rolling. He was covered in blood and where his right arm used to be was a mess of hanging flesh and stark white bone, even a couple of ribs sticking wildly through the sodden remains of his tweed waistcoat. How the man still stood with his entire arm and most of his shoulder bitten away was a mystery.

Caroline took one step forward, arms out as if to catch him, entirely uncertain of what she could do. Jeremiah stopped just inside the ruined wall, stood swaying, staring at the mantelpiece.

"Gone," he muttered.

Caroline glanced back, then returned her attention to Jeremiah. "The portal?" she asked. "The gateway to the past or whatever that was?"

Fotherington-Smythe nodded dumbly.

"I closed the box. It shut off."

He nodded again. "Good girl. Nothing else can come through." He seemed to make an effort of will and focus on her eyes for the first time. He grinned. "Quite a bloody story, eh? Make sure you spell my name right."

His eyes glazed and he tipped forward, stiff like a plank of wood. He crashed face-first into the floorboards, nose and mouth bursting with blood on impact, but made not a sound, and lay still. Blood poured from the enormous hole where his arm had been and pooled darkly on the wood.

Shouting sounded outside and Caroline turned back to the window. Callum Barker and Simon Grant ran past, both carrying double-barreled shotguns, on the trail of the T-Rex. The teenager had become the opposite of his previous lackluster self, animated and excited. She had to admire their bravery if they planned to hunt the dinosaur down. But then again, what else was there to do? They could hardly let a giant Cretaceous carnivore run rampant across the Yorkshire Moors. But shotguns?

She ran back through the study, gathering her things, and jumped out the window, calling after them. They paused, looked around. Callum grinned to see her.

"Glad you're okay," he said as she jogged up to them. "I was rather hoping you'd be in your car on the motorway back to London by now though."

Caroline chose not to mention that had been exactly her plan until the Rex had thundered by, cutting her off. "And miss this story?" she said instead. "Hardly." Then she pointed to the shotguns they held. "You plan to bring it down with those?"

Callum shrugged. "It's all we have." He showed her his pockets bulging with shells. Simon had a similar hoard.

"Uncle Jer had a pistol, a big old Magnum thing, but the Rex rounded on him and took it, along with his arm." Simon grinned, like that was the coolest thing he'd ever seen.

"Yes," she said. "I saw him. He didn't survive it."

"We figured," Callum said. "But he took out most of those small dinosaurs that flooded through, we got a couple too. I think there might still be some around, in the house or around the grounds. But we'll have to leave those for now."

Simon nodded towards the woods across the manicured expanse of Fotherington Manor's lawns. "Bigger fish to fry."

As if on cue, the T-Rex's bellowing screech echoed back from the trees.

"Not boring any more, is it?" Caroline said.

Simon gritted his teeth dramatically, then said, "If anything, a little too exciting now. I'd like some middle ground."

Callum Barker was staring at the trees, eyes narrowed. "I say," he said in a soft voice. "That's south, yes?"

"I think so," Simon said.

"That means only a mile or so away, on the other side of those woods, is the village of Tilting Sodbury."

Caroline's eyes widened, a memory coming back to her of the drive up early that morning. "I passed a sign on the way here. Tilting Sodbury summer fete. It's on today, from 10am." She glanced at her watch. "Now it's just after twelve noon. The place will be packed."

"And the fete is on the village green," Simon confirmed. "Which is the first thing you come to should you go through those woods."

"Bloody hell!" Barker said and broke into a run.

Caroline pulled her phone out as the three of them pounded across the lawns and into the trees. She opened the video and held the phone in front of her, staying behind the two men with shotguns. The footage would be terrible, jerky and messy, but far better than no footage at all. Maybe it would look thrilling, like one of those ridiculous found footage movies. She still doubted that shotguns would be any use against the beast, but perhaps they might at least deter it. Drive it away from the village if nothing else. Perhaps they should call someone. The Army, maybe?

Simon had said it was a mile through the woods, but it seemed like no time at all until they burst free of the trees and saw the bright colors of the fete on the village green. A low fence, old and moss-covered, marked the edge of Fotherington Manor's grounds. Simple wood, barely over three feet high. Country security at its finest. A shame Jeremiah hadn't installed twelve-foot high electrified fences all around, though she wondered if that would have stopped the beast anyway.

Across the grass stood the Green Lamb Inn, thatched roof and rustic red brick. To either side, the village of Tilting Sodbury spread out. A variety of thatch and slate and tile roofs, stone and brick construction, narrow roads and high hedges. Everything an English country village should be. What tourists would call quaint and what the locals would simply call home. And between them, on the green, were hundreds of people in their summer finery. They milled and talked and laughed, threw wooden balls at coconuts, tried their strength with a huge hammer, lobbed rings over rubber ducks. Kids ate candy floss and hotdogs, stalls sold cakes and jams and pickles and embroidery and crocheted toilet roll covers. On one side, screams and laughter came from the multiple impacts of bumper cars, bright and colorful as their drivers gleefully rammed each other. The sun shone down from a cloudless blue sky, everything bathed in gold. Red, white, and blue bunting fluttered in the soft breeze. Idyllic was the word that leaped to Caroline's mind. But there was one thing missing. A furious, carnivorous dinosaur. Perhaps that was a good thing. Maybe it had been distracted by game in the woods. Were there deer in these parts? Her questions ended when the screaming started. The three of them jumped the low fence and ran out into the fete.

At the far end of the green, where it met the churchyard of St Andrew's, was an open space reserved for donkey rides. Along with the screaming, the three donkeys began braying in terror as the giant reptile burst from the trees hauling leaves and branches with it. The thing stood more than thirty feet tall, dark scales overlapped with striated feathers of black and brown. Its amber eyes flashed in the sun as it swung its huge head left and right, then split its fanged maw to bellow its rage. It took earth-shaking steps forward as it roared and a mother snatched her wailing young daughter from the back of a donkey and ran as the Rex surged forward and grabbed the braying ass right around its middle. The braying turned to shrieks of pain and horror as the Rex stood tall and shook the donkey like a dog with a stick. Grey fur and blood and guts rained down across the bright green grass as the donkey fell in two halves. The T-Rex ducked its head to snatch up the hindquarters and gulp them down.

Stunned shock turned to panic and the village green erupted in terror. Families ran, grabbing gaping children as they went. They dashed in every direction except towards the carnivore and perhaps that bought some of them some time, as the T-Rex stood and swung its head left and right once more, watching the random activity.

Against the tide, Callum and Simon raced towards the beast, Caroline right behind them filming everything. The two men raised their shotguns, but before they could fire, the Rex made a decision and stampeded to its right. It leaned down as it ran, snapping up people too slow to dodge. Screams and blood filled the air.

Callum and Simon skidded to a halt between a cake stall and a funny-shaped vegetable competition and raised their weapons. The shotguns boomed simultaneously from only a few yards behind the Rex. It bellowed as feathers and scales burst up from its side and spun to face the men. A leg in blood-soaked jeans and the entire head and torso of an elderly woman tumbled from its jaws to land wetly in the grass as the beast screeched again. Callum and Simon each fired their second barrel, this time up in the soft tissue under the dinosaur's jaw. More blood rained down, but the shots seemed to cause little damage. But they must have caused some pain, as the beast flinched and took a step back, howling.

As Callum and Simon scrambled to reload, a flash of black and white shot between them with an accompanying wail. The local vicar raced across the green, yelling something about God's graces and the evil behemoth begone. He carried with him a glittering gold cross, some six feet long, presumably snatched from the altar of his church. In an impressive display of strength, he held it wedged under one arm as he powered forward like a rugby winger with the ball, rushing for the try line. Caroline had a moment to notice that the cross had a kind of spike at the top, a design feature to make it more interesting perhaps, then, with all his weight behind it, the vicar drove that point and then a good two feet of the huge crucifix itself, in the T-Rex's belly. Only the crossbar, where allegedly Christ's palms had been nailed, arrested the impaling of the beast.

The T-Rex roared again and rose up. Its tiny forelimbs scrabbled towards the cross as it shook itself but couldn't reach the Crucifix of Tilting Sodbury Church buried in its gut. But though wounded and clearly in terrible pain, it wasn't to be defeated. It raised one huge rear leg and stomped down on the hapless vicar and the man was crushed into the grass, his white and black vestments billowing and instantly crimson.

Heart slamming into her ribs, Caroline lowered her phone as Callum and Simon raised their shotguns and fired again. More blood, more bellows of rage and pain, but still the creature didn't fall. Bodies lay broken or half-eaten all around it, stalls and attractions crushed and overturned. People ran wild through the streets trying to get away while others wailed and sobbed where they lay, injured or refusing to leave their dead. Callum and Simon began loading again and the T-Rex leaned forward and bellowed, flesh and clothing hanging from its teeth.

They were enraging it, not killing it. Their weapons would not work. They needed something far more deadly. A horn blared behind them. Spinning around, Caroline managed to dive aside as a seven-ton truck came skidding across the village green, tearing up the grass in its wake. Crouched over the wheel, a grey-haired woman in dark blue overalls stared the T-Rex down, her teeth bared. The creature turned to meet the onslaught and the truck slammed into it with a bone-shattering impact and a wail of tearing metal. Truck and T-Rex slewed across the green and crashed into the grey stone walls of St Andrew's Church with a jarring crunch. For a moment, everything was still. From her angle, Caroline saw the woman in the overalls slumped over the steering wheel, blood running freely from her nose. Then a dull roar as the T-Rex sucked in a shuddering breath and drove its powerful hind legs against the church wall to push the truck off itself. It staggered side to side, the crucifix falling free of its abdomen followed by a flood of thick blood. It shook its head and bellowed.

Callum and Simon frantically scrabbled in their pockets to reload again, but Caroline ran over to them, pulled on Simon's sleeve. "Those aren't enough," she said. "I have another plan."

They looked at her in confusion. "What?" Callum asked.

From her bag, Caroline pulled the Amazonian puzzle box. She held it up in front of Simon. "I grabbed this on the way out. Can you solve it again? It reset when I slammed it closed."

Simon nodded. "Sure, if I have a few minutes."

"Good." Caroline handed it over and pointed across the green. "See there? That gap between the pub and the butcher's?"

"Yeah."

"Solve it there. We'll drive the T-Rex to it. Be quick."

Simon looked from the gap between the buildings to Caroline, then grinned. "You got it." He bolted off, long, pale fingers already sliding at the puzzle's buttons.

Callum stepped up to Caroline as the T-Rex righted itself and roared again, the stun of the truck's impact wearing off. It strode forward, picking up the remains of bleeding victims, swallowing them down, scavenging.

"And how do we get it there?" Callum asked.

Caroline pointed across the green at the bright colors of the inert bumper car arcade. "Ever driven the dodgems?" she asked.

The woman in blue overalls staggered from the cab of the truck, blood all over her face.

"What the bloody 'ell'll it take to bring that fecker down?" she demanded.

"Can you still drive?" Caroline asked her.

The woman looked affronted. "I'm Rose Tingle. I've driven for a livin' my whole life, lass. Since afore you were born!"

"Good, come with us."

"Dodgems?" Callum asked.

"Yes. But for real!"

Caroline ran to the edge of the green where a few rubberneckers driving past had slowed to an astonished crawl. "Get yourselves a car!" she yelled at the others, then pulled open the driver's door of the Range Rover she had approached. "Out!"

The man was so stunned by everything he witnessed that he obeyed without question. He slipped from the driver's seat, agog. Caroline jumped in, dropped her phone on the passenger seat, and gunned the engine. As she revved hard up over the curb and onto the green, Callum and Rose Tingle each pulled up alongside her in commandeered cars of their own.

Caroline led them between the fete's stalls, arcing around behind the T-Rex. They formed into a semi-circle and drove at it as it took long strides back towards a huddle of people near the church wall. Blinding brightness flashed from across the road and the vertical eye of the portal leapt into being once more, taller than the buildings. Unrestricted, perhaps, by Jeremiah's study as it had been before. Simon stepped aside and gave them a double thumbs up.

Caroline flashed the lights and blared the horn as she bore down on the dinosaur, to scare it into a run. Callum and Rose stayed either side, lights and horns matching hers. But Caroline's stomach clenched when the beast turned and ducked towards them instead of running away. At the last instant it whipped its enormous back end around, the thick tail slamming into Callum's borrowed Ford Sierra. The car lifted sideways and rolled over and over to smash into a collection of gravestones. Rose shot past on the other side and Caroline hit the brakes, slewing aside and barely avoiding the creature. If Rose's truck hadn't hurt it, a Range Rover wasn't about to. The beast looked around and started pounding across the green after Rose's wildly skidding stolen Mercedes.

Another idea came to Caroline. As Rose described a wide circle on the green, trying to lead the T-Rex back around, Caroline drove to the panicked donkeys and jumped out. "Sorry about this!" she said, and meant it. She grabbed the lead rope of one donkey off the fence and looped it a couple of times around the Range Rover's tow-bar. She jumped back in and powered away. The donkey ran hard the first few yards, braying and screeching, then it staggered, then went down. It sailed along on the grass like a toboggan, legs cycling madly in the air. If a donkey could scream, this one did so, the noise entirely unlike anything the beast should have been able to emit. Caroline cut right behind Rose's car, across the path of the T-Rex, blasting the horn again.

"Come on, you fucker!" she yelled out of the open window.

The T-Rex slowed briefly, saw the screaming donkey slide by, and turned in pursuit.

"Yes!" Caroline punched the air and turned towards the road. She floored it, mud and grass spraying up behind, driving hard directly for the incandescent portal. The T-Rex pounded after, leaning forward in an attempt to snap up the wailing donkey.

"Come on, come on, come on!" Caroline begged, then the Range Rover bounced over the curb at the edge of the green, found better traction on the asphalt, and shot across the street. The donkey left a smear of grey fur and blood as it was dragged behind, and Caroline drove directly through the portal, into a prehistoric realm. Heat and sulphurous odors assailed her as she went, bouncing over rocks and loose shale. The donkey screamed on, the T-Rex followed. Caroline opened the door and, praying for her own safety, dived out of the Range Rover, tucking and rolling as she hit the ground with a breath-exploding impact. Rocks spiked into her, she felt a couple of ribs crack, and agony blossomed through her left arm from the elbow. But as she skidded and rolled, she forced her feet to find ground beneath her and came up running. She had little time to register the majesty of the landscape around her as the donkey on its rope tumbled past and the T-Rex pounded after.

Caroline ducked and sprinted back the other way, desperately dragging air into tortured lungs. Simon's face, wide-eyed, appeared at the edge of the portal and Caroline focused only on that as the donkey's screams reached a pitch almost beyond hearing then abruptly ended. She didn't look back, and leaped through the portal, back into the balmy summer air of Tilting Sodbury. As the T-Rex's voice bellowed out again, she hit the road surface, tumbled over once, barking a noise of pain at the further torture to her arm, then scrambled back to the impossible gate. She reached under it for the puzzle box, gritting her teeth against the sparking shocks, and slammed it closed. The portal snapped away as if it had never been. Caroline tossed the box away from her and silence but for the moans of the injured, fell across the Tilting Sodbury village fete.

"Bloody hell," Simon whispered, eventually. "That. Was. Intense."

Caroline smiled, tears from the pain rolling free, but the adrenaline and sure knowledge the T-Rex was back where it should be kept her from complete collapse.

"A Range Rover in the Cretaceous," Simon said with a smile. "That'll fuck up the archaeologists one day."

"And my phone!" Caroline said, despair washing through her. "The footage of it all!"

Simon looked at the box lying in the road a yard or two away. "We could give it a little while for the T-Rex to wander off and go back for it," he said. "Recover the car too, for that matter."

Callum Barker limped over to them, his shotgun hanging along his thigh. He approached the box, put the two barrels against it, and fired. They winced back from the boom and thousands of particles of ebony and shiny filigree. The box was gone. "Fuck that," Barker said. He gave them a weak smile. "There's no place in our world for something like that. Jerry should have left it well the fuck alone."

Sirens wailed in the distance.

"You did an amazing job there, Caroline," Callum said. "But I suggest we all claim complete ignorance of what happened here. We were just at the village fete, yes? None of us have seen old Jeremiah Fotherington-Smythe for a few weeks."

Simon nodded. "He was supposed to meet me at the fete, then I was going to go and stay with him for a while, but he never showed up. Then this happened."

"And I got all I needed for the story by phone and mail," Caroline said. "I never even left London."

Callum nodded. "Good. Go on then, back through the woods, you two. Simon, get your stuff and sneak back here like you've been here all along. Caroline, you get in your car and head back home."

"And you?" Caroline asked.

Callum Barker looked across at the Green Lamb Inn. "I need a bloody drink."

In the woods of Fotherington Manor, a creature with a high, wide head and iridescent feathers of blue and green, ran in pursuit of a terrified rabbit.

The End

MANTLE

By Rick Chesler

Part I: Straight Down

Bardarbunga Volcano, Iceland

Kane Eisenberg stepped out of the custom designed motor home he'd lived in on this site for the last month. Like everything else in his life, it was top of the line, since he had financial resources most people could only dream about. Founder of a popular online retailer, Kane had the good fortune to become a billionaire through stock options exercised while in his forties. Having just turned 50, the internet mogul turned his sights to personal goals and aspirations that went above and beyond normal career dreams. Or in his case, below and beyond.

Unlike the handful of his peers in his elite group who focused their own pet projects on outer space, Kane decided to put his considerable wherewithal into probing the opposite direction--straight down into the Earth. No one had ever penetrated completely through the crust into the inner region of the planet that surrounded the core, known as the mantle, a sea of liquid magma that may also contain an ocean of water. It represented The Great Unknown, a true frontier of Earth exploration that, with a little luck, he would be the first human to explore, to personally plumb the depths of the planet in a quest to boldly go where no human ever has.

The internet mogul faced into an icy early morning breeze and told himself to enjoy the chill while he could, for later today, if everything went according to plan, he would be surrounded by unimaginable heat in the form of liquid magma. He gazed at the marvel of engineering that would allow him to do this—a ten-foot diameter titanium sphere that was built to withstand not only the heat, but also the immense pressures that existed underneath the Earth's crust.

Supported by a tower of scaffolding, the metal sphere was the capsule that would transport Kane into the Earth's mantle and back. Already Kane's team had broken records and made international news by lowering the sphere unmanned to the edge of the Earth's crust—forty miles deep—before retrieving the capsule, dubbed the "MagmaSphere," in full working condition. The massive cable that allowed the MagmaSphere to be raised and lowered by a computer-controlled winch was also made from titanium and designed to withstand the pressure and heat of inner Earth.

But it had yet to be attempted with a person inside, and not only was Kane Eisenberg to be that person, but today was the day. Some were critical of his intent to ride inside the metal ball deep into the planet, calling it a reckless publicity stunt at best, a boondoggle waste of resources at worst. Numerous requests for Kane to donate his fortune to various causes should he die during the stunt poured in. He ignored them all, keeping his mind focused on the task ahead. The inside of our own planet is less understood then the surface of the moon, his press releases went in response to the criticism. My colleagues have space covered, I'm trying to help us learn about the insides of our own home, planet Earth.

To that end, the MagmaSphere, compensating for its windowless capsule, was outfitted with an array of scientific instruments that would give a picture of the environment surrounding the capsule. Why was a human needed to ride along like, in the famous words of test pilot Chuck Yeager, "spam in a can?" Why not just let the instruments give us their data? To this, Kane replied, "Knowing that a human has never actually been to a major part of our planet is something I think is worth changing."

Still, as Kane stared at the MagmaSphere now, next to an active volcano, he would be lying if he didn't admit to having second thoughts. He had an awful lot to live for, after all—a wife, kids, a business empire, a lot of quality years ahead of him…and yet, the adventure called him like a siren's song from deep within the globe. He'd seen the failure statistics and was well versed in what could go wrong. The integrity of the MagmaSphere itself wasn't what worried him. The titanium sphere could handle the depths. He was aware of other technical concerns but pushed them to the back of his mind for now.

A small army of Eisenberg's employees scuttled about the base of the MagmaSphere's scaffolding and the nearby row of modular trailers that had been set up to monitor the Bardarbunga Volcano into which the capsule would be lowered by winch in a controlled descent. The volcano itself was what made the entire operation possible. It represented a unique spot on the surface of the planet. The Earth's crust was thickest on land, and yet this active volcano represented a portal straight to the mantle over forty miles below. Instead of costly and time-consuming drilling, the volcano itself was already connected deep underground to the upper mantle. So, the MagmaSphere would be craned out over the mouth of it and lowered inside.

A hardhat-wearing employee holding a computer tablet trotted up to Kane and nodded good morning. "Tests indicate all systems are go, sir." Patrick Sevald was the Operations Manager for Project Mantle. He had sat through countless team meetings with Kane and other members of his inner circle. Kane had no doubt that Patrick found the fact that this day was finally here as surreal as he did. All the work, preparation and planning—the blood, sweat and tears—now came down to this.

"Good deal."

"I'll have the crew start the launch countdown at T minus 60."

Kane smiled at the use of the space program terminology. It made for a good media show, and when a screen adjacent to the MagmaSphere scaffolding began showing a digital countdown accompanied with a female automated voice announcing that there was one hour until launch, the media on site came to life, aiming their cameras at the display and live streaming it to their respective websites.

"I'll be ready." Kane picked up the backpack at his feet that contained the few things he'd be bringing with him on the trip. Then he walked toward the tower of scaffolding, slowly, feeling like an odd combination of a condemned man taking his last steps to the electric chair, and someone about to embark on an exotic vacation.

∗∗∗

Forty-five minutes later, Kane Eisenberg rode an elevator up the scaffolding, which offered a commanding view of the top of the volcano's insides, the bubbling, seething orange lava looking like the least inviting place on Earth. He climbed down into the MagmaSphere. The sphere had been designed with only one passenger in mind, both to keep the size small and because, with no windows and an array of autonomous instruments, human payload wasn't a priority.

"Last chance to back out, buddy—you good?" Sevald breezed out of the elevator at the top of the scaffolding and peered down the MagmaSphere's boarding ladder as Kane dropped through the hatch.

"See you at the post-mission briefing, Pat." The billionaire crouched inside his "earth ship," as he thought of it. Although he'd spent countless hours inside a mockup version intended to simulate the exact same physical dimensions as well as controls, being in the real thing while it was poised over an active volcano was sobering.

They went through a systems check, including testing the radio link, even though it would only work for the uppermost layers of the trip. The entire inside of the dome, the cabin, was filled with electronic equipment, save for the bucket seat in the middle of it all. Kane sat in it, laid back in a semi-reclined posture. He pulled the safety harness across his torso and clicked it in place.

"Attaboy, Kane," a "mission control" operator's voice came over the radio. "Lifting into position now, hold tight." A massive crane arm lifted the MagmaSphere from its cradle of scaffolding and swung it up and over the volcano's rocky rim. He could just barely hear the rumbling of the crane's engines outside the thick walls of his protective cocoon, but he could feel the sway as he was dangled through the air. After a few minutes the noise stopped, and the swinging of the sphere grew more pronounced.

"Topside to MagmaSphere," came the radioman's voice again. "You're far enough out over the middle now, but we're waiting for the sway to calm down."

"It's all about the angle of the dangle," Kane joked.

"It's more about the plop of the drop." This from the crane operator, who sat in the control booth of the massive machine while he suspended the billionaire in his subterranean exploration sphere.

"Ready to pay out cable in three...two...one...commencing descent."

With those words, Kane Eisenberg was lowered into a bowl of lava inside an active volcano on live international television. For his part, encased in a titanium sphere, nothing looked or felt much different. He did have a closed-circuit video feed on a small monitor in front of him from two cameras fixed to the outside of the sphere, but it was expected that they would fail sometime after immersion in lava. But right now, the video showed a ring of spectators clapping and cheering him on as he was lowered into the volcano. He watched the people until splashes of lava covered part of the lens, and then, as the MagmaSphere sank into the lake of lava inside the volcano, the camera was submerged in liquid fire and the view on screen went dark.

"You're in it now," came the familiar voice of Patrick Sevald over the radio.

"I feel warmer already," Kane replied with a smile.

"Not funny, Kane." They both knew that the titanium cocoon was designed to be impervious to the heat of lava, and that while the temperature may increase slightly inside the cabin, with the computer-controlled climate inside, it shouldn't be noticeable to the passenger. Kane glanced at the temperature gauges on his console to confirm this fact. Inside was a balmy 76 degrees F, while outside an astounding 1,800 degrees Fahrenheit.

"All temp readings normal on my end," Kane said.

"Copy that, Kane. Holler if you need anything. Remember to expect—"

"Yeah, I know, radio blackout around ten miles. I'll miss the sound of your sweet voice, let me tell you."

Kane settled in for the descent through the volcano's lava, picturing himself as if watching from above, disappearing into the swirling orange maelstrom. He couldn't believe he was really doing this. He took a couple of deep breaths and settled in for the ride, which he knew would take about an hour to reach the bottom of the volcano itself.

The controlled drop was surprisingly smooth considering his environment, with only a small amount of jostling. Once he felt a thud as something hard—no doubt a chunk of ore that managed not to be liquified—impacted the titanium hull of the MagmaSphere—but by and large it was a noneventful ride considering he was literally dropping out through the bottom of an active volcano.

Kane fell into a kind of meditative trance where he relaxed while monitoring the MagmaSphere's instruments. He saw nothing but green lights, for the oxygen and carbon dioxide scrubbing systems, the fire suppression system, the internal and external temperature systems, etc. There was sporadic chatter with topside, as predicted until the MagmaSphere passed beneath the volcano itself, deep into the Earth's crust.

He heard Sevald say, "….cutting out…luck…then." And that was it. He knew he would not have any other communication until he was back inside the volcano again.

He stared at the instruments, trying not to imagine the countless tons of fiery rock bombarding every square inch of his little craft.

***

Kane wasn't sure when he'd dozed off, only that he felt embarrassed at having done so on the actual mission and was glad for the fact he was out of comm range. He checked his Rolex Submariner and sucked in his breath upon seeing that almost six hours had elapsed. Then he eyeballed the depth readout, astonished to see that the MagmaSphere was now thirty-eight miles below the surface of the Earth, truly in uncharted territory, what Project Magma's Public Relations team had referred to as, *The real last frontier. It's a shame I'm trapped in here like a hamster in a ball.* He wished he could see outside.

Down, down he went until he heard—and felt—something most unusual in the context of this sojourn. Contact. The MagmaSphere had hit rock bottom, solid rock, not the molten variety. He could tell by his instrument readings that the cable was still paying out, meaning he had hit an actual stony slope, but when slack was present in the cable, the sphere would roll downhill until once again suspended in a sea of magma. At that point, the cable would be paid out and the capsule would drop straight down. This process was repeated several times over the course of the next few hours, until one time, the MagmaSphere came to rest for good.

Kane tensed as he waited in his command seat (that was a laugh, though, wasn't it, he thought—he had no command of this metal ball, without the crane he was helpless) for the jostling to cease. It did for a couple of minutes, just long enough to where he was about to click out of his seat harness, when the titanium sphere began moving again. But this time the motion was different—faster, more chaotic—like nothing he'd ever experienced before in the MagmaSphere. And yet somehow it felt familiar.

With a cold shock to his gut, he realized where he'd "experienced" this before: in the simulation training. They'd built a mockup of the MagmaSphere with software that provided a realistic "physics engine," and the only one of the scenarios that caused the entire capsule to shake, rattle and roll like this was the dreaded Cable Snap Scenario.

Oh God, no, not that… Cable Snap was a death sentence. Plain and simple. There was no other craft on the planet capable of plummeting through miles of lava and molten rock to reach the capsule. He would die down here, beneath a mantle of fire, when his oxygen supply was exhausted.

Where was *here*, anyway? Kane checked his gauges and instruments. Video still down, of course, he wasn't expecting that. How about the radio? He spoke into the transmitter, but knew it was hopeless. The signal couldn't penetrate. The gyroscope showed that the craft was tilted at an angle relative to the cabin floor.

He was about to admit that the instrumentation didn't really have much to tell him when he cast a sidelong glance at an LED readout to his right: external temperature.

Something must be wrong, he thought, staring at it. It only displayed two digits: 95. *Maybe that's the inside temp of the pod,* he thought, but then dismissed the idea; *it's not 95 degrees in here.* To confirm this, he glanced at the internal temperature readout: 79 degrees F, and that felt about right.

So, what was up with the external temp? It should be around 1,800 F out there. He pressed buttons to confirm the units—maybe it wasn't set to Fahrenheit, but when he did that he found that it was. His external thermo-sensor was telling him that outside his sphere it was 95 degrees F. He let that sink in while he unclipped his seat harness.

Must be a sensor malfunction. He rose from the pilot's chair. He still thought of himself as a pilot. He moved to an area of the hull that was free of instrumentation and put his palm against it. He'd done this earlier and then he could feel a slight warmth through the thick titanium. Now, however, it was cool to the touch.

He couldn't explain it, so with not much else to do, he laid back down in the pilot's seat to think about his situation, and the next thing he knew, he dozed off again. When he awoke, he was terribly thirsty, groggy, and his head hurt. Carbon dioxide headache was the first coherent thought that circulated through his brain.

He had to get out of the pod, but he wasn't so far gone yet to think of that as a real option. He went over the oxygen and carbon dioxide systems, to make sure it wasn't something he could fix. Then he tried the radio again, to see if maybe they could give him some diagnostic help, but no signal there. Finally, he checked his temp gauge again, but it still showed 95 F outside the capsule.

Afraid he would pass out for lack of oxygen, the giddy Kane Eisenberg made a fateful decision. He would open the hatch. What did he have to lose? He was going to die if he didn't open it, that was certain. If he opened it, he would die too, but at least he'd see…something…besides the inside of this godforsaken metal ball before he punched his ticket to the next world.

Kane wobbled unsteadily to his feet and looked up at the hatch, the only portal to the world—whatever world that currently was—outside the sphere. He reached up and twisted the wheel counter-clockwise until he felt something give and it began to turn.

Outside the hatch he saw dry rock. Everything was cast in an orangish glow, but he couldn't see any magma, lava, or molten rock of any kind. Wherever his sphere had come to rest, there was air—or at least an atmosphere of some kind. Warm, hot even, at 95 F, but certainly preferable to molten rock. He recalled that he had a gas mask aboard, in the case of a malfunction with the carbon dioxide scrubbers, to buy time to fix it. There was no guarantee the atmosphere here was not poisonous sulfur clouds, so he donned the mask and poked his head out of the hatch…

…into another realm.

Part II: Hidden World

Kane Eisenberg, face obscured by a gas mask, slowly climbed out of the MagmaSphere's hatch until the upper half of his body protruded from the sphere. It had landed such that he was tilted at a forty-five-degree angle, so he could only see off to his right. But that was enough to take his breath away.

His ship had come to rest at the bottom of a rocky incline lined on both sides by streams of flowing magma that bubbled and sputtered with little popping sounds all around. Mists or vapors drifted through the air, if it was air. He was afraid to take off the mask to find out. All he knew was that he was about forty miles below the Earth's surface, in the upper mantle.

He turned around and looked at the cable attachment for the MagmaSphere, shaking his head. The cable was gone, the bolts which had held the shackle keeping it in place sheared off. The entire surface of the sphere was burnt black and smudged from its ordeal of plummeting through fire. He looked around to see if he could find the cable; maybe he could reattach it. But it was nowhere in sight.

He was stuck here. He pushed back the feelings of hopelessness at being stranded, of impending death, and dropped back into the cabin. He'd signed up for this. He had wanted to explore, and now he was in an incredible place to do just that.

He scrounged up the supplies he had with him—a flashlight, a thermos of water, a digital camera, and put them in a small pack. Then he climbed out of the hatch again and this time descended the boarding ladder until he could jump to the ground. But he hesitated. It looked like rock, but what if it was only burnt magma and he sank right through into a pool of lava? He took off his pack and tossed it to the ground first, breathing a sigh of relief when it plopped onto solid ground. Safe enough. He jumped and landed on the rocks next to his pack.

That's one small step for man, Kane thought, surveying his new surroundings. He and his ship had come to rest on a tongue of rock situated between two swift-flowing lava streams. The flows disappeared into small holes in the rock wall, which itself rose to form a high cavern ceiling with glittering stalactites.

It occurred to Kane that it should be completely dark in here without either natural light or a flashlight on, but the orange glow from the twin lava flows was enough to see by, so he decided it best to conserve his flashlight batteries for now. First he snapped a photograph of the MagmaSphere's final resting place, and then he picked his way carefully down the rocky strip, taking extreme care with his footing. He did not need to trip and stumble into a lava river. Near the bottom of the slope the ground levelled out and curved to the left. He followed it and held his breath as he walked into the new space.

He was greeted by a majestic cavern, its floor pockmarked with lava pools, its ceiling supporting stalactites that had to be at least fifty feet long. The area was vast, acres, he didn't know how large, but he could not see the other side. He took out his camera again and snapped more pictures. Maybe someday someone would see them. In the back of his mind a faint hope tried to sprout—that he could somehow find a passage back to the surface without the ship, that he could climb his way out. But he crushed that sprout, dismissing it as unhealthy wishful thinking. Miles of liquid magma churned between him and the surface. Somehow he'd dropped into a dry pocket, but that didn't mean it led all the way up. The ceiling looked solid, with no fissures or cracks leading anywhere.

He walked on, threading his way through the lava pools until a new sound arrested his attention. Running water? After looking around, he saw a stream of some kind a little further on. He moved to it and his eyes narrowed as he examined what looked like regular, clear running water. A stream. *Amazing!*

Despite his perilous situation, Kane's curiosity was piqued by what appeared to be fresh water and so he bent down at the edge of the stream to take a close look. It was deep, too, he could see. Although narrow, he could not see the bottom of it. He moved over to a more placid area between three boulders, where the water didn't flow so swiftly, so that he could see more clearly into it. He saw something fuzzy on one of the rocks but was unable to say for certain what it was because his gas mask was fogged over from his own breath.

What the heck, he thought, and tipped the mask up on his forehead. He sat there a moment without taking a breath, waiting to see if his eyes would sting in this atmosphere, but they didn't. He took a shallow breath, as if tasting the air in case it was bad. But it felt normal. He stood there, sipping the strange air while waiting to see if he would keel over into this bottomless stream because of some odorless, tasteless poison gas, but a minute passed, then two, and he felt invigorated from breathing air that didn't come from a recycling system or was filtered through a mask.

Kane put the mask in his pack in case he needed it later and then turned his attention back to the stream. He bent down to get an even better look and spotted a patch of coloration on a rock. Sort of a bluish color. Moss? Lichens? Mold? He didn't know, he wasn't a biologist, but any kind of life at all down here would be groundbreaking. *What the heck is that?* As he leaned over even farther, his face only inches from the colored mass, he saw a small object moving fast, darting in and out among the strange patch. It took him a moment to realize that it was a small fish about the size of his pinky finger, white in color, with red eyes.

Life! His inner voice screamed in triumph. Higher life forms living within the mantle of the Earth! He was startled out of his revelation by a sizable splash. He jerked his head up and to the left, where a big fish, about the size of the largemouth bass he remembered catching in his stocked pond in Kentucky, gulped down the little fish he'd been observing.

Kane pushed himself to his feet and turned around. He heard an even larger rush of water behind him. He turned in time to see a monstrous head—he only had time to process lots of dull green and yellowish spikes in the mouth before rolling away from the edge of the stream.

What the—

Kane saw another splash, larger than the last, toward the middle of the stream. He regained his feet. He saw a tail of some kind slap the water once, and then the beast was gone with a ripple of water.

What was that, a crocodile?

Whatever it was, it meant that there were large animals down here, predators. Kane glanced around at his surroundings. The lava pools interspersed by the flowing stream seemed endless, like a brown field pockmarked with orange as far as the horizon. Too late, he raised his camera to get a photo of the creature. But only the barest trace of a ripple still marred the water's surface.

Kane turned around, looking for the passage that led back up to the MagmaSphere. Where was it? Everything looked the same. For some reason he didn't want to become separated from his ship, his only connection to the humanity that had no rightful place down here. There it was, right over there. *Got it now.*

Feeling better at knowing where his ship was, Kane walked deeper into the plain of streams and lava pools. Now that he knew to look and listen for them, he detected more stream creatures. This place was full of life. A shadow tracked across one of the lava pools. He whipped his head up in time to see a dark, winged shape passing between columns of hanging stalactites. The beast angled in lower as it approached Kane. Instinctively, he took cover behind a clump of jagged lava rock that was twisted into a thick spire.

The animal swooped lower until Kane could hear its wings flapping. Not the soft flutter of birds' wings, but a rough, raspy leather-like sound that implied an animal with strength and size.

A pterodactyl.

The winged reptile landed one lava pool away from Kane and stamped around the ground on two feet. It reared its elongated head back and forth multiple times while making high-pitched clicking sounds, like a dolphin. Kane fumbled with his camera until he could raise it to his eye, aimed it at the creature's head, and clicked the shutter button. The flash tripped, capturing the reptile in blinding white light. It screeched in response and took to the air again, flying away from Kane, who slumped against the rocks, sighing in relief. There wouldn't have been much he could do if that pterodactyl had decided to attack him. He decided he better get closer to the MagmaSphere, which would offer shelter.

As he picked his way across the field of lava rock and magma pools, he became more attuned to the sounds of this subterranean hell. For that's what this is, he thought, *I'm in hell. Fire, brimstone, bubbling hot lava, monsters, cut off from the outside world...Maybe I'm hallucinating the whole thing and I'm really passed out in the capsule?*

But as he began to walk, and another pterodactyl winged its way into his peripheral vision, he knew that he was not imagining things, that this was real, and that his own actions had brought him to this place. He began to move at a trot, as fast as he dared, while the flying predator passed overhead and circled back around. He tripped over an uneven lava rock formation and went sprawling to the ground, palms flaying open on the jagged rock.

Before he could even push himself back to his feet, he felt a tremendous impact on the back of his neck. His nose was smashed into the ground and broken, a geyser of blood staining the lava rock. If not for the fact that his backpack had been pushed up around his neck, the impact of the pterodactyl's beak slamming into him probably would have broken his spine.

He felt himself lifting away from the ground, staring at the pool of blood from his face growing smaller beneath him, like he was floating out of his body after death. But he was still very much alive, at least for now. The airborne lizard shrieked, its call deafeningly loud and frightening; Kane could feel it vibrating in his skull.

He was now in the air, being carried in the mouth of a pterodactyl. Surely it can't fly for long like this, the billionaire thought, and then he understood that it didn't have to fly very long like this. It was a hunting strategy he'd seen used by birds at the beach in northern California, where they pick up a clam in their mouth, fly up high and drop it onto the rocks until the shell breaks. Then they fly back down and eat their treat.

Only now, *he* was the clam.

Unable to move his head while it was clenched tightly in the pterodactyl's jaws, Kane could only look straight down, watching a moving pastiche of bright orange lava pools and brown rock. When the creature dragged him over the freshwater stream, it whirled back around and reared up. For a second, Kane thought he would be dropped straight into a pool of lava, but the reptile did not release him, as he had predicted, until he was over rock. He felt the jaws of the predator relax around his neck and Kane plummeted to the ground.

He hit the jagged lava rock hard, his knees buckling fast so that his face slammed right into a hillock of razor sharp rock. Dazed and barely able to see through the blood pouring down his forehead into his eyes, Kane had to move fast unless he wanted to become a meal for this horrid creature. He clenched his teeth through the pain as he staggered to his feet, and then felt something slam into his back, hard. He no doubt suffered whiplash as his head was jerked forward and then back, and before he knew it, he was airborne once again in the beast's beak.

This time, the pterodactyl didn't try to gain altitude, but instead stayed low to the ground, threading its way through the towering spires of rock and lower-hanging stalactites. He passed horrifyingly close to solid rock towers, the surface of which were not smooth but jagged with razor edges, moving at high speed. He swung his legs to one side to avoid shattering a kneecap, only to have his face graze against a lava rock wall, peeling the skin off on one side like the rind from an orange. Somehow during this chaotic misery, Kane noticed movement below. He watched a crocodilian of some type—thirty feet long if it was an inch--slither into the stream.

What kind of hell is this? But he had no time for such ruminations as the predator body-slammed him into a boulder, releasing him while it cleared the obstacle. While Kane crumpled to the ground, struggling to stay conscious, the pterodactyl made a lazy circle around the cavern on the way back to its prey. Its flight became less lazy when it sensed competition for its meal.

The crocodile Kane had spotted lurched up out of the stream and waddled toward the entrepreneur. *It's coming for me!* He had no idea what to do, or whether he could outrun this giant. He could climb the boulders, but up there he'd be a sitting duck for the pterodactyls.

He stayed close to the boulder and began to move around it as the crocodile drew nearer. He had no illusions that the beast wasn't capable of a quick burst of speed that would end it all for him. He got a glimpse of the open mouth, imagining the festering bacteria that must lurk between the inches-long, curving teeth. It disgusted him to no end to have his fate lie in the gullet of this monstrosity, so he began to climb the boulder.

As the crocodile made a leap toward its prey, the pterodactyl dive-bombed the massive croc, jamming its beak between the lizard's eyes. The croc rolled over and lashed out with its jaws, seeking purchase against its foe.

Kane knew that while these two mega-beasts were fighting it out, he had to make an escape unless he wanted to be the spoils for the victor. He ran in the nearest direction that didn't have a lava pool blocking it. He looked back once, wiping the blood from his eyes, to see the two prehistoric creatures still grappling with each other.

Where was the MagmaSphere?

He took precious seconds to get his bearings. *That way...right?* This cavern was so vast and it all looked the same. He heard a booming *thump* and looked back to see the crocodile's head bashing the pterodactyl's leathery body on the rocks. Knowing that the croc was the one that would be eating him if he stuck around, Kane sprinted toward where he thought the MagmaSphere was. He leapt over small rocks and crevices through which bubbling magma pumped, until he reached one of the wider parts of the freshwater stream.

The water flowed fast here, and he followed its course with his gaze. It moved in the direction in which he needed to go. He would travel faster if he jumped in and swam with it than he would on foot up here. The sound of scaly foot pads padding across the cavern floor decided it for him. He didn't know what else was in the water, but he knew what was on land.

Kane executed a shallow dive out into the middle of the stream and swam fast, a messy crawl stroke. Coughing and sputtering, he looked up to see the rocky shore of the stream rushing past him. He kept swimming, too scared to look back at his reptilian pursuer.

Part III: Fossilized

About the same time as Kane could see the passage that led to the MagmaSphere, the stream began to veer away in the opposite direction. He swam to the right-side bank and planted his feet in a shallow crevice. As he prepared to haul himself out, he felt something with teeth bite into his calf. He kicked at it with the foot of the other leg, but whatever it was, it was latched on. He climbed out, and in the process, felt whatever beast it was scrape off against the rocks as he swung his leg over. He could still stand on it, and that was all he cared about as he started to run while the mega-croc rampaged toward him like a wobbling freight train of death.

The explorer jumped across a small lava pit and sidestepped around a boulder on his way to the last stretch of open ground between this hellish cavern and the MagmaSphere passage. He could still hear that dastardly slithering, though farther away now. Still, it was coming for him, relentless in its pursuit of what had to be a rare meal. *It doesn't even know if I taste good,* Kane thought, staggering on toward his capsule. *It's never eaten a person before, probably no warm-blooded creatures at all.*

But that didn't seem to matter as the beast lumbered on toward its prey. As Kane entered the upward sloping passage with his ship resting at the top, the ground seemed to be moving. *Now what? Bad, bad, bad idea to walk around out here...* He willed himself to run faster up the hill, even as he realized the cavern floor was alive with a herd of tiny lizards, each one no larger than a sparrow. But there were thousands, maybe millions of them. As he parted their masses, they pecked and scratched at his ankles, clinging onto his pants with their clawed feet while piledriving their triangular beaks into his flesh.

By the time Kane reached the MagmaSphere it was all he could do to keep moving. He felt the bird-beasts hopping on his shoulders now. This place would consume him, he knew, devour his entire body leaving nothing, not even bones. He was not meant to be here, no human was ever meant to be here, and this was the fate that awaited those who dared. He thought back to the dinosaur books he'd devoured as a kid, that had fired his imagination with their illustrations and short, punchy descriptions of what the "terrible lizards" ate and how they lived. He wished he had never seen those books now, as he scrambled up to his fateful capsule, a ball of technology into which he had poured hundreds of millions of dollars along with his own fate.

The birdies started to overtake him as he paused to climb the boarding ladder, tipped over at an angle. But he kept scaling the ladder. Near the top of the sphere, just before reaching the hatch, he glanced down the slope to see the mega-croc—now it looked like it might even be fifty feet long—charging toward his capsule, mouth open to hoover up the bird-beasts along the way.

Kane had seen enough of this inner-Earth freak show. He jammed first one leg, then the other down the open hatch, thinking how it was probably a mistake to leave it open. Sure enough, a few of the birdy-beasts were already inside, with many more now tumbling in along with him. He climbed part way down the ladder until he could pull the hatch closed over his head. He expected to hear a loud metal clang but instead was met with a soft, giving thud. He looked up at the hatch and saw the head of a serpent-like animal peering down at him, the skinny, forked tongue still darting in and out of the mouth while its eyes bulged out of the crushed skull.

Kane climbed back up a rung, lifted the hatch enough to gain some clearance, then yanked it down on the creature's head again, this time decapitating it. The severed head dropped into the cabin with a wet *plop* while Kane screwed the hatch closed.

What else is in here with me? He looked about the confines of the cabin, eyeballing it for predators, but all he could see were perhaps a dozen of the sparrow-like bird-lizards. He stamped them out with his feet like a drunk carnival worker at a jamboree on his night off, screaming *Yeehaw, take that ya sonofabitch* as he killed them. No sooner had he neutralized that threat than he heard a loud thump on the side of the ship, followed by a prolonged scraping sound.

The gator or croc or whatever it is…it's here…

After checking around once more to make certain he was the only living creature in there large enough to see with the naked eye, Kane took the only place to sit available, the pilot's chair. Like a captain going down with his ship, the explorer monitored his instruments. He had maybe a half-hour more of air supply remaining, if he was lucky. He felt the entire MagmaSphere wobble and shift as it was nudged by the primitive crocodilian.

Kane buckled his seat harness into place just as the sphere broke free from the rocky depression which had cradled it in place. The craft began to roll down the inclined passage, back to the magma cavern below.

Kane wished he could see outside as he rolled to his ultimate destiny. He knew this was the end for him; already, the air was harder to pull. He was breathing, but it wasn't doing anything, since most of the oxygen had already been sucked out of it. He wasn't worried about his craft being dislodged from its resting place. The thing was indestructible. If anything, this journey had proven that. The retrieval system, on the other hand, left much to be desired. *I'll have to make sure that's on the agenda for the post-mission briefing*, he joked to himself.

But the fact was, he was about to die in this titanium contraption, regardless of where it ended up. And after seeing what awaited him out there, he was fine with suffocating in here. A minute or so of *ohmygod I can't breathe*, and it would all be over. Compare that to outside, where he would be consumed alive piece by piece while being dragged around razor sharp rocks.

He settled back in the chair as the sphere picked up speed and rolled downhill, faster than the croc-o-saur could keep up with. But the animal had time, it was in no hurry, for it knew the sphere would still be there a few minutes, a few hours, a few days, later. Like the planet itself that it was now a part of, the ship would be here a few decades, a few centuries, a few millennia later, with Kane trapped inside of it. He, Kane Eisenberg

II, would essentially be fossilized down here in the Earth's molten innards, crushed for eons under bedrock and magma, inside the very mantle of the planet, until one day he would be belched up by some cataclysmic geological process, and humans would find him again.

Kane smiled as he thought about how he was about to become a fossil, to be slowly yet inevitably transformed into one of the things that had led him down here in the first place. What had once been a mere curiosity to him, a *Gee wow, isn't that cool?* type of thing, had now *become* his existence.

The MagmaSphere rolled out across the level lava rock ground until it hit an outcropping and ricocheted to the right, like a titanium ball in a *Journey to the Center of the Earth* pinball machine. Suddenly the motion of the vehicle changed dramatically, from a steady rolling over bumpy ground punctuated by hard hits, to a slower bobbing motion that saw him tipping this way and that in his seat.

A smile overtook his features as he understood what had happened. He checked the external temperature gauge to confirm it: *yep, outside temp is only 75 F instead of 95 F.* The reason for the sudden temperature drop was simple.

His ship had rolled into the stream, and now floated along with it, curving away from the inclined passage where Kane had gotten out after his swim. There was the occasional *thunk* as the sphere bounced off a rocky overhang on one of the banks, but mostly the ride was smooth.

And then the MagmaSphere passed through the opening in the wall, drifting on into the dark unknown. Kane tried to draw his next breath but found he couldn't, that the one before that had been his last. He held his breath, staving off the inevitable as he took out the camera and aimed its lens at himself. He would document his own end, the pilot of the MagmaSphere operating inside the cabin to the last second.

The flash went off, blinding him at the same time as the sphere flowed over a high waterfall, freefalling for hundreds of feet. When it impacted a pool of lava below, the last remaining breath Kane had been holding was knocked from his lungs, escaping his mouth with a pitiful *pfft....*

That was it, that was all you had...

As Kane Eisenberg's mind shut down, the MagmaSphere drifted away on a current of lava, the ship a protective mantle around his body, entombing it for eternity,—*fossilizing* it like one of the prehistoric animals known for leaving behind their remains.

The End

CLOSURE

By Tim Waggoner

Jason runs through green hell – thick fronds slapping his body, cutting him with edges sharp as razors – air so heavy and hot he can barely breathe. Sweat pours off of him like salty rain, streaming into the cuts on his skin, mingling with blood, making the thin wounds blaze like fire. Insects – longer and nastier-looking than the ones back home – swarm around him, biting and stinging. It seems everything in this nightmarish jungle wants to kill him – plants, bugs, animals . . . *especially* the animals.

Between the buzz-thrum of the insect and the thrashing of fronds as he shoves past them, he can't hear if anything is pursuing him, but he's sure there is. In this world, you're either predator or prey, and he's neither strong enough or swift enough to be the former. His sweat-sodden shirt is stuck to his body like a second skin, and his equally sweaty jeans are heavy with moisture, so much so it's like running with his legs encased in iron armor, but without anything of the protection that metal could offer.

Where is it? Where's the door?

He hears his father's voice in his mind.

Once you go through, there's no coming back. It's a one-way trip, my son. And believe me, it's a trip you don't want to make.

Jason bursts through foliage and into a small clearing. He stumbles and nearly falls, but he knows to do so would likely mean his death, so he fights to remain on his feet and succeeds, but just barely. He keeps running, and he's halfway across the clearing when a large shape emerges from the thick wall of plants behind him, slipping between them with silent grace, as if they are water and the creature a sleek fish. He senses the thing's presence, and although he doesn't want to, knows that by doing so he'll probably be signing his own death warrant, he slows and looks back over his shoulder.

The animal is larger than him, almost as large as a car and it walks on its two hind legs, hunched over, head jutting forward. It's covered with spiky greenish-brown quills that resemble feathers. Its mouth is filled with dagger-like teeth, and its hands and feet terminate in wicked curved claws. Its eyes are orange with large black pupils, and when they fixate on Jason, the creature lets out a low chuffing sound. Prey is near and it's excited. It races toward him, speed increasing with each step, and Jason – knowing that there's no possible way he can outrun the thing, faces forward and tries anyway.

* * *

Southwest Ohio is normally unbearable in August, but this year is especially bad. An all-time record for heat and humidity, at least according to the meteorologist he'd heard on the radio during the drive here. The cabin – Dad's cabin as he's always thought of it, although it originally belonged to Grandma and Grandpa – looks the same as the last time he was here, almost a decade ago, as if the years have had no effect on it whatsoever. They've had plenty of effect on him, though. Yes, they have.

He drives his Prius up the gravel driveway and parks behind his father's pickup. He turns off the engine and removes the key from the ignition, but he doesn't get out right away. He sits there for several moments, thinking. Remembering. Dad started bringing him to the cabin – which had been in the family for several generations – since before he could walk. Mom came in those days, too, back when she was still around. Jason spent a lot of happy hours here, exploring the woods, walking on the shore of the lake, feeling the sun on his skin and the wind in his hair. He was alone a lot of the time – no siblings, no friends – but he never minded. Being alone wasn't the same as being lonely, and he liked solitude, found it peaceful and comforting, at least up until the time he was fourteen. After that, not so much.

He gets out of the car and heads for the cabin. His dad doesn't know he's coming. He didn't bother calling. He knows his dad would've made up some bullshit reason why he shouldn't visit, and Jason is determined not to be put off this time.

His father was older than his mother by close to twenty years, and he was near retirement age by the time Jason graduated high school. He left the engineering firm where he'd worked since before Jason was born, sold the house, and moved into the cabin full time. Jason was an only child, and his father is the only family he has left. He has an aunt in Arizona and a few cousins scattered around the country, but he really doesn't know any of them well. But then, he can say the same thing about his father, can't he?

If his dad is inside the cabin, then he heard Jason pull up and park. But if he's out fishing or hiking, it could be hours before he's home.

Days, if he decided to camp somewhere. But as Jason approaches the cabin, the front door swings open, old hinges protesting, and Arthur Montrose's thick, sturdy form fills the doorway. The man's in his sixties but looks ten years younger. His hair is a bright white, but there are no obvious lines on his face, no liver spots on his hands. Brown eyes that seem to blink half as often as they should, jaw so square it doesn't look quite real. He doesn't smile when he looks at Jason, and there's a wariness in his manner, as if he's not sure what his son might do.

"Hey, Dad."

Arthur stands silent for a moment, as if he's having trouble forming an appropriate response. He finally settles on, "This is a surprise."

Even though he quit smoking almost a decade ago, his voice is still raspy.

Not a *nice* surprise, Jason notes.

"I hope this isn't a bad time."

As far as his dad's concerned, there's probably no good time for him to visit, but he says, "It's fine."

He doesn't invite Jason in, though, doesn't step aside so his son can enter what is, for all intents and purposes, his second childhood home.

"I thought we could talk."

Dad's eyes narrow, but otherwise his face remains expressionless.

"Sure."

Dad hesitates several seconds before finally moving back to make room for Jason to enter. It's Jason's turn to hesitate then, but eventually he steps inside.

* * *

Jason first learned about the cave – and what lay beyond it – when he was seven. It was early July, and his parents came to the cabin to watch the Fourth of July fireworks. The woods were located roughly equidistant from three different towns, and people would take boats out onto the lake and watch three separate lightshows occurring more or less simultaneously. Mom and Dad brought him last year, and he'd loved it. The best part for him was seeing the fireworks' reflection on the water's surface. It had felt like he was gazing into another world. But the fireworks weren't until tonight, and Jason – wound up with excitement – was running off his energy in the woods with Trixie, the family's German shepherd. She was only two years old, basically still a big puppy, and her manic energy matched his. He'd told Mom and Dad that he was taking Trixie to the lake. She loved going into the water, and Jason would throw a tennis ball as far out as he could, and she would jump into the lake and swim to fetch it. But he'd lied. What he'd really wanted to do was explore. Doing so was forbidden by his father, though.

These are big woods. We don't want you getting lost now, do we?

Dad had showed him a handful of trails – including one that led to the lake – which he was permitted to us, but the rest were off limits.

You don't know what you might find if you take one of those other trails. Bear, wolves, cougar . . .

Jason would be an adult before he learned that none of those animals lived in Southwest Ohio. But rather than be scared off by Dad's warning, he was excited by it. He'd love to see animals like that, and he had Trixie. She'd protect him. Normally, Jason would never lie to his father. If he got caught, Dad would punish him – bad. But he just had to *see*, and there was no way Dad would ever find out, right?

So he picked one of the forbidden trails at random, and together he and Trixie set out. It didn't take long for the thrill of disobeying his father to wear off. There was nothing special about the trail. It was the same as all the others: trees, bushes, weeds, rocks . . . And the only animals they saw were birds and squirrels. Trixie would chase the latter, barking frantically, but the squirrels always managed to scurry up trees before she could come close to catching any of them. Jason was completely at a loss as to why Dad thought this trail was so dangerous, and he was about ready to put it down to adult weirdness and turn back when Trixie stopped and lifted her head, ears raised. She sniffed the air, head cocked slightly to the side as if whatever scents she'd caught confused her. Then she left the trail and plunged into the underbrush, not barking this time, but moving swiftly and with purpose.

Jason called her name and ran after her, but the brush was thick, and he had trouble moving with any speed. But before long the brush thinned out, and Jason found himself looking at a stream, beyond which lay a rocky slope with an opening in it. A cave.

Trixie stood before the cave's entrance in a half crouch, teeth bared, growling. The entrance was roughly triangular in shape, and it was taller than the cabin, if not as wide. Jason didn't pay Trixie much attention at first. He was too enthralled by the sight of the cave. This was the single greatest thing he'd ever seen in his short life, and he was even more confused about why Dad didn't want him to come here. Why would he keep something this awesome a secret? It didn't make sense.

Except it did, and it was Trixie who made him realize this. The way she stood before the cave – growling, feet planted firmly, hackles raised – said that there was something inside the cave. Something that Trixie didn't like. He remembered his father's warning then. Bear, wolves, cougar . . .

"Trixie! Come back!"

He meant for this to come out in a strong, commanding tone, but instead it was little more than a frightened whisper. Trixie didn't turn to look at him, gave no sign she'd heard him. She continued growling at the darkness inside the cave. And then, without warning, Trixie took off like a shot and ran inside. Jason was horrified, and an image leaped into his mind of Trixie being torn apart by a huge bear. He was seven; there was absolutely nothing he could do to help Trixie if there was a bear inside the cave, but he didn't think, just reacted. He ran toward the cave, splashed through the creek, and threw himself into the dark.

Enough light filtered in from the entrance for him to see a little, but he still put his hands out in front of him to keep himself from running face-first into a wall of rock. He called Trixie's name again and again, but she didn't come to him. He continued running. The light diminished the farther he went, and then it was gone, and he found himself in total blackness. But that only lasted for a couple seconds, and then it began to grow light again. But this light was of a different quality. It seemed brighter and somehow thicker, and the air was hot, much more so than it had been outside. Weren't caves supposed to be cool inside? There were strange smells, too: the fresh green of plants combined with a musk that made Jason think of a reptile house at the zoo. Some primitive part of his mind that was only concerned with survival shrieked a warning. Something was wrong here, *very* wrong, and he should turn around and haul ass out of here right now. Trixie was a big, strong dog, and she was capable of taking care of herself.

He didn't listen to this voice, though. He loved Trixie. In many ways she was his best friend, and he could not abandon her. So he kept running. The cave curved to the right ahead, but there was more than enough light for him to see, and he negotiated the way without difficulty.

And then he stopped.

Trixie stood in front of what looked like another opening in the cave, this one rounder and larger than the one behind Jason. But the world outside was not the one he'd left behind. It looked like some kind of jungle, and things moved between thick-fronded plants. Things that looked like

– dinosaurs –

Except they weren't like the kind of dinosaurs that he'd seen in books or movies. These creatures were covered with feathery hair or hairy feathers, and they moved like giant chickens. This should've made them seem ridiculous, but it made them far more alien and horrifying than they might've been. Jason didn't question the reality of the world outside the cave – the *Otherside*, he thought. All of his senses, including perhaps ones he didn't know he possessed, told him it was real. It was obvious Trixie thought so, too, for she stood at the opening to this end of the cave, growling as if she was ready to tear the throat out of anything dumb enough to come near her.

Jason wanted to move forward, take hold of Trixie's collar, and pull her away from the *Otherside*, but he was too awestruck by what he was seeing and he remained a dozen feet back. He watched, unable to move, unable to even breathe, as something from the *Otherside* – a bipedal creature with striking orange eyes – walked past the cave opening with a jerky chicken-like gait, turned its head, and looked at Trixie. Its head cocked to the side, reminding Jason of the way Trixie did the same thing earlier. The bird-thing – Jason wouldn't realize it was a velociraptor for many years because it didn't look like the ones in *Jurassic Park* – jumped into the cave and began ripping into Trixie with its hind legs. The creature had prominent curved claws for slicing that protruded from the middle toes on its feet, and it employed these claws with surgical precision to catch hold of Trixie's side, flip her over, and open up her belly. Trixie howled in agony as her guts spilled out, and the creature stabbed its head downward, opened its tooth-filled mouth, and began to eat, greedily snapping up Trixie's innards as if they were delicacies.

In his mind, Jason screamed *No!* but in reality he stood silent as the feather-haired monster devoured his dog. The creature was a fast and efficient eater, and within moments all that remained of Trixie was blood and a few tufts of fur. The thing had even eaten her bones. As the beast licked blood from its mouth, Jason came to understand what this place was. It was a passageway, not through rock – at least not just through rock – but through *time*. One end was attached to the present, the other to the far distant past. And it was possible to travel from one to the other simply by walking. He had no idea how such a thing could exist. Was it a natural phenomenon? The result of some sort of science experiment? Some kind of magic? He supposed it really didn't matter. The creature was here, and it had killed his dog. *That's* what mattered.

He hadn't realized he was holding his breath until he opened his mouth and drew in a long gasp of air. The creature – no, the *dinosaur* – looked up from its grisly repast and fixed its orange eyes on Jason. Those eyes – gleaming with emotionless hunger – broke Jason's paralysis. He turned and fled, running for all he was worth. The birdlike monster let out a low rumbling sound, and Jason heard its claws scrabbling on the cave floor as it came after him. He had a couple things going for him. One, the cave – while large enough for the dinosaur to move through, wasn't large enough for it to do so comfortably. It sometimes had to squeeze through places where the cave narrowed, slowing it down and giving Jason time to lengthen his lead. Jason passed through the dark area so fast it was little more than a flicker in his vision, and then he was in *his* half of the cave, back in his own time. Or maybe in a place where the two time periods overlapped, somewhere between here and there, now and then, a place where anything could happen.

Jason had nearly made it to the cave's entrance when the dinosaur caught up with him. It gave a rumble-roar, and Jason glanced back over his shoulder to see it hunker down as it ran, as if in preparation for a jump. He faced forward, put on a fresh burst of speed, and shot out of the cave, running faster than he ever had in his life. He collided with something big and solid, and he would've bounced off and fallen to the ground if a hand hadn't reached out and caught hold of his shoulder. He looked up at his father's stern visage, and for an instant, he forgot about the dinosaur. In his own way, Arthur Montrose was equally as terrifying, not least because he was holding a gun in his other hand. A *big* one.

Dad scowled. "When I didn't find you at the lake, I knew you –"

He broke off when he saw the dinosaur approaching the cave entrance. He stepped in front of Jason and raised his Magnum, but he didn't fire right away. The dinosaur slowed as it drew nearer the entrance, then it stopped and drew in on itself, almost curled into a large feathery ball. Its nostrils flared, and it shook its head back and forth, as if it sensed danger but had no idea what direction it lay in. Dad kept his weapon trained on the creature the entire time it was like this, but after several moments it turned and scuttled away, claws scratching on the rocky floor, the sound growing fainter, diminishing, then gone.

Dad lowered his gun and turned to Jason.

"They don't like it on our side. Too cold for them. Probably smells wrong, too. Come. We should get back before your mom starts to worry."

Dad started to walked away from the cave. He'd said nothing about Trixie.

After a moment, Jason followed.

* * *

Jason stood rigid as Mom hugged him.

"How *horrible!* You must have been so scared!"

She had gone to her knees in the kitchen to wrap her arms around him and pull him close. Dad stood at the sink, arms crossed, watching the two of them, expression unreadable.

Jason didn't respond to Mom's words. He couldn't tell her the truth. *Dad and I lied to you. Trixie wasn't killed by a wild dog she got into a fight with. We didn't bury her in the woods. She got eaten by a dinosaur with feathers.*

Dad knew about the cave, knew where – *when* – it led. He told Jason that he'd found it when he wasn't much older than Jason was now, when Grandpa and Grandma used to bring him and Uncle Jim here. The brothers were exploring the woods when they found the cave and went inside. Uncle Jim was killed by a dinosaur not much different than the one that killed Trixie, although Dad told Grandma and Grandpa that they were playing in the lake and Jim drowned. He lied because he was afraid that no one would believe what really happened.

Jason had lied to Mom because he was afraid of his father. Dad had made him promise not to tell anyone about the cave, including Mom – or else.

"Stop babying the boy, Sarah."

Dad's voice was soft, but his tone was low and dangerous. He had very specific ideas about how things should be done – how *everything* should be done – and he wasn't happy when they didn't go the way he wanted. And when he wasn't happy, he got mad, and when he got mad, he yelled. Sometimes that was all he'd do. But other times – too many – he did worse. Dad hadn't given him a good ass-beating for disobeying him because, he said, he figured seeing the dinosaur kill his dog, and almost getting killed himself, was punishment enough. But Jason wouldn't be allowed to see the fireworks tonight, which was okay. Jason didn't feel like celebrating.

Mom tensed at Dad's words, but she didn't let Jason go. Instead, she squeezed him tighter.

"He just lost his best friend, Arthur. That isn't something a person can just shrug off."

Her voice was calm when she said this, but she didn't look at Dad as she spoke.

Dad leaned back against the sink and gripped the counter's edge with both hands, so hard his knuckles whitened. He said nothing more, and Mom went right on comforting Jason. But later that night, when Jason was lying awake in his bedroom right next to his parents, he heard Dad tell Mom that when he told her to do something, such as stop babying his son, he damn well expected her to do it, and without any backtalk. And then Jason heard other sounds, sounds fists make on flesh, and he thought about how people could be scarier than dinosaurs.

* * *

Jason sits at the kitchen table opposite his father. Both of them have bottles of beer in front of them, beads of condensation collected on the glass. Dad's is half empty already, but Jason's only taken a sip of his, and a small one at that. There are only two air-conditioning units in the cabin – one in the front room and one in Dad's bedroom – and despite the fact that both are running full blast, the cool air hasn't managed to reach the kitchen, and the room is stifling. Dad doesn't seem to notice the temperature, but then he's always been an expert at hiding his thoughts and feelings – until what he feels is anger. Controlling that particular emotion has always been problematic for him.

"How's your job going?" Dad asks after another sip of beer.

Jason wonders if Dad remembers what kind of work he does. He works at a company that sells and installs water heaters. Not the most glamorous of jobs, but one with low stress. After the childhood he'd had, stress of any kind is the last thing he wants. And yet he's here.

"It's okay." Jason takes another small sip of his beer, more to stall than anything else.

"What's on your mind, son?"

Jason doesn't reply, and Dad goes on.

"I know how you feel about this place . . . about *me*. Whatever motivated you to come back has to be pretty important. No way you'd come for just a casual visit."

Jason would like to deny this, but he's never been any good at lying to his dad. When he was a kid, he'd learned what would happen if Dad caught him lying, and although he's in his late twenties now and hardly helpless, that kind of conditioning goes deep.

"I want to talk about Mom."

Dad's lips tighten. After a moment, he says, "What's there to talk about? She walked out on us when you were fourteen. She was almost twenty years younger than me, and I guess she wanted to be with someone her own age."

"Why didn't she say goodbye to me? Why didn't she want to share custody of me with you?" *Or take full custody of me to get me away from you?* "Why didn't she try to get in touch with me as the years went by?"

"I don't know. Sometimes when people make a break from their past, they want to make it clean. Leave it all behind them, no matter who it hurts."

Jason nods as if accepting Dad's words, but then he says, "There are other reasons people disappear and are never heard from again. None of them good."

Dad finishes the last of his beer and slams the bottle down on the table so hard that Jason's surprised the glass doesn't shatter in his father's hands.

"If you've got something to say, boy, just say it." His voice is like a tightly coiled spring.

Jason takes a good-sized swig of his beer now. He needs it.

"We were here right before Mom left. You don't know this, but when you were out – hunting or fishing, I can't remember which – she came to me and told me to pack a suitcase when we got back to the house. We were going to leave the first day you went back to work. Except she never made it back to the house, did she? For some reason she decided to take off early, and she left by foot. By herself. At least that's what you told me. I think I knew even then what really happened, but I couldn't bring myself to face the truth. I knew what kind of temper you had, but you were still my father. I didn't want to believe that you could hurt Mom – not like that. And as long as I kept denying what happened, I could imagine that Mom was out there somewhere, safe, living a new life, and maybe – just maybe – she'd come for me one day."

Neither speaks for a long time. Finally, Dad says, "Why are you coming to me about this now, after so many years?"

"Because I met someone. Her name's Aubrey, and we've been dating for a year or so. And during that time, I made an unpleasant discovery. I inherited your temper. Or I was infected by it. Maybe a combination of both. I didn't want to treat Aubrey the way you treated Mom, so I started seeing a therapist. I wanted to learn how to deal with my anger in ways that wouldn't cause pain to the people I love. And I did learn that. But something else came up during my therapy sessions. I was carrying a lot of resentment toward you, of course, but I was also carrying a lot of guilt and shame. I didn't have any idea why. Over the years, I'd managed to convince myself that what happened at the cave – what I saw there – was just a nightmare. I came to believe that Trixie really had been killed by another dog. *Made* myself believe it. Just like I made myself believe it when you told me Mom left us. But during the course of my therapy, I remembered everything. And once my memories were restored, I had to come see you. It's not the sort of thing you discuss over the phone."

"What are you implying? That I found out your mother was planning to leave, and I killed her and took her body to the cave to dispose of it?"

"No."

Dad's eyebrows raise in surprise.

"A sadistic fucker like you would've wanted Mom to be alive when you took her to the *Otherside*. Did you lie to her, trick her into going with you? Tell her there was something beautiful and amazing inside the cave that she just *had* to see? Or did you just hold a gun on her and force her to march to her death?"

Dad says nothing.

"I suppose it doesn't really matter how it happened, just that it did."

"What do you want from me? A confession? A tearful apology for the terrible thing I did?"

"Were you angry at Uncle Jim, too? Grandma told me how you two used to fight. When Jim and you discovered the cave and realized where the other end led to, did you shove him through so you could get rid of him?"

More silence, then, "Do you feel like a big man for figuring it all out? Do you feel like you finally scored a point against your old man? Well, you haven't accomplished dick. No bodies, no crimes. And if you try to tell the cops what happened, they'll think you're crazy. They won't even come out here to investigate. They'll probably slap cuffs on you then haul your ass to the nearest loony bin."

Jason can feel his own anger rising, and he fights to keep it under control.

"That's not how I'll do it. First I'll find people willing to check out the cave, and when they see it's real and father enough evidence to convince others, these woods will be crawling with scientists, reporters, and people who just want to get a look into the prehistoric past. Your peaceful retirement will be ruined, and *then* I'll start telling anyone who'll listen that you fed my mom to the dinosaurs because she'd grown tired to your abuse. Some will believe me. And who knows? Maybe there's some of Mom's blood still in the cave, enough for forensic scientists to collect and analyze. And even if there isn't any evidence and you don't go to jail, the world will know the truth about what kind of man you really are, and that's all I –"

Jason's father moves swiftly for a man in his sixties. He stands, grabs his empty beer bottle by the neck, and swings it at Jason's head. Glass shatters as the bottle connects with his temple, and then everything goes black.

* * *

Jason starts to come to as his father carries him slung over his shoulder into the cave. He's barely aware of what's happening, and he can't make his body move yet. He can't even open his eyes. The next thing he knows, the air is hotter than blast furnace, and Dad drops him onto the ground. The landing drives the breath from his lungs, but it jolts him further awake, and this time he manages to open his eyes. He sees his father push his way through a thick wall of green-fronded foliage, and then he's gone.

Jason pushes himself into a crouching position, head pounding. He reaches up to gingerly touch his head where Dad hit him, and his fingers come away tacky with blood. He continues to get to his feet and hopes to follow after his father, maybe sneak up from behind and take the sonofabitch down. But that was when he hears the rumbling sound, one he hasn't heard since he was seven, and his instincts tell him to get the hell out of there – *now.* He jumps to his feet and starts running.

* * *

Where is the fucking entrance?

If he didn't panic and start running blindly, he probably would've found the entrance right away, and he'd be safe on the other side, back in his time, where the velociraptor pursuing him – who might not be the same one that killed Trixie but was almost certainly the same species – couldn't get at him. But if he can't find the cave, it will only be a matter of time before he begins to tire, and the velociraptor will catch him and tear him to pieces.

But a moment later, he sees the cave entrance right in front of him, less than a dozen yards. He must've run in a circle or something. He doesn't care how it happened, only that it has. He runs for the opening, head pounding like it might explode any second, legs heavy and numb, heart racing, lungs burning, sweat flying from his skin. He reaches the cave and runs inside, but although he wants nothing more than to fall to his knees and gulp air, he knows the velociraptor is right behind and will follow him into the cave, at least partway. He needs to keep going, needs to make it all the way back to his world if he hopes to live.

He keeps running, not allowing himself to slow down, although he desperately wants to. He hears the dinosaur's foot claws scrabbling on the cave's rocky floor, hears the harsh bellows-like breathing of its lungs. He feels a prickling on the back of his neck, an atavistic warning that his pursuer is closing in, and he wonders what it will feel like when the monster catches up to him and starts cutting into his flesh with its curving foot talons.

Then suddenly he's through and out the other side – and there's his father, standing ten feet from the entrance, Magnum in hand. Dad raises the weapon, and for an instant Jason allows himself to believe his father had a change of heart, that he isn't able to let his only child die, that he'll shoot and kill the velociraptor when it reaches the entrance. But then he understands the truth. Arthur Montrose was keeping watch in case his son survived. If that happened, he'd put a few bullets in him and then carry his corpse back into the cave to dispose of it. He expects to hear the gun roar, to feel heavy blows strike his chest as bullets strike him. But Arthur doesn't fire. Instead his eyes go wide with shock, and Jason knows why when he hears the velociraptor approaching behind, still running at full speed and showing no signs of slowing down.

It's the hottest summer on record, he thinks. *Hot enough even for a dinosaur.*

He throws himself to the side as the velociraptor comes racing out of the cave, heading straight for his father. Arthur gets off a single shot before the dinosaur leaps into the air and falls upon him. The man's screaming is one of the sweetest sounds that Jason's ever heard.

While the velociraptor is occupied with eviscerating his father, Jason gets to his feet and begins walking away. He's exhausted and he's hurt, but he's deeply satisfied. He supposes the dinosaur will finish its meal and then return to its own time. Or maybe it will stick around, at least until autumn draws near and the temperature starts to fall. As for Jason, he figures he can stop going to therapy now.

He smiles as he continues walking, accompanied by the sounds of tearing flesh and splintering bone.

The End

PREHISTORIC AUTHORS

David Achord: After being honorably discharged as a Sergeant in the United States Army, David Achord found his true calling in law enforcement. His twenty-five year career included stints with the Rutherford County Sheriff's Department and the Metropolitan Nashville Police Department. A lifelong Tennessee native, he is a graduate of Middle Tennessee State University and Cumberland University.

Jeff Brackett is the author of "Half Past Midnight", "The Road to Rejas", and "Streets of Payne", as well as a variety of short stories and novellas published in magazines and anthologies. After having lived almost his entire life in and around Houston, 2014 presented several life changes that brought him, his wife, and two dogs (Bella and Cricket) to Claremore, Oklahoma. There, they found a nice little house with a much larger yard, and are all adjusting to the new lifestyle quite well. Jeff has even begun

Hunter Shea is the author of over 20 books, with a specialization in cryptozoological horror that includes The Jersey Devil, The Dover Demon, Loch Ness Revenge and many others. His novel The Montauk Monster, was named one of the best reads of the summer by Publishers Weekly. A trip to the International Cryptozoology Museum will find several of his cryptid books among the fascinating displays. Living in a true haunted house inspired his Jessica Backman: Death in the Afterlife series (Forest of Shadows, Sinister Entity and Island of the Forbidden). He was selected to be part of the launch of Samhain Publishing's new horror line in 2011 alongside legendary author Ramsey Campbell. When he's not writing thrillers and horror, he also spins tall tales for middle grade readers on Amazon's highly regarded Rapids reading app.

An avid podcaster, he can be seen and heard on Monster Men, one of the longest running video horror podcasts in the world, and Final Guys, focusing on weekly movie and book reviews. His nostalgic column about the magic of 80s horror, Video Visions, is featured monthly at Cemetery Dance Online. You can find his short stories in a number of anthologies, including Chopping Block Party, The Body Horror Bookand Fearful Fathoms II.

Living with his crazy and supportive family and two cats, he's happy to be close enough to New York City to see the skyline without having to pay New York rent. You can follow his travails at www.huntershea.com.

David Wood is the USA Today bestselling author of the action-adventure series, The Dane Maddock Adventures, and many other works. He also writes fantasy under his David Debord pen name. When not writing, he hosts the Wood on Words podcast. David and his family live in Santa Fe, New Mexico. Visit him online at www.davidwoodweb.com.

Jake Bible Novelist, short story writer, independent screenwriter, podcaster, and inventor of the Drabble Novel, has entertained thousands with his horror and sci/fi tales. He reaches audiences of all ages with his uncanny ability to write a wide range of characters and genres. Jake is the author of the bestselling Z-Burbia series set in Asheville, NC, the Apex Trilogy (DEAD MECH, The Americans, Metal and Ash) and the Mega series for Severed Press, as well as the YA zombie novel, Little Dead Man and the Teen horror novel, Intentional Haunting, the ScareScapes series, and the Reign of Four series for Permuted Press.

Brad Harmer-Barnes is a British horror author who grew up watching 1950s "creature-feature" movies and 1980s action and slasher movies, as well as reading H.P. Lovecraft, M.R. James, Stephen King, Brian Lumley and Clive Barker. Outside of writing, he enjoys tabletop gaming, collecting obscure soundtracks on vinyl, and trying to get through as much of his "To Read" pile as possible. Outside of writing horror, you can find him on various podcasts and YouTube shows at www.emotionally14.com, and he is a regular host of TalkStarWars (www.talkstarwars.co.uk). Praise for VIETNAM BLACK: "'Vietnam Black' might be one of the best examples of the 'creature feature' genre that I've ever encountered, and certainly one of the best titles ever published by Severed Press" - Sci Fi and Fantasy Reviewer.

William Meikle is a Scottish writer, now living in Canada, with more than thirty novels published in the genre press and over 300 short story credits in thirteen countries. He has books available from a variety of publishers including Dark Regions Press, Crossroad Press and Severed Press, and his work has appeared in a number of professional anthologies and magazines. He lives in Newfoundland with whales, bald eagles and icebergs for company. When he's not writing he drinks beer, plays guitar, and dreams of fortune and glory.

One of the premier storytellers of our time - FAMOUS MONSTERS OF FILMLAND

Scotland's Greatest Horror Writer - GINGER NUTS OF HORROR

Rich Restucci is a practicing chemist living in Pembroke Massachusetts. He resides with his lovely wife, three children, and a permanent hangover. He enjoys drinking beer, stocking up on weapons and supplies, playing with explosives and reading/writing anything zombie related. An up and coming writer, Rich is currently working on two series set in the same undead world: The Run Series, and the Theories Series.. Rich's work can be found on the fiction section of Homepage of the dead.com, or you could check out his blog on Zombie Fiend.com. Rich's novels can be found wherever books are sold.

Tim Curran hails from Michigan's Upper Peninsula. He is the author of the novels Skin Medicine, Hive, Dead Sea, Resurrection, Hag Night, The Devil Next Door, Long Black Coffin, Graveworm, Skull Moon, Nightcrawlers, and Biohazard. His short stories have been collected in Bone Marrow Stew and Zombie Pulp. His novellas include Fear Me, The Underdwelling, The Corpse King, Puppet Graveyard, Sow, Leviathan, Worm, and BLackout. His short stories have appeared in such magazines as City Slab, Flesh&Blood, Book of Dark Wisdom, and Inhuman, as well as anthologies such as Dead Bait, Shivers IV, World War Cthulhu, and, Vile Things. His fiction has been translated into German, Japanese, and Italian.

Alan Baxter is a British-Australian author who writes supernatural thrillers, dark fantasy, and urban horror, rides a motorcycle and loves his dogs. He also teaches Kung Fu. He lives among dairy paddocks on the beautiful south coast of NSW, Australia, with his wife, son, and two crazy hounds. He's the multi-award-winning author of several novels and around eighty short stories and novellas. So far. Read extracts from his novels, novellas, and find free short stories at his website – www.warriorscribe.com – or find him on Twitter @AlanBaxter and Facebook, and feel free to tell him what you think. About anything.

Geoff Jones is the author of <u>The Dinosaur Four</u>, a sci-fi adventure about ten people trapped in the Cretaceous. He lives in Colorado with his wife, two daughters, and a dog named River. Geoff is currently working on a post-apocalyptic thriller about a group of everyday people trying to survive the end of the world.

"The First Man on Earth" benefited from the astronomical and geological insights of Andrew Caldwell, who operates the Stargazer Observatory in Fort Collins, Colorado. Any errors should be attributed solely to the author. Additional thanks go to the LocoSpecFic critique group for tremendous help polishing the story. (Dani Coleman, Heidi Farmer, C. R. Hodges, Steven Johnson, Margot Romary, Jason Rush, and James Shade) Look them up and read their work. Finally, my heartfelt appreciation goes to Romana Baotic and the fine folks at Severed Press.

Rick Chesler holds a Bachelor of Science in marine biology and has had a life-long interest in the ocean and its mysteries. A certified scuba Divemaster, when not at work writing he can be found diving, boating or traveling to research his next thriller idea. He currently lives in the Florida Keys with his family.

Tim Waggoner has published close to forty novels and three collections of short stories. He writes original dark fantasy and horror, as well as media tie-ins, and his articles on writing have appeared in numerous publications. In 2017 he received the Bram Stoker Award for Superior Achievement in Long Fiction, he's been a finalist for the Shirley Jackson Award and the Scribe Award, and his fiction has received numerous Honorable Mentions in volumes of Best Horror of the Year. He's also a full-time tenured professor who teaches creative writing and composition at Sinclair College in Dayton, Ohio.

CHECK OUT OTHER GREAT DINOSAUR BOOKS

PRIMORDIA
by **Greig Beck**

Ben Cartwright, former soldier, home to mourn the loss of his father stumbles upon cryptic letters from the past between the author, Arthur Conan Doyle and his great, great grandfather who vanished while exploring the Amazon jungle in 1908.

Amazingly, these letters lead Ben to believe that his ancestor's expedition was the basis for Doyle's fantastical tale of a lost world inhabited by long extinct creatures. As Ben digs some more he finds clues to the whereabouts of a lost notebook that might contain a map to a place that is home to creatures that would rewrite everything known about history, biology and evolution.

But other parties now know about the notebook, and will do anything to obtain it. For Ben and his friends, it becomes a race against time and against ruthless rivals.

In the remotest corners of Venezuela, along winding river trails known only to lost tribes, and through near impenetrable jungle, Ben and his novice team find a forbidden place more terrifying and dangerous than anything they could ever have imagined.

PANGAEA EXILES
by **Jeff Brackett**

Tried and convicted for his crimes, Sean Barrow is sent into temporal exile—banished to a time so far before recorded history that there is no chance that he, or any other criminal sent back, has any chance of altering history.

Now Sean must find a way to survive more than 200 million years in the past, in a world populated by monstrous creatures that would rend him limb from limb if they got the chance. And that's just his fellow prisoners.

The dinosaurs are almost as bad.

CHECK OUT OTHER GREAT DINOSAUR BOOKS

FLIPSIDE
by JAKE BIBLE

The year is 2046 and dinosaurs are real.

Time bubbles across the world, many as large as one hundred square miles, turn like clockwork, revealing prehistoric landscapes from the Cretaceous Period.

They reveal the Flipside.

Now, thirty years after the first Turn, the clockwork is breaking down as one of the world's powers has decided to exploit the phenomenon for their own gain, possibly destroying everything then and now in the process.

A MAN OUT OF TIME
by Christopher Laflan

Five years after the Chinese Axis detonated an unknown weapon of mass destruction off the southern coast of the United States, Special Ops Sergeant John Crider and the members of Shadow Company have finally captured what they all hope will lead to the end of the war. Unfortunately, the population within the United States is no longer sustainable. In an effort to stabilize the economy, the government enacts the Cryonics Act. One hundred years in suspended animation, all debt forgiven, and a chance at a less crowded future are too good to pass up for John and his young daughter.

Except not everything always goes as planned as Sergeant John Crider finds himself pitted against a land of prehistoric monsters genetically resurrected from the fossil record, murderous inhabitants, and a future he never wanted.

CHECK OUT OTHER GREAT DINOSAUR BOOKS

THE FOUND WORLD
by Hugo Navikov

A powerful global cabal wants adventurer Brett Russell to retrieve a superweapon stolen by the scientist who built it. To entice him to travel underneath one of the most dangerous volcanoes on Earth to find the scientist, this shadowy organization will pay him the only thing he cares about: information that will allow him to avenge his family's murder.

But before he can get paid, he and his team must enter an underground hellscape of killer plants, giant insects, terrifying dinosaurs, and an army of other predators never previously seen by man.

At the end of this journey awaits a revelation that could alter the fate of mankind ... if they can make it back from this horrifying found world.

HOUSE OF THE GODS
by Davide Mana

High above the steamy jungle of the Amazon basin, rise the flat plateaus known as the Tepui, the House of the Gods. Lost worlds of unknown beauty, a naturalistic wonder, each an ecology onto itself, shunned by the local tribes for centuries. The House of the Gods was not made for men.

But now, the crew and passengers of a small charter plane are about to find what was hidden for sixty million years.

Lost on an island in the clouds 10.000 feet above the jungle, surrounded by dinosaurs, hunted by mysterious mercenaries, the survivors of Sligo Air flight 001 will quickly learn the only rule of life on Earth: Extinction.

Printed in Great Britain
by Amazon

44379362R00125